Isreda 61

Elaine D. Sal⸺
January 3rd
'Sal-Mur⸺
10 Twain Avenue,
Stenhousemuir
Larbert.

D1140745

Household Ghosts

In outline, but not in treatment, *Household Ghosts* is a simple story. Set in the Lowlands of Scotland, a landscape which forms an important but unobtrusive background for the mood of the book, it concerns the tensions that arise when a young married girl attempts to find with a lover the satisfaction she cannot achieve with her husband. But the ghosts of family and childhood loyalties, everything that has contributed to make her what she is, prove too strong; she is unable to break away; there is no solution to her dilemma in unfaithfulness. A situation that starts with brittleness and deceit ends, not with tragedy, but with tender amazement.

This story is told with originality and style, and with that strength of compassion for which James Kennaway was praised on the publication of his first book, *Tunes of Glory*. This is a serious novel, not without humour, distinguished for its depth of insight and for the excellence of its writing.

By the same author

TUNES OF GLORY

Household Ghosts

JAMES KENNAWAY

LONGMANS

LONGMANS, GREEN AND CO LTD
48 GROSVENOR STREET, LONDON W1
RAILWAY CRESCENT, CROYDON, VICTORIA, AUSTRALIA
443 LOCKHART ROAD, HONG KONG
PRIVATE MAIL BAG 1036, IKEJA (LAGOS)
44 JALAN AMPANG, KUALA LUMPUR
ACCRA, AUCKLAND, IBADAN KINGSTON (JAMAICA)
NAIROBI, SALISBURY (RHODESIA)

LONGMANS SOUTHERN AFRICA (PTY) LTD
THIBAULT HOUSE, THIBAULT SQUARE, CAPE TOWN

LONGMANS, GREEN AND CO INC
119 WEST 40TH STREET, NEW YORK 18

LONGMANS, GREEN AND CO
137 BOND STREET, TORONTO 2

ORIENT LONGMANS PRIVATE LTD
CALCUTTA, BOMBAY, MADRAS
DELHI, HYDERABAD, DACCA

© *James Kennaway* 1961

First published 1961

PRINTED IN GREAT BRITAIN
BY EBENEZER BAYLIS AND SON, LTD.
THE TRINITY PRESS, WORCESTER, AND LONDON

For
SUSAN

PART I

A Country Dance

1

THE gymnasium at Dow's Academy that night was a monumental patch-up of ugliness and joy. Fifty tables covered by hand-stitched linen cloths were squeezed into the shadows, at one side, hard against the climbing bars; and at the other side, beyond a huge square mirror (in front of which, in term time, flat-footed grammar school boys performed remedial exercises) all the instruments of torture or of glory—the horse, the horizontal and the parallel bars —were crowded into the corner and inadequately covered with a huge Union Jack, as if for a mass burial at sea. Sad streamers were looped across the hall but all they succeeded in doing was to draw the eye to the two climbing ropes strung up like giant nooses. Amongst the climbing bars by the mirror pale ribbons were inter-woven and tied in pussy bows. Framed in the middle of these was a coloured photograph of the Duke of Edinburgh on his wedding day, provided by the local confectioner whose best pre-war line had been boxes of George V chocolates. Above the platform, at the end of the hall, set against blue sackcloth curtains was a big banner which shouted VOTE UNIONIST and carried, one each side, prints of Sir Winston Churchill and Sir Anthony Eden, both wearing confident smiles.

Around the tables sat a hundred Auntie Belles ('Gin and ginger, thanks, pet') and Mary, brilliant, red-haired Mary moved amongst them, expecting the answer yes. Hardly had an Uncle Harry or a Douglas time to reply—to say 'Hello there, Mary', with joy, because no man was anything but pleased when Mary touched their sleeve or laid the flat of her hand on their lapel—before she moved on again. Mary bending forward, listening keenly; Mary leaning right back and laughing; nodding worriedly to one or sympathizing with the next; she talked to practically all of them.

And there was a phalanx of square-shouldered fur-capes to talk to; a great aroma of bath salts and moth balls and a loud tinkle-crash of jewellery.

At the top of the hall, beside the platform but not directly below the band, a table for some guests and parents of the Committee or Landed added the Kitzbuhl and Consolidated Steel touch. Below the band, some perched on the stage, others standing biting their nails or holding each other's hips, were many girls in pretty cotton frocks with full skirts; pinks and greens and whites. These girls were anything from fifteen to a rather raddled, on-the-make elder sister of twenty-eight, and they darted glances at the unaccompanied young men who were standing by the main entrance flattering each other with obscenities and loud, long laughs. Most of these seemed, at least at first, reluctant to dance. Two of them were dressed more or less as Teddy boys but they were unteddied by their own pink cheeks. In the end, the younger of the two forgot his grimace and assumed a leery grin confirming that he would have come in a cow-boy's get-up, if only he had had the nerve. The other boys were all in blue or brown suits and they looked as if they had shaved in a circular movement along the chin and around the back of the neck. They were sharply critical of the girls in their pretty frocks, of the bar prices, of the band and of the old bags sitting at the tables; but polite, abashed and confused as soon as Mary said:

'You must be the crook who sold us short on coke——'

And she talked to the important townsfolk too. Each one jumped to his feet, from the provost to the clerk's assistant. But they did so not only for Mary. It was as if they were desperately canvassing votes not for any political cause but for some imaginary, competitive election to be decided on the basis of obituaries in the local Press and on the market-day epitaphs collected on the week they should die.

A few gaps at the tables where men should be looking after their wives betrayed the group who moved between the bar and Classroom III. These were the Boys from the Queen's private bar; the vet, half a dozen farmers, the potato merchant, the town's second solicitor and estate agent, the golfing pro, the undertaker and building contractor, and a couple of others. But somehow the women who had been abandoned looked happier than those who had managed to hang on to their husbands, diverting their appetites from whiskies and Exports to soft biscuits, sweet tea and creamy meringues. ('Will you not have another, pet?')

Mary, jokingly, held her hands against her ears to dull the blasts of laughter and the noise of the smart-Alec concertina and fiddle band with Flying-Officer Kite type on the Kettle Drums, then slipping past a couple of young girls who were dancing together at the corner of the floor she went to the table where an absurdly good-looking little man with white hair was staring into the middle distance. She approached and spoke in his ear and he was obviously very fond of her. He put a hand on her shoulder. She said quickly and seriously:

'Daddy, darling, you don't blame me, do you?' He leant back and against the noise of the band he mouthed a long 'No'. She began again:

'For God's sake, darling, what does it matter? It's too idiotic. It's a silly joke, even if he has fallen for me which I don't suppose he has. I can tell you he's never really said a friendly word. And if they think I've fallen for him they're absolutely batty. He never smiles at me. He never says a kind thing. Not to me or anyone else, I bet, except when he's laying on the charm. But don't blame me. I just met him at this bloody silly cocktail party, only down in London it seems to be after supper when they throw about the gin.' She sighed and shrugged. Again her father reassured her with a shake of his head. She persisted:

'I've told them about a hundred times—So he glared at me? I didn't hide my wedding ring or anything like that. We danced to some ghastly Rock and Roll, and that wasn't much of a pleasure I can tell you. He's the world's worst dancer. He rang and rang, and all right, so I did have lunch with him. After all, I was there for a holiday.'

She flung out her hands.

'Well, since then he's followed me about, even to the extent of turning up here.' She referred to a man called David Dow, a physiologist approaching middle age who was the son of the first headmaster of the Academy, and that is why she added, 'After all, I can't stop him. This place is more home to him than me.' Her father was a little deaf. He cupped his hand round his ear. She finished, 'You know? Let's not make a situation. That would be too boring for words.' Then quickly she kissed him on the cheek, said 'Big official stuff' and hurried away. At the bar she touched her husband and her brother, and as she led the way through the swing doors to the quiet of a corridor lined with classroom doors she said:

'Come on, you slobs.'

The two men she touched were of very different kinds. Stephen, her husband, correctly, almost fastidiously dressed in kilt and black Highland jacket, had the look of a man who expects the answer no. He was very pale and thin to be a farmer, with dark wavy hair, blue eyes and a long thin red line for a mouth. He was somehow like one's mother's idea of how a young barrister (not a farmer) should look. But closer examination made one less confident of his success. His eyelashes, almost girlishly long, fell on his cheek with the softness of failure. There was intelligence but also resignation in his expression; it was as if he were mocking himself very gently all the time. He did not seem to dwell on his success, which was considerable. He had managed Mary's father's farm for four years —married for two of them—with pessimism, but had achieved superb results. He was known all over the county as the most effective of the young farmers, and of this reputation he once said, lugubriously, 'Even cheated of failure by limited success, that's me.'

Brother Pink—Charles Henry Arbuthnot Ferguson—needs altogether less description. He was balder and fatter than a man should be at thirty. He wore a single-breasted pin-stripe suit, that he had long outgrown. It pinched his shoulders and was tight at the cuffs. He took extraordinarily short steps for such a big man, and his feet were almost ludicrously small.

He answered his sister's call, 'Come on, you slobs,' with a vague, 'Oyez, oyez, tea-break: a bracing cup of chah,' not because it was tea-time or even because he intended then to drink tea, but because it was one of his formulae, and Pink and Mary had talked in a private and complicated language made up of just such phrases since their night-nursery days.

He paused and looked back at the hall. He closed out the talk from the bar, refusing to listen to the heifer prices or the advantages of Wolseley cars and heeded only the voices of the wives and

Auntie Belles. They spoke of common sense and cookies, and Pink could imitate them all.

('I don't fancy the South, dear, you can have your San Tropez or Brighton. My skin's too delicate. I fancy Troon myself.')

They lived on the land which the first farmers in Scotland had defended again and again from Highland thieves and clans. But Rob Roy and Montrose and the anti-Jacobites are well buried now.

('She was three up and two to go, pet, but I beat her on the bye. And that's not counting her lost pill. I beat her on the bye; so I did.')

Voices of tidy angels fading into tidy graves; the names do not matter. They were part of Pink's myth, and therefore of Mary's too.

Then, at last, Pink pulled himself away, saying 'Oyez, oyez, there's a great-time coming. You can ring those bloody bells.' He trundled after his sister, checking his fly buttons as he went.

2

Even out of term-time a junior classroom smells of something other than chalk dust and scrubbed wood. There was an inseparable but unmistakable ingredient which both Mary and her brother Pink seemed to recognize as soon as they came into Classroom IV, even if they could not define it. They had overtaken Stephen in the corridor.

Mary smoothed the skirt of her party frock and taking short steps crossed swiftly to the table on which rested sandwiches, glasses, soft drinks and a bottle of Gloag's Old Grouse Malt Whisky. She said, very quickly:

'It's rather smelly, but never mind. They seem to have organized the eats.'

Vaguely, Pink looked round at the pine panelling, the scrubbed floorboards, the glassy blackboard and the narrow Gothic windows set safely above boys' eye-level. He tried to define the missing ingredient.

'Sex?' he suggested, sniffing once or twice and looking up at the

11

dark space between the overhead lights and the high vaulted roof. Mary, grabbing a sandwich, shook her head, then spoke with her mouth full.

'We're jolly lucky to have it.'

Pink put his thumbs in his pockets. He was still sniffing the air. He made a further suggestion.

'Sex cruelly denied?'

Mary said, 'You eat this one, it's horrible,' and placed the bitten sandwich on the white linen cloth. As Pink obliged, her husband, Stephen, followed into the room. Apparently she did not think he was so close behind because she blushed a second after she had said:

'We've got David to thank for that. He went and talked nicely to that horrid headmaster who could hardly refuse old Dow's flesh —not in Dow's Academy.' She started thumbing through the sandwiches, announcing the choice. Only she did not do so accurately. Instead, in broad Yorkshire, just for the hell of it, she quoted from a Priestley play. She was almost like a child whistling to cover her guilt.

'Salmon, salad, trifle, two kinds of tarts, lemon cheese tart, jam tarts, two kinds of jelly . . .'

But her husband did not listen. He ignored or pretended to ignore her. He too seemed to be affected by the room which contrived to be both damp and dusty at once. His smell-suggestions were more abstract.

'Of nervous anxiety?' he asked, looking over the desks that had been shoved up the far end of the room. 'D'you think?'

The grandeur of this comment drove Mary back to the sandwiches. She tucked her head down and the light shone on her thick red hair.

Her husband continued, solemnly, 'Perhaps the smell of being laughed at?' and brother Pink nodded enthusiastically at that.

'Absolutely, old man,' he said firmly. 'Of the extraction of urine. You bet. That's the stink-a-bomb.'

'Ugh,' Stephen said, then smiled faintly. He raised his eyebrows and protested gently, 'Honestly, I'm not a fastidious man. Really I'm not.' But this denial did not ring true. His hair was carefully brushed, his nails were perfectly clean.

Mary walked over to the desks and began to play with a china ink-well, pushing it up and down in its socket. Pink, meantime, examined the bottle of Gloag's as if he had never seen whisky before. He went through a dumb show of discovery. In the gymnasium they were now dancing a reel, but the gym doors muffled the sound of the fiddles. The only noise that reached Classroom IV was the thumping of feet on the floor. It sounded like distant gunfire.

'Of cut-throat competition for brainy, swatty boys like me,' Stephen said with a quick, shy glance at Mary, and then he stepped up to the master's dais. He strolled as far as the blackboard where he picked up a copy of Kennedy's *Revised Latin Primer* and he drew an isosceles triangle on it with his finger then blew the chalk dust away. Mary said:

'Oh, come on, boys and girls, everything's going swimmingly. You are a couple of damp cloths. Do open up that bottle, Pink, I swear the others won't mind. Anyway they won't have to. They always do as I say—or does that sound rather horrid and bossy?'

'A bit on the boss-eyed side, old flesh,' Pink replied after he had assumed an intensely thoughtful expression. It seemed that he felt bound to mime every thought that passed through his head. He therefore squinted.

Stephen ignored this. Just before he opened the primer he said, with his eyes closed:

'A right-hand page, about the middle, *Mensa, mensa, mensam, mensae, mensae, mensa.*'

Duly finding page seventeen he smoothed it with long fingers and said:

'I'm right.'

'I'm so glad, old man,' Pink replied affably and reached out for a couple of the cheap, fluted tumblers, mumbling, 'Gloagers.'

It was cold in Classroom IV, even in September. Gusts of wind occasionally rattled against the narrow windows, but Mary still looked warm. She put the back of her hand against her cheek which was glowing pink. Hers was a very small hand with freckles of which she was ashamed. Every gesture seemed to be calculated to imply that this was just another Young Conservative dance; nothing out of the usual.

Stephen, still turning over the pages, said:

'It's just the same. I confess I find that reassuring. *Tristis, tristem, tristis, tristi.'* Then he turned over some more pages and smiled again. He said, 'Here's one for Pink. *Vomo, vomere, vomui, vomitum.'*

'Oh, do shut up spouting Latin and enjoy yourself, darling,' Mary said, a little edgily.

Stephen looked up innocently.

'But I haven't enjoyed anything so much for years. Perhaps I'm not the scholar your friend David is, but I'm strictly the serious type.'

Mary let the ink-well drop into its socket. As if she meant something quite different, in the same firm tone in which one might dismiss a servant forever, she said:

'If you lean back on the board like that you'll get your jacket covered with chalk.'

Stephen looked back at her, his eyes wide open.

'Does that matter?'

And when she shrugged, he asked:

'Do you mind?'

This was Pink's cue, as fool. He at once grasped the phrase, repeating it cockney style as if he were a typist finding a hand above his knee.

'Do you mind?' And as Stephen did not react he turned back to his sister and spread his arms wide.

'For God's sake,' he pleaded. 'The boy's doing his best.'

She said suddenly, to Pink, in one breath, 'Don't worry, it's only Steve. I'm laughing like anything.'

Pink's method of blowing her a kiss was to stick his finger in his mouth and make the noise of a cork being extracted from a bottle. The imitation was loud and successful.

'Right up,' he said, and his sister replied:

'I'm so glad I only understand half the things you say. They get fouler every day.'

Stephen closed the book. Looking round again, he said 'Of guilt,' and sniffed.

'Oh God,' Mary said, dropping her head and gripping the edge of the desk.

'Of ambition,' Stephen went on, quietly, with a nod, as if he still had a list of alternatives.

'He only does it to annoy,' Pink said, and added, instructing himself, 'Do stop fumbling with that bottle, old chum.'

But Stephen continued:

14

'I think it really makes rather an appropriate sitting-out room. . . . Odd to think it used to be your friend David's home.'

'Oh, come on,' Pink said quietly, warningly.

'But correct me if I'm wrong——'

'Stephen!' Mary pleaded.

Pink drank his whisky, then spoke again to Stephen.

'My chum and I,' he said, with a gesture towards Mary, 'are rooting for you. What Moo has joined together let no black-eyed intellectual expatriate Dow put asunder—it's in the Book. All right?'

'Please,' Stephen insisted. 'I just said it was his old home. And he was at school here. You've told me so yourself. D'you suppose his initials are carved on one of the desks?'

'I haven't looked,' Mary replied, staring him straight in the eye, and there was a moment's silence, broken only by that noise like distant gunfire. The top half of Mary's face was in the deep shadow cast by the bakelite shades, like Chinese hats, above the bright bulbs, but her eyes shone.

She then persisted, 'D'you want me to make a search?'

'Why should I do that?' Stephen replied, turning his head to one side, almost as if he were showing his neck.

Mary shrugged and said, 'You raised it,' and another sticky silence was only broken by the noise of the ink-well dropping in the socket again. Mary spilt some ink on her fingers. 'Bugger the thing!'

Pink said, 'The world's your oyster, Lilian.'

'Can I borrow your hanky?' she asked, and Pink pretended to be shy. He blushed and gave a very dirty laugh.

'Well actually, old girl,' he began. 'Farmers' hop and all that——'

'Oh, do stop being foul and give me the thing. I'm covered in ink.' Then, still furiously trying to rub the ink off her fingers, she rushed across to her husband, saying:

'Poor, poor Stiffy,' and she put her arms round his neck. 'But we do root for you, honestly we do.'

She leant back a little and smiled, then adjusted his jaw so that he grinned more broadly, saying:

'Light up the lantern.'

For a second she looked seriously, almost sadly, at his white face. Just before she turned to Pink she said:

15

'Old chum?'

'Old chum,' Pink replied.

'A tiny triple old chum.' She stepped away from her husband.

'For Madame.'

'Absolutely, old chum,' she said, still seriously.

'No sooner said than done.'

He poured her an enormous whisky, and sliding some sandwiches on to a Dundee cake that looked like a fighter, he put the tumbler on the plate and carried it across to her, speaking once again in their curious code, a language drawn from anecdote and limerick; from family jokes and nursery rhyme; from a lifetime spent together; from a myth they had had to weave for themselves.

'At the Savoy,' he said, 'we do it with a warm spoonerooni,' and at once understanding, she hauled up her dress, which since she raised her arms to hug Stephen had begun slipping down her breasts.

For the first time she smiled warmly.

'I love Pink,' she said, 'L.U.V. Mary loves Charles Henry Arbuthnot Chuff-chuff Ferguson,' for Pink had been 'Chuff-chuff' before he was old enough for gin.

The only bright things shining in the two brutal arcs of light were Stephen's silver buttons and the table-cloth. Then, as Pink moved, there was a third reflection which Mary increased by poking her brother in the middle. His remarkably white shirt which did not quite button up at the neck had escaped between waistcoat and pin-stripe trousers. Mary pulled the shirt out further.

'You haven't even buttoned it,' she complained.

'Dress optional, old Dutch,' Pink said, tucking it in again.

In a loud and false voice, Stephen answered a remark which Mary had made only with a doubtful look. 'My darling, I promise I'm being perfectly reasonable.'

'Then why did you mention his name?'

Stephen shrugged.

'I thought this was a great family for jokes . . .'

Mary blinked and Pink, his chins folding into each other as he gave a little burp, recommended his sister to lift her elbow. He did this, of course, by signal; a signal which he could not resist developing into an imitation of a big dog lifting his leg. He was answered more or less, in code. This time Mary spoke in a strongly respectable Kelvinside accent.

'The elbow?' she asked. 'D'you think that's wise, Bun?' And they went into one of their acts.

Pink was convincing as a respectable spinster. He blinked as he plunged into the imitation.

'A little of what you fancy, Belle—it'll do you the world of good.'

'Is that a fact, Bun?'

'That's a fact.'

Stephen's dislike of the Kelvinside 'respectable' game seemed to be out of all proportion. He groaned, said 'No' and screwed up his face as if he were experiencing physical pain. His fists were squeezed tight. It seemed possible that it was not the act itself that annoyed him. The act merely provided him with an excuse to express some of the feelings of nervousness and irritation which until then had only just been kept under control. Laughing quietly, as if it hurt him, and as if he were about to break into tears, he said:

'No, please. I don't think I can bear it if you go on like that. I know what it's like once you've started. We won't hear a sensible word all night.'

'Oh dear,' Mary said, taking a big drink. 'It's ages since we've done Bun and Belle. We used to do it for hours on end.'

'I know,' Stephen said; and Pink said, very sentimentally:

'Always on a rainy day.' Catching his mood, Mary answered:

'And it always rained.' She gave him a very sweet smile, then they all drank again, quickly. A second later Mary was frowning, and Pink picked up her hand and kissed the back of it before he returned to the table for a sandwich. They could still hear the thump of the floorboards.

Stephen sat down on the bench along the wall and pushed his legs out in front of him. He said:

'We're very nostalgic, suddenly. The story changes, as you grow up. I thought you used to spend your time smoking cigarettes or lying in the loft, watching the bull at work. That was much more convincing as a picture of country childhood.'

Mary was still sitting dreaming and she did not listen to Pink as he said:

'You wait till we write our book. We will write one, won't we?' Then, polishing the imaginary screen in front of Mary's eyes, he said much more loudly:

'Won't we?'

'That's it,' she replied, swinging her feet on to the floor. 'Children of the Caledonian Forest.' Suddenly she started laughing, and dropping her head to her hands on the desk she said, 'Dear me!'

'What?' Pink was half smiling. It was as if he did not know what exactly she was laughing at, but knew at once the nature of it.

Stephen had moved towards the classroom door. Down the corridor he could see the reel being danced in the gym. He pretended not to hear Mary, as she began to giggle, hopelessly. It always irritated him. In the pitch of her laughter he recognized an oblique attack.

Her eyes were sparkling. She put her fingers over her face as she began to blush as well as giggle. She managed to blurt out:

'Those competitions in the bunkers—— No, they were too bad.'

Pink imitated her frown.

'Too bad,' he agreed. 'Strictly Wolfenden stuff. I've always said it. Children ought not to be brought up in the country. It's altogether too near to Nature. The things we did on that golf course would turn Bank Lizzy green.'

'With horror!'

'With envy,' Pink said.

Stephen still did not turn round and it was perhaps the sight of his thin neck (14½-inch collar) with his dark hair cut just so, neither too short nor too long, that drove her to continue the conversation.

'And in the loft,' she said. 'In the spare room, on the bridge, in the rhododendrons and the attic and the black shed——'

'Even in the garage,' Pink agreed.

'Dear!' She was again horrified by some memory, but still could not stop herself laughing. 'I swear to you, Steve, one time we——'

She ignored Pink's long face of warning.

'Steve?'

For a second it was doubtful how she would cope with him. Then she put the point of her little finger, her pinkie, into the ink-well and said:

'Steve's huffing.'

When he turned, pretending that his thoughts had been miles away, she said, warningly:

'Darling——'

18

'Me?' Stephen said. 'I'm not huffing.' He walked over to the table and said, 'I'm pouring myself another drink.' Mary was once again furiously trying to remove the ink stain from her skin, with Pink's handkerchief.

She said, 'You won't huff, will you? After all you started it.'

'I?' Stephen said. Pink's eyebrows jumped up.

'I, Mother?' Mary asked very grandly. It must have been another of their library of private jokes. If it was not marked under 'huffy' it could be found under 'stuffy'.

'I'm sorry, darling,' she said, seeing the tiny muscle in his jaw, which always worked when he was angry. 'But you did start it, you know. About the loft and the bull. Oh dear, how awful. Now you're really huffy.'

Stephen said, 'I don't know why you choose to use these childish expressions whenever——'

'Blame it on old Pink,' Pink said, trundling back to the table, since the cork was out of the bottle again.

'That's it,' Mary said, swinging her legs again. 'He's the eldest.'

Pink turned to his brother-in-law who had wandered as far as the corridor again, and said, 'Tell us, old fruit, was childhood in the Doctor's house just about the same?'

'I can't say I found it so.' Stephen, by a turn of his head, implied that he was still listening to the music. He had spent most of his childhood south of the border, and it made him very sensitive to things Highland and regimental. At last he said, rather stiffly:

'I do wish they wouldn't play Cannon Woods. They don't seem to know it's originally a German tune. It was never played here before the war.' Mary glanced at Pink as if to say, 'Don't tell me he's pompous.' But Pink knew how far to go. He did not embarrass her. Instead he turned back to Stephen, saying, as affably as ever:

'Oh, come clean, Stiffy. We're all chums, we're all girls together.' When he toasted his drinking companions he raised his glass to eye level rather formally. He held the tumbler between finger and thumb and his other fingers splayed out in mid-air. Then, literally, he lifted his elbow.

'Astonishing good luck,' he said.

Stephen said, 'I'm sorry to disappoint you, but I really have nothing to hide. Perhaps it was the English influence, or living in

19

a town. Even when we were in the country, hay-making meant a ride in the buggy, not a day in the loft.'

'Really?' Pink sounded serious and amazed, but it was doubtful if he was thinking what he was saying. He seemed to be more worried by the tumbler in his hand, which he emptied in one gulp.

'Perhaps it was just me,' Stephen went on pleasantly, then suddenly, coldly, with one remark, he killed the conversation. It was at an end, as soon as he said, 'Sex was never my strong subject. It isn't now, as we know.'

Mary moved across the room. She spoke seriously, as if someone had suddenly, unnecessarily displayed an ugly open wound.

'Darling, why must you be so silly?'

Stephen seemed perfectly cheerful. His voice and his manner were bolder again.

'My dear, it isn't I who needs sympathy. It's you. There.' He smiled, put an arm round her shoulder, and kissed her cheek. She dropped her eyes. Pink's stomach seemed to grow bigger. He almost stood on tiptoe, and he stammered slightly as he said:

'Come on, my loves. Blame it on Pink. Old Pink started it.'

'Not true,' Stephen said, depressed again, and Pink was irritated. He took it out on the plates and glasses which he clattered about as he said:

'Damn it all, chum.'

'Pink,' Mary said softly, and Stephen's voice rode over hers as it so often did.

'I'm afraid I am a bit of a cold sponge at——'

'Darling!'

But Stephen went on. 'A fact's a fact, for heaven's sake.'

Pink said, as nicely as he could, 'Okay, chumbo, but don't let's go on about it at a farmers' hop.'

'True.'

Mary had sat down on a bench at the side of the room. She looked straight in front of her, over the desks, towards the panels covered with carved initials, and the long cords falling down from the small, high windows. She said to Stephen:

'Nobody is as ruthless with himself as you are. I don't know whether to admire it or——'

'Shudder,' he said, in the icy tone of someone who not only has the courage to admit to others that he is no good in bed, but braver still, to confess it to himself.

'No.' She was angry for a second, as she looked up at him. 'Not shudder—I never felt that.'

Pink took a couple of steps backwards. Stephen ran his finger round the rim of his glass. He said very calmly:

'Tell me, does your friend David know the situation?'

'No,' she answered sharply. 'Of course he doesn't. You know he doesn't. Unless you've unburdened yourself to him.' She drank a little of her whisky.

'That's hardly likely,' he said and at once, in a low voice, she replied:

'I'm not so bloody sure.'

'Bab—Ba—Bambinos!' Pink moved softly forward, but Mary kept her head away from him. She was looking firmly at the glass in her hand.

'He's not my friend, anyway, I told you.'

'Darling,' Stephen said, 'I trust you implicitly.'

Mary looked at Pink, not Stephen, but Pink also turned away.

Stephen swallowed and still talking of marriage and of bed, he went on:

'Whatever happened, I could hardly blame you when the fault is so patently mine.'

But Mary, perhaps to his surprise, did not rush to deny this. She remained perfectly still, and silent. Pink, putting one foot in front of the other, walked carefully up the line of one of the floorboards, and then the gym doors opened, and Young Conservatives came flooding in saying, 'Really, Charles? But I thought there was a pile to be made in broilers' and other more ornate and surprising Young Conservative things, like 'I said, "Jack, I careth not for thee." '

3

With an astonishing lack of hard evidence, the mind-benders insist that the dreams we forget are the important ones. But at least we can each prove to ourselves that the letters which we never send are the revealing ones. And for months, in a corner of a bench in

David Dow's laboratory in the Medical Research Council building in Mill Hill there lay scores of these; letters which went back over all the scenes with Mary; letters of love, of protest, of explanation and angry letters too. Some spread themselves so far as to become something beyond a letter, striking out from specific apology to woolly confession. Some were addressed privately and passionately to Mary, others seemed to be directed to nobody, prepared carefully and laboriously for the waste-paper basket.

The first letters, some no more than torn scraps of paper, are written in a spidery hand, corrected and recorrected, advancing painfully, inch by inch, as if reluctant to reach the kernel of their relationship. At the end, the handwriting grows bolder and grammar itself seems to oblige and bend to the material. These last pages will be quoted, but the first ones, laboriously pursuing minute events in Classroom IV and the gym, matter too.

The first does not directly concern Mary and David, but David's observation of Mary at work that night; Mary as she was then but is no longer; Mary, oblique and hysterical. She played for David that evening, involving herself at first neither with poor Pink nor with Stephen but with the steadiest member of the Ferguson family, Flora Macdonald, the huge Nanny, housekeeper, nurse and rock.

*　　*　　*

Mary, Mary, cousin as you are now, you've told me [David writes] that I looked that night, in my white tie and tails, like a mixture between a second-class pugilist and Deacon Brodie on the prowl, just because I watched silently the performance that you put on for me and forgot to speak to your friends who *you*, remember, called harmless and I called kind. And though I write always, other, countless, unpostable and unposted letters only to be forgiven, in this one scene at least, it was you who behaved badly. Promise.

Just reconsider it. Forget all the talk *to* your Conservative friends, *at* me; forget the loudness of your voice. Forget the brassy laugh, and that comment, advertising yourself, as you filled your glass, about yourself but put, horribly, in the third person, 'Well, her father was a card-cheat and her mother was a drunk. . . . Ha-ha-ha!'—Suggestions, incidentally, which you had denied

22

with such a show of passion in London only a week previously that you successfully reduced a cocktail party to embarrassed silence.

Remember only poor Macdonald coming in—poor, huge, gloomy, loving Macdonald who you had told me not once but many times was (your phrase) 'a guardian angel in your life, not a Nanny but a foster-mother'. I always remember her, perhaps the one person who comes out of the story with credit, as she looked that night, in a dress that was more like a toga. I imagine her now as six foot four but perhaps she was shorter than that. It was as if all the expression in her features had been swept back with the gold-grey hair to that big bun at the back of her neck. She had huge, chicken-killing hands and feet made for plough. Yet she was gentle.

If I had not known by then the extraordinary amount of alcohol you were capable of holding I would have sworn that you must be drunk to be so cruel. I may not have all poor Macdonald's lines right, but it was the look on her face that mattered. On the other hand I have, as you can judge for yourself, an unerring memory for Mary lines. Proof? You greeted her, as she loomed through the door, mauve dress and square fur cape, by turning more than half away from her, addressing one of your girl-friends who was (please note) on my side of the room, 'Lerwick's answer to Cassandra. Whistler's maiden aunt.' This announcement, needless to say, was made in a voice loud enough not only for me to hear but for poor Macdonald to hear, as well.

'Can I speak to you, Mary?' I think she said, at the door, and with a whirling turn and a kind of enthusiastic rush of innocence, you grasped both of her hands and said:

'Yes, *darling* Macdonald,' and I saw the 'darling' make its mark on wary Macdonald's face. What invited 'darling' now, after twenty years without?

I could have told her. I was flattered, I confess.

'Darling Macdonald, do come and have a proper drink—you've been doing marvels through there, I know.'

'Heavens,' one of your dairy-minded friends gave you away, 'from all the darlings and that I thought it must be a man coming through the door.'

'Goodness, don't look so grim,' you were now saying irritably to Macdonald, as if suddenly you had changed your mind and never wanted to see her again, then even as I watched, you changed back and stretching out your hands to her again said, 'Dear, lovely Macdonald, Rock of Gibraltar only much prettier and nicer really —you are so MI5. It can't be all that bad.'

'A word in your ear, Mary.' One step forward. She approached the erratic animal.

'Oh, don't be so silly,' quietly from you. With your nail you picked at the Cairngorm brooch which she had clasped in her dress, then stopped yourself with a flick of the hand—a hand which you hated, so you told me; but you left it flat on Macdonald's shoulder for everybody to see.

You said to her, 'If it's so embarrassing you can tell me in a whisper,' and encouraged by a titter round about (and not my laughter, I assure you) you said, not exactly to Macdonald, 'Well, it's not a children's party any more. Not Mr. Reed's dancing class and bow to your partners. Pink and I have grown up on you.' Then directly to her face, 'I won't be shocked.' And to the brooch, quietly, but oh, so audibly, 'Has your sweetheart jilted you?'

God, she was patient. If I'd been her I would have slapped your face.

She said, wearily, 'Don't get so excited, Mary dear. I know the mood.'

'Well, what on earth have you come to say?'

Macdonald looked round then, nodded good evening to somebody, before she asked, 'D'you not think it's time you went back to your father, next door? You know what he is. He won't move away from the table at all.'

'Haven't you been there, for heaven's sake?' A pause. A sly glance to your yes-friends, with your eyes right round to the sides. Then you add, 'You and your sweetheart, I mean?'

Don't you blush to read this? Wasn't it obvious to you then? Surely everybody in the room must have seen what you were up to, attacking and teasing Macdonald while you kept me within earshot. I see you now, as you were at that moment, circling round like a brightly coloured bird, flapping a wing, fluttering the feathers in your tail.

Poor Macdonald bit her lip. She must have known how dangerous it was to mention her boy-friend's name. But she took the plunge, while you waited, ready to strike. She did not say Captain Gordon, but stuck to his Christian name.

'Jack and I have held the fort for over an hour now.'

Saying Jack she used his short 'a'; what you and Pink used to call his 'immaculate Edinburgh and Bombay'. I wonder if she did so as a sort of dare. But you didn't fail. You got another titter for your echo. 'Jack? Captain Jack Gordon? M.C., R.A.M.C.?'

Imperviously, Macdonald frankly confessed:

'It's the gay Gordons. That's Jack's favourite,' and you, pure bitch, threw back your head and laughed, then quickly, like a schoolgirl, clasped a hand over your mouth (fingers long and straight of that hand you hate so much) and said:

'Oh God, I'm sure I shouldn't laugh.'

It is difficult to keep up with you at this point. At once you followed with the short a's again, mimicking (not very well) poor Captain Jack Gordon.

'Tripping the light fantastic?' you asked and then swung round to your brother who, give him his due, was not enjoying this very much.

'Pink, darling, do say "Light fantastic Saturday, Jack." Do it properly. In Jack's voice.'

He was then gasping for air, trying to warn you what you already knew, that Macdonald, with great dignity, was leaving the room.

Then, by golly, you covered. I don't say it was for my sake alone, but certainly for my sake as well.

Sweetly and desperately, 'No, Macdonald, don't be so silly, don't take on so. Macdonald dear.'

Rushed after her. Caught her in the corridor and held her, not in front of *all* the guests but in front of some. In front of me, by the way. Held her again by the arms and looked imploringly at the big solemn face.

'So it was silly, on your part,' Macdonald said. 'I'd say you've got no reason to be unkind about Jack.'

A big shake of your head. A wag from side to side.

'It was just a joke.'

'What's the joke?'

You shrugged at that, but still clung to her arms. The alarmed spoilt child; contrite, insecure, cunning. 'Just ridiculous. I've said I'm sorry.'

'What's ridiculous, Mary? Are we too old, is that it?'

'No.' She had you there. 'Don't look like that, Macdonald. Don't ask questions.'

'Is it that he's small and I'm big?' [In my mind's eye, just as Macdonald has gained stature, I remember Captain Jack Gordon as only two feet tall.]

'No!' You looked a little afraid. 'No honestly, please forget it. You must forgive me. Otherwise it'll ruin my evening. I promise it will.' You were pinching her arms, now.

'Are you coming through then?'

'This minute.'

'Okay, toots,' she said, forgiving. You stood on tiptoe and kissed her. Then dropped on your heels again and leant against the wall pushing both the flat of your hands and that red hair, cousin, against the glossy surface. Frock? Short and pink. Legs? Well set apart. If you doubt me, cousin, it is for a good reason; remembering you are ashamed. But it is true enough. I'll give you another echo to prove it to you. But in proving, I give myself away: my own shame. There's not a moment of Classroom IV which escapes me, I've lived it so often again.

That farmer, of course, is the echo—the one who wandered down the corridor at just that moment. The big round moon-faced one in the brown suit who was so proud of his tenor voice. As you stood and watched Macdonald go, presenting me with the perfect side-face, he came by, insisting to his friends:

'I've got the technique I have. . . . Semi-trained.' Something like that. 'When I was just a treble my singing teacher said—she said I'd a most remarkable voice. So she said.'

You looked at your shoes as you came into the classroom again. You were ashamed even then, cousin. If not from your own heart then at least from the look on my face you reckoned you had over-played and you were very quiet as the Young Conservatives drained out. You leant your backside against one of the desks and stared at your tumbler, whirling the whisky round and round. I tried very hard, I confess, but you wouldn't look at me.

You weren't at all happy at being left behind with me, then. Not after you'd over-played.

Voices and gestures:—

Stephen, in your ear, 'Best if you follow us through, darling.

We'd better not delay.' He had both a dark look and a bright smile for me.

You were clasping the bridge of your nose as if your head ached.

'No,' holding your hand out to your husband, and for the first time, daring a look at me. 'I'll come through now.'

After that it's only voices for me. I turned to the blackboard then. There were only the three voices: yours, Pink's and Stephen's. The others were mere murmurs of complaint against taxation, echoing down the corridor.

Stephen's voice, without confidence: 'Give David another drink. No please do.'

A shifting of feet, a glass thumped on a table, then Stephen's voice again. This time bright and cheerful.

'Please do. One for all the good work he did with you on the flags and streamers next door. He helped decorate, didn't he?'

Stephen's voice again. 'You entertain him, darling.'

Then yours, sharp and clipped: 'Very well. We'll follow you through.'

Last of all, Captain Jack Gordon, R.A.M.C. (Indian Army), precisely, but it came, I assume, from poor Pink.

'Yes. Yes. "A bit of the light fantastic, Saturday." '

Then Pink in his own voice: "Oyez, oyez. You can ring those bloody bells.'

4

As Mary reached for the bottle of Gloag's she knocked over one of the fluted glasses and she only just saved it from falling to the floor. David watched her with dark and tender eyes as she picked it up and reached for the bottle again. He walked away from the blackboard to the far wall and played with one of the thin cords hanging from the tiny area of window which could be opened. The cord was low enough for the master to adjust, but high enough to prevent boys from hanging themselves without difficulty.

Mary said, 'I was told to give you a drink,' and when she drew in a breath it made a small wavering noise.

'Why did you stay?' he asked.

'Because my husband asked me to.'

She looked up at him. She was pale now, and not at her prettiest. When the colour ran from her cheeks her skin sometimes looked almost green. The effect had something to do with the tiny freckles.

She rested her hands on the table, behind her back. 'David, I do want to speak to you about yesterday.'

'No, that's really a wrong one——' he said, coming round to her, flicking his fingers and thumbs.

'Please, I'd like to explain.'

'Explain nothing. Forget what happened.' But as he laid a hand on her skin just where the neck curves into the shoulder she walked away and she said a little hysterically:

'No, please don't touch me.'

'Oh no,' he said, again snapping his fingers with irritation. 'This is snakes and ladders. Each time one has to begin at base.'

'If you really want to know, I feel I never really want to be touched again. It's all so complicated. But that's what I do feel.'

He had turned right away from her and going back to the window and the cord he said, very quietly:

'Please, miss. Don't tempt me by telling more lies. You're really on form tonight.'

At once she said, 'You mean about Macdonald? You don't know it but I was being kind. He's a dreadful little man. Her boy-friend, I mean. Jack Gordon. He's half her height.'

He simply shook his head, refusing the excuse and at once on a debby note which sounded almost an octave higher she said:

'I absolutely confess it, I was rather tough. . . . But Macdonald understands. It's just that I'm fearfully jealous I suppose. I'm that sort of person and I've always been bitchy about Macdonald's friends. It shows how much I love her, don't you see? Poor old cow. Anyway, I didn't tell any lies about her or anybody else. . . .'

He quoted her own words, ' "My mother was a drunk." '

'Oh, that was just a joke.'

'It's something you weren't so prepared to joke about in London.'

She answered quietly, 'No, of course not. Here everybody knows. I mean they know it's not true. That's why I can afford to joke.'

David raised an eyebrow. He was prepared to leave the subject as her mother had been dead for ten years anyway. Moreover when she was alive she was rather a pathetic, self-pitying invalid who later took to drink. David even could remember meeting her, once, in Forfar when he was a boy; a fussy, nervous, dumpy little woman wearing a hat and white gloves. His mother had introduced her as Lady Ferguson.

Contrarily, Mary had decided to talk about her mother. 'Anything to do with Mummy's complicated,' she said and drank a gulp of whisky. It was not easy to see what she was up to, but her movement across to the desks, back to little-girl land, seemed to give something away.

She said, 'I don't know why I get so worked up about her, sometimes, but it annoys me. People get such wrong impressions of what she was, and even if you did see her once, she was my mother and I know. It doesn't matter if they get a good impression or a bad impression, it's still the wrong impression and it makes me mad. It's probably very silly.'

'I'll buy it,' David said, a little mystified. 'Go on.'

'I'm not selling anything, David.' She turned back to the inkwell. 'Really I'm not. Absolutely the opposite. But I'd hate you to go away thinking I'm bloody about Mummy because honestly, honestly I'm not. She was awful and mixed-up, but she was a great woman really. Most people up here met her when she was at the end of her tether. Didn't even meet her, just heard about her, lying in her bed, drinking and that. Maybe she did drink, but she was a great woman; a very passionate woman.'

David watched her very carefully as she circled round and returned to the desk. The approach was nothing, if not oblique. He sat down and smoked. Mary, meantime, sat down on the desk and told her story with bright eyes.

'I could tell you things about Mummy almost beyond belief that nobody knows—I mean outside Pink and Co. And it's only lately, really, since I was married that I added it all together. Not just the card cheating, the scandal and their coming back north: not about that at all. Until a year or two ago I just used to frown when people asked me about Mummy. She was just a washed-out woman in bed. We never used to see her get drunk, but we'd hear her sometimes at night, shouting and often laughing, saying the most extraordinary things. Pink and I never could make out whether

29

she was talking to Daddy or one of the dogs. Whichever it was they never answered. Then there would be a long silence and Pink and I would hold hands.'

She moved the ink-well again. She did not look at him for a moment as she spoke. Very quickly she went on:

'You've been home, you know where—just by the top of the stairs by the nursery gate, there's a linen cupboard there. We'd hide in it. Then another silence or perhaps a click of a door and we'd dash back to bed, shivering cold. I wonder we weren't more frightened. She came in once and found us in the same bed and I thought there would be an awful rumpus. Macdonald never used to allow us in the same bed. She said that's how keely children slept. But Mummy wasn't really angry at all. She put on all the lights, she blinked, then she moved across to us. I remember it like yesterday. Then she sat down at the end of the bed and pitched forward and her hair was all undone. She kind of pushed us through the bedclothes as if we were the dogs under the blankets. I kept my eyes tight shut until I heard her. I thought she was laughing, but she wasn't. Tears were pouring down her cheeks. I don't think she was drunk at all. We were scared stiff. We didn't move or speak, even after she went out. We stayed like that until it was light outside, and the sun was shining on the floods.'

David sat patiently. Nothing could have stemmed the flow. Mary talked and went on talking for about half an hour, with hardly a pause for breath. Her eyes were here and there and everywhere; for a second staring honestly and emphatically into David's; then looking up at the light; at the ink-well; at her white, pointed shoes. She still talked of her mother.

'Another time once she got out of bed. She took us into Dundee right down by the docks and the tenements there, it's almost as bad as Glasgow. We didn't know then much what it was all about. There were a lot of men standing about at the street corners. There must have been some strike or something like that. They'd got banners, some of them, God knows what they said. . . . We'd done something wrong, I think. We'd put our rice pudding under the chest in the dining-room hoping the dogs would find it, and when she discovered it hours later, it was a day later, I think, she bunged us into the back of the car and took us into Dundee. I suppose she was pretty high. She shouted, "Open! P.N.!" That's what the kids

cry there at night when they come up the wynds and can't get in
the door. The Inas and Sheilas and Elspeths and Jeans. The
Cathies and Normas. She threatened to leave us there until Macdonald said, "For Heavens sakes, that's enough." Macdonald never
said, "For heaven's sake," it was always, "For Heavens sakes,"
with the "s" on both.

'We were very frightened then. Pink was a great weeper. I
didn't cry out but Pink cried all the way there and all the way
back in kind of short bursts. Macdonald told him he was a great
bubbly and that just made him worse.'

She walked over to the sandwiches again. She ate a lot. Speaking
with her mouth full of smoked salmon, she said:

'But we didn't know, then. We weren't told anything. Daddy
never said much to us beyond, "Old boy" or "Old girl", and
Macdonald's as secret as the grave. The only time we ever got
anything out of her was when she was bathing us. Soap seemed to
do something to her discretion. She'd cackle away.

'It's only lately I've kind of discovered, and now I feel awful for
all the things I used to say about Mummy. That's why I feel bad
now. I confess you've got me on the raw. Even as a joke. I feel
bad about saying she was a boozer. I probably was in the wrong.
I used to say awful things about her at school. Tell fibs.'

'Even then,' David interrupted quietly, and she looked at him,
a little puzzled.

'Yes . . .' Then she checked herself and said, 'What do you mean?
You never will say quite what you mean.'

David shook his head. He wondered if there was any truth in her
stories.

'Forget it.'

'That's a very womanish thing to say,' she replied, and frowned.
She scraped her nail against the wood of the desk and began again,
speaking even more quietly than before.

'Anyway. It's as I was saying. People don't really know about
Mummy. She was terrific, really. I mean she had an awful time. You
see that day in Dundee was awfully significant really. Her taking
us back there, because when she was very little, well, about eleven,
I suppose, until she was about eleven she lived there. Can you
believe it? It explains a lot. I mean, when she was younger, God
knows what she didn't go through.'

She moved away a step or two, then she turned round to him and smiled.

'Honestly, David, I do wish we could make it work as sort of friends. Cousin-type. I so adore talking to you.' She put her back to one of the old desks and jumped up and swung her legs again. Pointing her toes, she continued:

'There's a really terrifying background. This one Macdonald knows and nobody else. I don't think Mummy properly knew it herself. You can have a kind of block with these things, can't you? When she was eleven she was living in one of those horrid tenement things. Her father wasn't a labourer, actually. He was an actor or music hall or something, but at one time he'd had to do with the jute business . . . clerk or checker, I think. . . . You didn't know who you were cousin to, did you? All your long looks of the poor schoolmaster's son? God knows who my cousins are on Mummy's side, probably all sailors and drunks.

'Anyway, Grandfather doesn't come much into the picture. It was Mummy's mother looked after her and she was supposed to be redheaded but even littler than me. She used to go out and work up the Perth Road or one of those places, sometimes in a private house and sometimes in the Infirmary. You didn't get much as a cleaner in those days, so she had to kind of work all day and Mummy spent all her time in those gloomy streets, I suppose, skipping and playing peevers and all that with Ina and Sheila, and Elspeth and Jean and Cathie and Norma and all. Mummy never talked of it exactly but little things came out when she was plastered. They lived in two or three rooms up eighty-nine steps, and some people thought they did too well. There were ten people in one room below. And there was an old creepy man opposite, he smelt like a cat, or his room did. I don't know. Anyway he used to give Mummy jube-jubes and watch her until she ate them. He always watched her until she swallowed them right down. Mummy, when she was drunk, you know, whether it was to the dogs or Macdonald or me, she always used to give a great sweep of her hand and say, "You don't know very much."

'It's an awful story really, but it explains so much. I'm sure if things had gone the other way she'd have been so different. She'd got,' she clenched her fists here, 'she'd got a sort of passion. Did you notice that when you met her?'

But David did not reply and Mary went on in a lower, steadier tone.

'Mummy had a brother. My uncle, I suppose, if he'd lived, and that's actually where Pink gets the Arbuthnot. I know it sounds funny but they called him Arbuthnot, and my grandmother absolutely worshipped him. She couldn't see past him and he was delicate. Maybe that's why she was so fond of him. Worse than delicate. He had fits. He was epileptic or whatever they call it. Isn't it awful how life works? Get landed with a no-good husband and no money in a tenement in Dundee and you bet your son's an epileptic. And this wasn't all that long ago. That's what makes it more frightening. They had the whole works in the tenement.

'But it wasn't fits Arbuthnot died of. I don't think you do die that way, do you? Not unless you smother? He was evidently a terribly complicated, tidy sort of boy. It's too awful really, it makes me laugh. Pink does a splendid imitation of the scene. There was a bucket, you see. Uncle Arbuthnot was so tidy . . .'

She broke off and laughed. Then she clenched her fists.

'God please don't let me laugh,' she said. 'Please. I promise I don't really think it's funny. If I'm laughing when the wind changes perhaps I'll die of hiccoughs like that queen.'

She diverged for a few seconds, perhaps to gain control of herself.

She said, 'It's like a woman in the village, Bank Lizzy, in her new car, only last winter, in the snow. She wasn't very good with this car and she ran over the village cripple. That's bad enough, but then the poor dear panicked and instead of putting on the brake and getting out she jammed the thing into reverse and by mistake,' she began to laugh again. 'Bumpety-bump,' she cried and leant back with tears of laughter forming in her eyes. '. . . she went straight back over him and finished him off.'

She shook her head. 'When Pink and I are really blue we always think of that.'

She shifted her seat along a desk, toward David and asked for a cigarette. She smoked very ineptly, like a schoolgirl.

'Anyway,' she said, as she always did, resuming the tale. 'This poor Arbuthnot boy decided things were a bit much for him. One's been sixteen, but not in a tenement. One hardly blames him. So one afternoon he slits his wrists, only he does it very methodically,

33   HG—C

getting on to his bed, and holding the wrist over the bucket. Appalling, really. But there it is, and Mummy came up the eighty-nine steps back from school, or Salvation Army or Ina or Sheila or whatever it was she was doing—walks into the house and calls his name. She was about eleven, yes, just eleven. She hears nothing, but a moment later there's a clanking next door, and a groan.'

She had stopped laughing now. She looked quite pale.

'I mustn't go too quickly,' she said. 'I must get it right. . . . The first thing is that the boy has changed his mind and he's trying to stop the blood coming. In doing so he's knocked over the bucket which was about half full of blood, and oddly enough what strength he does have seems directed against the fearful mess around the floor and the rug—one of those woollen rugs you make yourself, you know. . . . In the space of two seconds Mummy's out the door again and across the gallery to the body 'lives next door. But they're all out working, the women at the Perth Road or Broughty Ferry, and old jube-jube and the rest at the jute or the ships. . . . Some of them worked on the railways, there. Well, by the time Mummy's tried some doors, and got no reply—"Open . . . P.N." for another reason, then—she sees she must go back herself. He has righted the bucket which is filling with red again. In doing so everything has got covered with blood. And he's dead.

'Now Mummy's got two hours before her mother's back. And what's so odd about life is that of course because her mother adored Arbuthnot, Mummy worshipped her mother. And she knew it would break her heart if her mother learnt how the boy had died. She's got two hours——

'She starts with the bucket. Then Arbuthnot. She heaves him until he's face downwards on the bed. Then with a big wet clout from the kitchen she starts on the floor, the chest of drawers, the wall, even the window pane. She's not sick—she's sweating. There's less than an hour to go. Downstairs she runs—"I'll play with you later, Sheila, Ina, Elspeth, Jean, Cathie and Norma, I'm in a hurry now!" Up comes the doctor, a funny kind of strip across his jacket at the back—a Norfolk jacket don't they call it? And he's quite good about things. He's worked in the tenements. He knows the family. He says nothing but plays the game, and when my grandmother came home he said it was one of the fits. "The boy's suffocated," he says, "it was a tragic accident. . . ." After that there were screams and yells, I suppose. I don't know. But anyway the whole thing was in vain, as might be expected. Of course she wanted to see her child and she found the open wrist. There are some horrid details there. She was half crazed with distress and she didn't even seem to remember Mummy's existence so the doctor did the right thing. More than that. He took Mummy home and later adopted her and all that, and that's another story, because he wasn't quite the angel he looked either. Not when Mummy grew a little older, anyway——'

David was still watching her very carefully. She suddenly stretched her neck and said:

'Oh God, now I feel awful and guilty and ashamed. I shouldn't have told you that. Mummy didn't remember half of it herself. It's only Macdonald and . . .' She frowned. 'I don't know why I told you. It's silly of me. I can't think what made me do that.'

Slowly David said, 'Are you meaning to sleep with me?'

She looked frightened.

'No. No. I don't understand.'

'Yes, you do.'

'I promise——'

He said, 'You are without exception the worst teaser that I've ever met. The ends you go to—the ornate—the——' He could not find words enough, so he leant back, saying in amazement, 'Lord help us.'

5

'It is true!' she cried. 'I promise it's true. Really, I can't think why I told you a thing like that. I'll never tell you another word of anything that matters to me——'

'I didn't say it wasn't true,' David slowly and quietly replied. 'Even if you expected me to. Your ear has recorded, even if you firmly reject another quite different comment which I made.'

'I heard it,' she said, on the move again, 'and it doesn't make sense. "Ear has recorded" and "rejecting"—God, if you knew how I hated the way you spoke you'd never say another word to me! That's if you loved me, which I don't suppose you do.'

She steadied and looked straight at his face. 'David, I promise it's true. Maybe not all the details. I've thought of it so often; so often I have to laugh about it, don't you see?'

'But you're still at work,' he said. 'It's perfectly amazing.'

She frowned deeply. 'You mean about teasing? I don't think I understand what you said. I never touched you at all—not today, I mean, and I was going to say about yesterday. I'd forgotten that. You must let me explain——'

'You've prepared a statement?'

'Don't look like that. Don't talk sarcastically.' Suddenly she spoke more slowly. 'Nobody likes sarcastic talk, you funny, ugly little man.'

'Help,' he said and shook his head.

'Why d'you say that?'

'I'm exhausted. Exhausted by your dishonesty——'

'But I told you, I swear——'

'Not your lies—if they were lies, I don't know about that. But by your dishonesty.'

She picked up another sandwich and seemed to try to collect her thoughts together, before he spoke again. There were rival noises in the distance now. Against the thumping from the gym there were odd phrases of songs being sung by some of the more cheerful farmers and locals, Pink's chums from the Queen's bar, who had encamped themselves in the classroom next door.

Mary said, 'They sound cheerful enough,' and she looked around the classroom as if she were a little amazed to find herself there. 'God knows what's happened to everybody else. I suppose they're wondering what's happened to us.' Her mind seemed to be flitting along like a fly on the surface of the water, as if she were very tired or had just woken up. She made no effort to leave.

'Some details may not be right,' she said. 'One had to piece the story together from shouts in the night, other things Macdonald has heard. Mind you, nobody else knows this. They don't even know Mummy was adopted. But I only told you because——'

'Because?' he asked. 'I'm very interested in this.'

'Because you said I was being unfair to Mummy.'

'It seems an odd sort of way to answer the charge——'

'No,' she said. 'I just told you. I don't have to pretend she's something she wasn't—not at all, she was pathetic, she drank, she gave up, she wasn't very pretty any more but if we'd had that life we'd be a bit battered too. I mean, after all that, just when she thought she was safe there was the card game too—you know, the scandal.'

'I think I remember this one,' he said.

'Oh, you must. If you lived there you must remember. It's the only thing people know about the Fergusons.'

She turned away from him again and he said:

'Remind me of the details.'

'Oh, they're not known exactly.'

'In outline.'

'Well, I shan't say whether Daddy was the scapegoat or not. Obviously I have an opinion. Let's leave that aside. Either way the result's the same as far as we're concerned. Instead of being in London in some stuffy house in Chester Square or something like that, here we are on our lovely farm. I don't complain about that. But it's true enough.'

'Facts,' David gently suggested.

'Not very original really,' she said, gliding across the room. 'A country house. Ascot I think it was. A lot of smart people. Daddy was in the Guards, you know. Well, there was one person there much smarter than the rest. There was evidently some sort of trouble. Anyway the men played cards half the night and argued what to do about the fact that somebody had cheated, for the rest of the night. Rumour has it that it wasn't Daddy who did cheat, but Daddy certainly took the rap. The very next day, you know, he resigned from his clubs.'

'What a dreadful hardship,' David said.

'Oh I know——' she said quickly. 'We're marvellously lucky really. Nobody cares up here. Nobody at all. Not in our generation anyway.'

'And in mine?'

'Oh, don't be so silly, you're not as old as all that. No, you mustn't get the idea that I'm complaining about things. And of course to us cheating at cards sounds such a little thing. I'd do it like mad, I'm sure——'

'I'm sure,' he agreed.

She went on, 'Resigning from clubs and all that. It's all terribly grand, but in those days, you know——'

He interrupted, 'D'you not think it's perhaps a little too grand?'

'I don't understand you.' She seemed alarmed again.

'I actually do remember this story. . . . I mean both the one you're telling and what was told at the time.'

'Oh yes?' very slowly.

'Yes. I can't remember why I learnt. I don't honestly believe that people were sufficiently interested——'

'Everybody knows the Ferguson scandal,' she replied firmly.

'I'm sure you're right. I wonder who could have told them?' He smiled. 'I confess I'd never thought of it in quite the same way as you. I didn't think the operation had quite the scale to merit the word scandal. What we gathered was that your father used to make quite a habit of gambling, even soon after he was married, and your mother put her foot down. It was one of several things of that nature. But she used to ring him at his club. I believe it was one of the St. James's Clubs. It was said, jokingly, I believe——'

'I don't think you've got it right.'

He persisted. 'Purely as a local joke, that your mother brought him north because he spent so much time in his club, playing bridge. I don't remember any suggestion of cheating.'

'Of course there was cheating. That was the whole point. And as a matter of fact,' she added, 'Daddy did cheat. He's wonderful, Daddy, really.' She snapped her fingers. 'He doesn't care that for what anybody says. Never did.'

David shrugged. 'I only tell it as I remember it. You may be right.'

'I am.'

'I didn't know your parents, myself. But I remember the farm being pointed out to me. That's when the joke came up. I remember it quite clearly because it was one of the most human jokes my father ever told me. And I remember my mother enjoying it enormously and pretending to be rather shocked.' He added, 'It doesn't really matter, you know.'

'Of course it matters. I know exactly what you're thinking. That I'm untruthful.'

'I think you may get muddled. There was quite a famous case called Tranby Croft, but that was at the turn of the century, I believe——'

'Of course I've heard of that,' she said, her colour rising. 'And

I don't muddle it a bit. In fact usually when I'm telling the story I mention Tranby Croft. The circumstances were quite extraordinarily similar—a different guest of honour—you know?' The way she added 'you know' with a childish haughtiness made it clear that he had caught her and he suddenly looked sad, too. He sat down on one of the desks and reached out both hands to her. If one suspects one's best friend of pinching things, there is, after all, no satisfaction in finding out that one's suspicions were well founded. She stood biting her lip, refusing, shaking her head.

'It doesn't matter,' he said very kindly. She came near enough for him to be able to reach forward and touch her only with his fingertips. Rather moodily, still with a deep frown she banged her hip again and again against one of the desks. She looked at him solemnly and bitterly. She was not afraid to meet his eye. He said, again:

'It doesn't matter a bit. And I won't tell anybody.'

She continued to stare at him.

He went on, 'But you ought to know why you did it. Why you exaggerated. Let's put it kindly—the Ferguson scandal and maybe the Dundee——'

'No,' she said. 'Not Dundee. That one's sacred. That's quite a different thing. Really it is. I confess the Ferguson scandal thing —it's a bit of a fib. Not really all fib. One's forgotten just quite what's right and what's wrong about it. Pink and I had lots of versions, once. Some better than others. But it doesn't do any harm. People like a good story. It brightens their lives.'

'Go on.'

'You know too much, don't you?' She looked at him, for a second, as if she had loved him for a thousand years.

'No,' he shook his head. 'I haven't said your story-telling didn't work. On the contrary, you'll remember that the basis of my complaint is that it works too well, if you don't mean to go through with it.'

'Did I tell you these stories just to make myself more attractive? Is that what you think?'

He nodded.

She laughed suddenly, and touched the ink-well again. 'Isn't that clever of me?' she said. 'You may be right. I'm amazed. I must say it would be nice to have you around, as a friend, cousin-style. We could employ you as a kind of fortune teller. Pink would love that too.'

She moved quickly away, laughing rather loudly while he sat still. But as she suggested, 'I think it's high time we went back,' and walked towards the classroom door, he said:

'Stop.'

She turned and actually arched an eyebrow in a little pose of dignified surprise.

He shook his head and rubbed his eyes, saying:

'I shall never learn. It doesn't pay to tell the truth. But I promise I'm not going to tell anybody. You don't need to feel guilt or shame——'

'Over fibbing about something that happened thirty years ago? Don't be so silly, David. I'm hardly likely to feel guilty about that. I am a woman, after all. Anyway, a girl. And they're allowed little lies.'

'Only when they know they're telling them. That's a very important point.' He smiled again as he raised a finger of warning and she returned his smile with real warmth. She came back into the room a few steps.

She said, 'I daren't approach more than this, else you'll go all grim again and call me obscene names and charge up and down, scratching your head to find new ways of making me feel small.'

He shook his head.

'Am I as bad as that?'

She said, 'You do seem to like knocking me about a bit.'

'No.' He shook his head.

She replied, 'Yes, you do. You're a kind of schoolmaster at heart. No, honestly, I'm saying something nice. Will you go up there and pick up Kennedy's *Latin Primer* and read me a bit?'

'If you want.'

'No, don't,' she replied quickly. 'That was a silly idea. David, don't bark at me and don't call me that other hateful thing even if you think it, because if I am what you said I am, then I honestly don't think I can help it very much.'

'Who's getting complicated now?'

'It's a plague,' she said. 'You should hear Pink try and tell someone how he feels. It always comes out backside foremost. David,

I was going to ask. We were having a love scene, weren't we? Just now, I mean, not just for the last minute or two. Even when I was telling you about poor Mummy.' She looked at her watch. 'God, we must go through.'

'That's what I was trying to tell you,' he said. 'You put it much more nicely. At least I know that I'm making love.'

'When you're cross-examining me? That's very modern living. Look, I won't make a speech, David. I'd got a little speech ready. About yesterday.'

'I could see that.'

'You tell me, then, what I was going to say.'

He thought and smiled slowly, then he spoke on her behalf.

' "Look, David, about yesterday. I don't want you to misunderstand. I'm not sorry that I said 'no'. I'm just sorry that I didn't say 'no' much sooner. I don't mean just yesterday afternoon. Not just in the car. I mean in London. From the very start." ' He laughed, pleased with his own performance, then grew more serious as he saw that there were tears in her eyes.

She said, 'But it's exactly . . . Darling David, do you know everything about me, as easily as that?'

'No,' he said thoughtfully, and he did not move towards her. She stared at him as she spoke.

'Anyway, I've made up my mind—it is "no". Because? Well, because it is, darling.' He still did not move, and she went on, 'But you've every right to bawl me out. I know that's why I hated the word as much as I did. I did encourage you and then said "no". It was a very bad thing to do. Please forgive me for that.'

He said, 'It happens quite often. I wouldn't feel too badly about it. In fact it always happens. It's just a question of how long you go on doing it. Beyond certain limits it slips from good technique to bad judgment, bad taste and then crime.'

She looked at him solemnly.

'David, am I doing it now?'

'Yes,' he replied.

'Yes, I thought I was,' she said. And turning quickly, she ran out of the room. As she did so, Peebles, the singing farmer, was returning to the gym with his friend. He was saying:

'I've been told on the highest authority that if I'd got the professional attention when I was younger I could have made my living that way. It was a conductor told me that. He said to me, "You have some remarkable pure tenor notes." He said that.'

6

As soon as Mary re-entered the gymnasium, which, in Pink's words, now smelt strongly of what your best friend won't tell you, she realized that she had stayed in Classroom IV too long. The group round the Ferguson table by the door had that particular look of indecision which follows some minor calamity. Macdonald was standing by the table staring in the direction of the band and alongside, her boy-friend the tiny Captain, Jack Gordon, M.C., R.A.M.C. (Retd.), who looked like a sick Mr. Esquire, was joking as he picked a green pill from his silver snuff-box.

'May I offer any one of you one of these anti-coagulatory pills given to me by the kind services of that bloody awful organization the National Health Service?' he asked, but Mary, as always, brushed him aside. Stephen was sitting back in the chair drinking some white wine and the blank expression on his face betrayed that he was up to his usual trick of contracting out of a scene. He was looking at Pink, but at the same time ignoring him.

Pink, meantime, was stuttering and sucking in air. Whenever he had words with his father there appeared an impediment less in his speech than in his brain. He was saying:

'Not just sitting in front of the nursery fire! Oh no! Not right! Fact.' He twisted his head in a little circle. 'Not the whole truth. Absolutely not.' He assumed a mysterious smile. 'No question of sitting-sickness these days. I may hang on a bit in the nursery alone, sometimes, you follow, but—but not just sitting. You may be very surprised. Things have changed. Pink's got pink plans. You may be very surprised indeed. I've come to my senses.'

To which Mary said, almost under her breath:

'Oh God. Guv'nor stuff,' and she meant that there must have been a row between Pink and her father. She looked at Macdonald. 'Right?'

Macdonald nodded but Pink interrupted again.

'Nothing to it, Nelly,' he said to Mary. 'Just a little ruffling of

42

the old feathers. I was trying to tell him to cheer up, it wasn't such a bad hop, he seemed to be a bit snobbish about it. You know what he is. He suggested rather snobbishly that it might suit me. Said it suited him too that I should hang on here as it would save me sitting up all night in the nursery drinking his booze.'

'Is that all?' Mary asked.

'More or less, old flesh.' Pink took a little drink. 'When I offered to buy him a bottle he said it was the sitting, not the whisky, that offended him. Then he pushed off.'

Macdonald said, 'It was just this minute,' and Mary ran into the hall. She caught her father on the steps. He wore a perfectly cut, rather gay dog's-tooth check coat over his dinner-jacket. He looked round with his usual blank, blue-eyed, flat-eyed stare when somebody said:

'You're being called, Sir Harry,' but he smiled at once when he saw that it was Mary.

She said, 'Darling, you're not huffing, not on my account? I couldn't bear that.'

He stopped with one foot a step higher than the other. He had a royal knack of pose. He smiled very slowly and kindly and took both her hands.

'I wouldn't dream of it.'

'Then do come back.'

He shook his head. He said, 'I've had the one dance I wanted,' referring, of course, to their dance. 'I'd only look what you call stony.'

'You'd still look the best.'

'Bed-time for old bones,' he said, plonking a tweed hat on his head. He always looked brown.

'Daddy, did you snap at Pink?'

'Snap?' He frowned, seemed puzzled. 'Not that I know.'

'He's a bit hectic.'

The Colonel shrugged. 'Well, then he's being too idiotic.'

He kissed her and moved off, careless of the others' transport problems, intending to take the family car.

The cars were parked in the school's ashcourt or playground, and when he arrived at his he found that it would be awkward if not impossible to reverse out. He stood for a moment, staring at it, and he did not turn round when one of the social secretaries of the

43

Young Conservatives, a boy called Alec, with long fair hair, suede shoes and enthusiastic manners came dashing out.

'This'll never do, Sir Harry. I'll just move Mr. Scott's car, here, and that'll let you out.'

The Colonel did not smile. He looked faintly surprised as he said:

'That's extremely kind of you.'

It was somehow never necessary for him to say thank-you.

*　　*　　*

Much as the business man blames himself unnecessarily for the deal that's fallen through, if he spends an afternoon with a tart, so Mary, tight-lipped and clenched fist, blamed herself as she returned to Pink and Stephen. Macdonald and the Captain were by then having what they called 'a difference' by the bar at the end of the room. ('My dear Flora, my dear girl . . .' the Captain said, again and again.)

Pink was still shaking his head and talking mysteriously and secretively of a public relations firm which he and some connection of a neighbouring family were going to set up in Montreal, or maybe Sydney. He had dark plans, but they rather petered out when Mary returned.

The hiatus that followed was suddenly, swiftly broken by Mary. She pulled in her chair and seeing David over by the bar she turned her back on him, firmly. She talked to Pink with her special kind of excited innocence; as if unbroken conversation would keep the bogey-man away. Stephen examined the label of the hock bottle throughout her next outburst, as if it had as much written on it as the label pasted on those tiny bottles of Angostura bitters.

'There's the most fascinating thing going on in Classroom III.' She drummed her fingers on the table in front of her and then quickly continued:

'It's all your chums, Pink. You're really missing something. They're all in Classroom III sticking pins into the effigy of David's papa. You know they're all his pupils, practically all of them, any-way——'

As she ran on, naming the group, Maclaren, Miller, Peebles, Davidson and all the rest, a sad smile passed across Pink's face.

44

'I promise. Honestly,' she said, which Pink knew to be the mark of pure fiction, then she went back to her story.

'All of them, about ten or twelve, and I couldn't quite see whether one was pretending to be old Dowie or not—they probably just imagined him.'

The music seemed loud as a new dance began. It was a dance called Hamilton House, which begins with the girl setting to one man, as if to dance with him, then quickly passing to the next and turning him. The girls were all enjoying it and some of the younger ones put great spirit into the rejection of the first man, twisting their heads away or even flicking their fingers in the first man's face before grasping the hands of the next.

Mary still talked.

'I honestly don't think there was anybody up there actually imitating him, but they were all acting as if they were back at school. I was riveted.' The heels of her hands banging against the table seemed to say 'It'll be all right, Pink, it'll be all right. Forget his bullying.' She ran on, as Pink covered his face with his hands.

'Can you imagine all the lads squeezed into desks, half of them laughing and poor old Bill Davidson [the proprietor of the Queen's], he'd fallen fast asleep at the back. They were shouting at him to wake up at the back and old Baldy Maclaren was standing up in his desk waving his arm about, asking the ghost of Dowie if he might be excused. He was quite funny, I must say, going "Please, please sir", flicking his fingers too.' She spoke more and more swiftly. 'Some of them were imitating Old Dowie too. And wee Peter Forbes was shouting the most of all. All glowing and red, the way he gets, though I must say he's kept his figure better than the others have, and he must be over fifty now. He's shouting at the top of his voice, "Aye, and I still feel the strap across my palm. I do. 'Peter Forbes, you're dunce!' Wham! 'You'll no do any good in this world or the next.' Aye and here's me," Peter shouts, "And the mill's never done better and that's a fact. It's me that's done it! Three thousand a year I make! Three thousand pounds and expenses on top of that! Bloody old Dowie! Bloody old man!" He was shaking his fist quite violently.'

She smiled brightly as she finished her story.

'Aren't men so silly when they get drunk? Especially the little ones. They get so aggressive. You must have heard Peter Forbes.

You must have heard him when he's drunk. Pink, darling, you're not sobbing really. And Peebles, too, going on about his tenor voice——'

But Pink had recovered. He dropped his hands and opened his mouth in what almost appeared to be a cartoon of a toothless, noiseless laugh. Then he laid his hand on the top of Mary's head and said cheerfully:

'As a matter of fact, kid, I confirm you as a member of God's Holy Church.'

'I do love Pink.'

Not very long after that, the band leader played the first bars of 'The Dashing White Sergeant'.

Mary said, 'Isn't that perfect? Just right for three sparrows on a wire,' and Stephen put down the bottle.

'Are you dancing, Belle?' Pink asked and Mary gave a skittish little giggle, as Belle.

She said, 'That's a fact. We'd better bring hubby too.'

Mary seemed prepared, as they moved to the floor, to ignore David. But Stephen was polite to him. He said, very pleasantly:

'Sit down at our table. There's lots of room.'

Mary looked at her husband furiously. As they moved into their first circle she said, 'That's a bloody silly thing to do.'

7

Cousin, d'you remember? All three of us felt badly about it, I'm sure. There were some sticky moments, at that corner table, after your Dashing White Sergeant and before poor Captain Jack Gordon diverted us.

Even the atmosphere had changed. It was vaguely Teutonic, when the squeeze-box man came down from the stand. All your Young Conservative friends tried to yodel. In my mind the scene is marked as a notable chapter in Scotland's war against taste. Burns had given way to Lehar. Somebody lowered the lights to that particular degree of dimness which makes the younger girls (and a few of your Auntie Belles) scream, yet fail to lose their inhibitions.

I remember your face, white, and your eyes looking darker than

46

I'd ever seen them as you hung on to Stephen, pushing your face against his arm. When you did look at me it was with hatred. Or is that quite accurate? With something resembling hatred, something a little sulkier. I can't get nearer it than that. And remembering it now, in a bright neon-lit laboratory, it's like something out of a dream. It was as if we were in a huge, unhaunted night club on the outskirts of Berlin. The wooden beams and the music lead me to Germany. The square mirror, the instruments in the corner and the giant nooses above added a macabre touch to excite the macabre; these take me to Hamburg or Berlin.

How did it start? I can't remember. Perhaps talking about Pink who had gone to join the Queen's bar cronies in that other classroom. Yes. Stephen mystified me, I remember now, with some reference to the antics in that classroom: something about their imitating my father, his former pupils abusing him, now that he was safely dead and buried. But of course, not having heard the story you wove for Pink, I was lost.

I remember your bracelet fell down your wrist as you watched the dancers creeping round, most of them, rolling Hunt Ball-Night Club style. You weren't drinking whisky any more. That added another German touch. Lager, now. You leant your head back until your hair pushed against the climbing bars, and there were dark shadows under your eyes, giving you, rather alarmingly, and suddenly, a great deal more sex. You blew some cigarette smoke that had drifted close to your eyes and then cut into our conversation, saying to Stephen, not to me (nothing was addressed directly to me), 'I made the story up. More or less.' You said it with a sort of shamelessness that added, perhaps you knew, to the sex. Before we said anything you ran on, 'I am rather worried about Daddy. Perhaps he was huffing because I was away so long.'

Then you twisted back to the classroom story. It was typical Mary.

'I just said it to keep old Pink afloat.' You never smiled. Then you said, 'David didn't rape me or anything like that.'

'That wasn't going through my head.' Stephen, on the other hand, smiled kindly at you.

'Prop me,' you said, and leant against him. He put an arm behind you and played with the back of your hair.

Two, three years ago?

I can't have taken my eyes away from you. I can live every second again. But I was already beginning the game I played so mercilessly for six months, pressing you for answers to the unanswerable. Stephen rather took my part, I remember, as we tried to examine what had made you make up the particular story about the Queen's bar gentlemen. You were not to be provoked. You shrugged and answered, looking into the lager glass:

'Even *my* nose is too small to get into this thing. I wonder what proper craggy Scotsmen do.' You looked at Stephen then, at his thin pointed nose and at my pugilist's job. 'You two are no good,' you said.

Gently, I remember coming in. 'Let's take that other story you told me about your mother,' I saw your grip tighten on Stephen's arm.

'He only does it to annoy,' you said lightly, but Stephen, oddly, was solidly on my side then, falling over himself to be generous to me, and friendly and fair.

'Answer the gentleman,' he said. 'Tell him what's true about all the stories you've spun him.'

Silence from you. A little superior laugh from me. I said:

'Come on, it's only a point of interest,' and you lifted your eyes to me then. It was not hatred. That is the wrong word. It was a sort of self-hatred. And yet an invitation of a sluttish kind. Then you sat up and pushing a finger into Stephen's cheek, you said, a fraction louder:

'I didn't tell any more stories. I hepped up the gambling thing a little, but I don't think that was such a bad thing to do.' To Stephen you said with a smile, 'I served him Tranby Croft.'

'Why do you do it?' Stephen asked. The lights grew lighter and then dimmer. I suppose some young farmer had found and could not resist the running control. The brown suits and green frocks were having their own back on the Hunt Ball-Night Club crawl. With Scottish accents they were singing Lili Marlene.

'If David was anything of a friend he'd go and fish out Pink, else he'll get sick drunk.'

Stephen said at once, 'I'll get him, darling.'

A shake of your head. You said:

'No, really,' as he began to move, then 'No' again, much louder.

'But it won't take a minute,' he said.

'No, please,' clenching your fists round his sleeve. 'Stay here.'
We knew by then, all three of us: of course we did. You looked
at me once again, I remember, when Stephen described your
mother as respectable Dundee jute. Silver teapot, I think he said,
and what are those paper serviettes called? Doyles or something
like that. It hardly fitted with the buckets of blood in the tenement
but I let another lie pass. I was playing the old dog's games now.
I did not even have the subtlety to bully you. Just looked at your
mouth. All the time Stephen talked coolly and disinterestedly as if
he were a little embarrassed that you should hug his arm so tightly
and press your head against his chest. You brushed your cheek
along the black cloth, from time to time.

Stephen, with prefect's authority now, put us right about the
Ferguson scandal. I don't suppose I listened to a word at the time
but it must have been a very important scene, this one. I only have
to close my eyes, and listen, and I can play him back. He smoked
rather elegantly as he talked of your mother.

'Pregnant at the time,' he said, and I remember your blink of
distaste at the phrase that followed. 'Carrying Pink.' Once or twice
you tried to stop him. I think you were always frightened of Stephen
being a bore. You tugged, but it made no difference. He did not
talk so quickly or irrationally as you so often did, distant cousin,
but he talked for the same reason. Talk takes the edge off a scene.
So long as conversation is suspended one can ignore the cave-man
stuff going on beneath. 'That makes it about 1926——' he went
on. 'For whatever reason the Colonel had started going back to
some of his bachelor habits and he was in one of the smarter jobs,
White's or Buck's or Boodle's or Pratt's, or one of those, when
Mona kept ringing him up to get him home; she became tearful
and evidently quite obsessional about his club life, nobody can quite
explain why. It got to the stage when she rang the club about every
five minutes and then she arrived in a taxi. There followed a scene
which sounds pretty farcical, whereby she was bundled out of the
place, weeping and yelling, but the Colonel evidently didn't think
this was such a joke. There's a missing link here, but it seems that
his friends and acquaintances behaved rather cruelly. They were all
very bright sort of men, most of them fairly idle, and one assumes
they must have teased the life out of him. Anyway, rather obstinately, and certainly very stupidly, as he had a huge future in front

of him—he was a colonel at thirty-three, after all—he tried to get his own back at cards. He cheated. It was discovered.'

At that, you interrupted sharply. Lifted your head to say, violently, 'He didn't care if he were discovered! That's the whole point. He doesn't care what anybody says. He's marvellous like that!'

Stephen ignored you again. He seemed to consider your outburst understandable but inaccurate. He went on, smoothly, as before:

'I fancy the other men would have done nothing about it but he felt he'd let himself down, he lost confidence, resigned from the club, resigned his commission, sold the Knightsbridge house—the whole lot. To Mona, from Dundee—and she'd done pretty well, for jute from Dundee—all this meant an end to a dream. Anyway, she was a nervous sort of type—rather plump. They came back and bought the farm and the family's been here ever since——'

I couldn't be bothered to tell him the story didn't fit together. Colonels aged thirty-three don't cheat at cards because their wives kick up a row at the club door. It's good for prestige to have a woman howling up and down St. James's, crying 'Bring him out'.

But the silence had to be broken. It was you, at last, speaking sleepily.

'Now he knows I'm a bloody liar. But some of the things I said were true. Mummy was adopted, you know. That's the point. Honestly.'

'Oh darling——' Stephen warned you.

'Yes, she bloody well was.' You spoke into his face and he betrayed you with an easy smile, saying:

'Yes, of course she was.' Then he laughed and patted you. 'Pappa understands,' he said, and to me, almost as if he were selling you, 'She's a remarkable little woman, my wife.'

'Christ,' right under your breath.

Even the music had stopped. People were shuffling about. Dishonest you were, cousin, but the least dishonest of the three of us. You sat yourself up to say, 'I'm in a cold sweat. I feel horrid and old.'

Then you took your handbag and said, 'Don't follow me, Steve darling. I'm hopping it to the loo.'

He knew as well as I did that you said that to me. Everybody knew everybody knew. That's why we all felt sick.

8

Pink was not the first to see Captain Gordon lumbered in the Gentlemen's lavatory, but because, in a mild sort of way, he was extremely observant, he took a good look and noticed a detail was wrong. Captain Gordon was sitting in one of the cubicles, with the door wide open. His elbows were on his knees and his head was in his hands.

Pink said, hesitantly and politely, 'Old knob, I'd take your trousers off,' and Captain Gordon swayed unhappily from side to side. He looked up and opened his mouth, once or twice, like a salmon on a rock. His collar was undone.

'Pissed, old chap?' Pink asked kindly, and perhaps because the Captain shook his head Pink said 'Never mind'. He then looked around, and seeing a sort of refuse bin, not quite as big as a dustbin and with a lid that opened by pressing a foot pedal, he dragged that across to the door of the cubicle and there, more or less comfortable, he sat down. 'As a matter of fact,' he said, banging his knuckles against the bin a couple of times, 'I'm fit for the human scrap-heap myself.'

Gusts of noise, of music and of laughter came from the corridors, the classrooms and the gym. They were like two boys in the sick-room, kind of poignantly out of things. It was doubtful if the Captain knew what it was all about. He seemed to have lost his knack for his semaphore of winks, belches and rubber faces, or at least the energy needed for its execution. When at last he did answer Pink he applied one of these Scotticisms, which mean nothing but which have a use. They keep friends along the bar from falling fast asleep, and save grandmother in the parlour, on a Sunday afternoon, from dissolving into tears. The one he used translates approximately as 'life is a labour', but curiously enough is seldom exchanged between men at work.

He said, 'It's an awful trachle.'

Pink, apparently delighted to get a reply, as the Captain's heavy breathing had been beginning to upset him, knew exactly the sort of thing to say to this. A thousand crawling hours at the bar of the Queen's made him answer, without hesitation:

'Absolutely, old man. But then the fun's in the ficht.'

'D'you think my collar was too tight?' the Captain asked. He referred to the pills he had to take, when he added, in a hurt voice, 'I took my coagulation Johnnies. I didn't forget.'

Pink said, 'I hate these bloody collars. You want to wear a soft job like this.'

'Yours looks tight.'

Pink did not like the idea that he was, weekly, growing fatter. 'Not a bit, old man,' he said huffily, 'perfectly all right.' Then added, 'They always shrink things in the laundry. And, by God, the price.'

'It was mixing drinks, I think,' the Captain said, recovering a little. 'Jack Gordon's all right. I hope.'

'Could be,' Pink said, pensively. 'Grain and grape.'

'I'm sure that's what it was,' the Captain replied. And then, *non sequitur*: 'I remember fine, at Territorial camp, it must have been 1913, anno domini, September I think. There was a big camp over Crieff way; I fainted that night. Now I couldn't have been more than seventeen then. I was a sprinter too. I was nimble on my feet. It happens sometimes, with people. In adolescence too. Fainting, like that.' He breathed noisily and shortly, two or three times.

'Good Lord, yes,' Pink said. 'You bet. There's a chum in my house at school, Blinkers somebody. We used to make a book on which Collect it would be. "Lighten our darkness, we beseech Thee, O Lord" used to crack him most times. Real Blinkers' Beechers. "Lord have mercy upon us".'

'Christ have mercy upon us.'

' "Lord have mercy upon us" and bonk, there's old Blinkers hooped over the stall in front, like a rag doll. Out for the count. As much as twenty-five bob would slip through from the first treble to the altos. It whiled away the time,' he said.

'I'm Episcopalian,' the Captain said, swallowing.

'There's more music,' Pink said. 'Am I right, old man?' But the scenes from his schooldays demanded his attention. He said, in the pause that followed, 'Old Blinkers' eyes used to shoot up before he went. I remember the whites of them. We didn't like him for it, you know, poor chum.'

The Captain rested his elbows on his knees again. He dropped his head for a second, then lifting it again, he said, with a curious, uncertain little smile:

'You panic, you know. Anything to do with breath. I was a doctor, I should know. It's not that there's real danger. . . . I still go to the kirk.'

'Good for you,' Pink said. 'It's good for the—it keeps the thing together.'

'I haven't the same faith, you know. Not now.'

'Not?'

'No. You'd think someone's been to death's door. I've been to death's door. I do not joke, Charles. You'd think it would go the other way. It's not what's happened to Jack Gordon. My mother was a great believer, a hat on every Sunday morning and down the road—I've always been to the kirk. And now, mind, at the eleventh hour. I don't hear a peep. No angels' trumpets——'

The look in his eye was one of blank fear.

Pink said affably, 'You're still this side of the door, what?'

'I know it——' The Captain spread out his hands. He seemed bewildered in a curiously practical sort of fashion. It did not look as if he were saying that his most fundamental beliefs had crumbled. He resembled a man who had been done out of some money. Seeing his face and hands alone, Pink would have imagined that he were saying, 'I've known this man Moo for years: I've been in there to put a bet on every Saturday, regularly. And here, he says to me, no ticket, Captain Gordon, no divvy.' His smile broadened, and froze on his face. In a tiny voice, he went on, about himself:

'It's the other way about with Jack Gordon. There's just nothing. I can't explain it more than that, Charles. A kind o' tidal wave of nothing coming hellish fast.' He said 'fast' with a very short 'a'.

After a pause, Pink said, 'I never was much of a God-botherer myself, old chum.'

The Captain looked at him again. It was difficult to know whether he was anxious to find out if he had got his point across, or whether he wanted Pink to find some sort of comfort for him.

'Mind,' the Captain said at last, 'it wasn't always like this. I was at Passchendaele, and——' He looked at Pink uncertainly. 'You've heard of Passchendaele?'

'Absolutely,' Pink answered him. 'It's in the book. Part of the myth for me. Don't you worry, chum. A kind of Golgotha for me.'

The Captain frowned. 'I wasn't there,' he admitted, about Golgotha. 'But Passchendaele——' He managed one of his gay little whistles. 'Boy, you don't get nearer to death than that, no—and the mud? The mud! Up to here. I do not exaggerate. No. I tell my stories, maybe, but I would not exaggerate about that day. It was a week really. Mud above the knee. Some places it was higher, but to the knee was far enough for Captain Gordon, R.A.M.C., Lieutenant, as he was then.' He frowned. 'I can't remember what I thought.' He sounded frightened by his own forgetfulness. 'I can't remember it clearly now. But I'd a Bible in my pocket. I can tell you that. A photo of my mother and another of a lassie I never saw in my life. She was somebody's sister, I think. I don't remember.' He tried to pull himself together a little, but he did not have the courage to take a drink of whisky from Pink's flask. 'No, no,' he said, and paused for a long minute. 'Up to the knees!' he repeated, and then added vaguely, 'My knees are awful cold now.' More firmly he continued:

'When we got there, Jerry's machine-gun——' He relapsed into semaphore to mark a thousand of his countrymen dead. He put his hand flat on his forehead. 'When we got there the boys had no fight left in them.' His eyes suddenly filled with tears. 'Oh my goodness me,' he said. He brushed his forehead with the sleeve of his black Highland jacket and one of the sharp silver buttons scratched his cheek, but he did not seem to notice it. He put the cloth to his nose again.

He said, 'This thing smells of moth balls. It's most unpleasant. That's my dotter's doing. And I don't think you get moths in a caravan at all.'

He sat back and closed his eyes and then, almost in slow motion he tipped forward, and Pink let him gently down to the floor.

'All right, old man?' Pink asked anxiously, and moved forward to help pick him up again. But he lay where he fell and Pink said to himself, out loud:

'Cheri—cheri—bim, by God. A regular thing.'

Then he went to look for John the policeman. Shouts of laughter still rang through the corridors, coming from the gym.

* * *

It was a few moments after this when Macdonald and Mary arrived. Although she had been near to tears herself when she met Macdonald, Mary now played it gay. Her laughter tinkled a little falsely as she came down the corridor, accusing Macdonald of respectability and false modesty for not having ventured into the gentlemen's lavatory and further for having refused to accost any men on their way in or out. But then she did not see herself blush and laugh gaily as she led the way into the same lavatory saying 'Good heavens! Look at those awful stalls!'

But the lavatory was by then as busy as a railway station. People were hauling the poor Captain this way and that. Around the body there were twenty pairs of legs, and six or seven people were talking at once. Somebody other than Macdonald, who came edging through, recognized that perhaps the Captain was something more than drunk, but John, who was a very young policeman, seemed determined that drunk he was, and badly confusing his duties, as he had himself drunk an illicit pint, he seemed further determined to make some moral judgments. He had his cap off and his short hair stuck upwards and outwards. His only concession to civility at this point was to name the person he was talking to as often as a comma turns up in a sentence. Each clause was punctuated by a Mr. Miller, a Miss Macdonald, or in the end, a Miss Ferguson, which anyway was incorrect, as Mary's surname was now Cameron.

Somehow or other, action continued in spite of the confusion of argument, medical advice and a general atmosphere of clumsiness and indistinct focus. The groaning Captain was lifted to his feet and Mary, with unthinking annoyance, tore a strip off John the policeman, who could not have had better intentions as he said again and again to one person or the next:

'A good evening's one thing, Mr. Hogg, but this is no' right at all, Mr. Hogg. This is the sort of thing that spoils a party. This is tantamount to public nuisance, Mr. Hogg. So it is. I'm not at all sure that it shouldn't go down in the book.'

'It's in the Book,' Pink sang to himself. 'Oyez, it's in the Book.'

A moment later a flaming argument grew up, the same points being put again and again, as John the policeman refused to let Peebles, the singing farmer, take Macdonald and the Captain home.

By then, half the dance and all the boys from Classroom III were involved, but perhaps for reasons of class as much as personality they inclined to back Mary who dictated the following course of action. If the only car big enough to take the Captain in comfort was Peebles' massive fawn Humber, then that was the car that should be used. Pink would drive it, Macdonald would go with the Captain, and John the policeman, himself, must also go to help carry the Captain from road to caravan, should this be necessary.

The Captain himself had offered only one positive note. He was not going anywhere except back to his burrow, namely the Captain's caravan. John seemed doubtful about this, but as the body of spectators were solidly behind Mary, he at last agreed. There were two amendments, or additions, to the plan. The Captain himself, with a guilty look at Macdonald, asked that Mary should come, too. Somewhat to everybody's surprise, after an important two seconds of thought (or better, forethought) Mary announced, and announced particularly plainly, that she was willing to do this. And as soon as she had said so she looked round the heads at the back of the crowd. There was no sign of David, but Stephen was there. He signalled, at once, that he had heard and understood. The other last-minute addition was that Peebles said he had a sheep-dog, named Flossy, in the back of the Humber. He was careful about the name. He said that as she was nervous he had better come along too. At last, the whole nebula of confusion gradually moved from the lavatory to the hall and then to the ashcourt. The description of the Captain's embussing would be as laborious as the procedure itself. Somehow they squeezed him in (and he was looking very ill, now), then the car drove off. By some disturbing reflex, the crowd gave a little cheer, as if it were the send-off at the end of a wedding.

In the hall, meantime, Stephen told David, who had emerged from the gym, what had happened. He added, turning away, 'Mary's gone along too.' Then at the gym door he paused, and said, 'Want a drink?'

David shook his head. For a moment he seemed about to explain himself, then he decided on a simple 'No, thanks' and with a flick of his fingers about turned and made for the room where all the coats were kept. The crowd of well-wishers sauntered back, knocking their feet against the top step, as if they were used to mud. Most of them then decided that it was long past time to go. Some looked rather angry with themselves. But the hard nucleus of the Queen's bar boys sidled back down the corridor, while the younger couples, shouting nonsenses at each other on a slightly high pitch, went back to the dance floor and tried to recapture the mood of the clinch.

But the country dance was at an end. Patchy music was provided by a rather dreamy young farmer who played the piano as if he had only one hand: the left being an automatic pump. Satisfied by this, several young couples dragged out the proceedings by dancing more or less in the dark, in front of the mirror. They swayed very slowly in their twos, looking only at those strangers, themselves.

Stephen did not stay in the hall to watch David run down the steps to his car. He returned to the gym and sat on the platform where all those girls had sat; those who were now being taken home in little cars or walked through blue, echoing streets. Stephen looked calm enough but he was then obliged to talk to one of the leading Young Conservatives, a nice boy, without looks, without money and without talent for games, dancing or sports, who for some reason spent all his time, outside the estate agent's office in which he worked, doing everything in his power to preserve, or more accurately to recreate a society in which looks, money, field sports, games and dancing would have importance. This young man affected a Highland pose, with arms crossed and one foot splay, and he enjoyed talking to Stephen. He told himself that he found Stephen sympathetic because he was one of the most intelligent young men in the district. Stephen himself thought how awful it was that he should sit discussing politics and crops with the dullest man in the area, and how inevitable. Soon he looked bored stiff.

Five or six minutes after the pianist had packed up, the couples drifted away and Stephen was in the gym alone. He sat a little while longer then, confirming that nobody else was there, he walked as far as the big square mirror. He stood for a few moments seriously considering the nice-looking dark young man in Highland dress who there confronted him, so passively. He seemed bewildered by the image's inaction under provocation; puzzled by the flatness of jealousy. Then he took a step or two forward and looked very carefully at the blue eyes almost as if, having found himself so unconfident of his sex, he felt confused about his identity.

9

The caravan was not particularly clean or comfortable, but it was tidy. The books, but for *Treasure Island* and *Journey's End*, which rested on the ledge by the bunk, were neatly clasped between a pair of stirrups which had been made into book ends. The Captain's silver hair-brushes were carefully aligned with his comb and stud box. But the final scenes of his life were played clumsily. His own appearance was pathetically untidy, and even his clipped speech deserted him, because in the end, one half of his face was paralysed.

Pink, as soon as he had helped the Captain as far as the caravan, funked it, and saying something, weakly, about Peebles' dog which had woken another at the cottage nearby, he hastened back to the car where Peebles lay snoring, sprawled half along the back seat.

Mary, when she was still shouting orders, had lost her nerve. At first, as if she were dealing with a drunk, not an invalid, she shouted to the policeman to undress him.

'We'll have him into bed and he'll be right as rain.'

She smiled uncertainly at the Captain, but he could not reply. As he arrived at the caravan he was once again gripped with a pain that went across his chest, to his shoulders, even down his arms: a hollow and burning pain. In the car he had not attempted to speak. It was the policeman who had done most of the talking. He had protested all the way that the Force was the best career, Miss Macdonald, for a man such as himself coming from a big family like he did. He had done well at the Police College. 'The Force offers the opportunities', he said as the little Captain swayed and fell against his shoulder. Macdonald was in the back of the car and she reached forward and grasped the Captain's shoulders. She spent half of the journey crying and the other half adjusting him in his seat as if he were a ventriloquist's dummy, and for a moment, until he regained balance, holding him firmly there. Rabbits' eyes shone in the headlights when they approached the river. At the sight of them Peebles' dog began to bark, and Peebles, waking from a noisy sleep, hit it on the nose.

In the caravan, Macdonald, as they began to undress the Captain, clicked her teeth at Mary and said, 'There's no need to shout.' They took off his shoes and his stockings, they unbuckled his sporran, then with difficulty undid his kilt. His legs were almost the same thickness all the way up, and white as the sheets. They took off his Highland jacket, and with his handkerchief, Macdonald dabbed the scratch on his cheek, but it was already dry. They removed his collar but they did not manage the shirt. The scene flared up for a moment as they tried. The Captain groaned in protest. He was sitting on his shirt tails and he could not lean forward and stand up. Mary said, 'Well, lift him up then,' her voice again rising to a shout. Macdonald stood back and the policeman could not manage on his own. His whole face was aglow with sweat. Mary's hands moved in sharp nervy circles. 'Go on, go on.' Effortlessly, like a baby after his bottle, the Captain was a little sick and Macdonald took his hand towel and mopped it up. The policeman had stepped back and even Mary grew silent. For a second they did not seem to be friends helping the sick, but accomplices stripping the body.

Mary said suddenly, 'Well, just leave him like that, for God's sake, it doesn't matter if he's got his shirt on.'

'He's real bad,' Macdonald said.

'He's half asleep,' Mary retorted. 'He's tired out. Of course he is.'

They laid him in his bed in his vest and his open, boiled shirt. A meticulous Highland officer to the end, the Captain wore nothing under his kilt. As he rested against the pillows the front of his shirt pushed up against his chin, and curved like a board. Macdonald pulled up the sheet and blankets.

She said, again, 'He's bad,' and Mary bit her nail.

She turned to the policeman who was putting on his cap and said:

'Don't just stand about then. Get over to the farm and use the phone.'

'Who'll I ring?' he asked, and Mary's impatience overwhelmed her. She clenched her fists as if she were going to scream. Macdonald moved back to the door of the caravan and in a low voice, like a voice from another room, she told him the numbers of the doctor and of the Captain's daughter. By the time the policeman had noted them down, the Captain had momentarily recovered enough to indicate to Mary the syringe by his bedside. There was a tiny sealed phial of morphia in the drawer beside it. With a smile, the last smile that was not crooked, he said, 'Jab.'

Mary, with an outward show of courage and appetite for action, removed the syringe from its case and shakily fitted it together. Her hands did not tremble. They were steady for a second, then leapt two or three inches at a time. She fumbled several times before she had the syringe fixed together. When she was trying to break the seal of the minute phial, because she did not understand that it was rubber to be pierced, her hand slipped again. The phial slid along the hard surface of the table and fell with a crash on the floor.

Mary cried out, then she shoved the syringe away from her.

'Oh, damn the thing,' she said, pushing her knuckles into her brow.

Macdonald, picking up the phial, saw that the contents were spilt.

The Captain said, very faintly, 'It'll not matter,' and Mary did not dare look him in the face, lest she saw pain.

Macdonald, suddenly, for personal more than practical reasons, was determined that Mary should leave them. She stood over her and said, 'There's no point in both of us staying now. You've had a day of it. I'll stay with him.'

Mary might have obeyed. She looked up at Macdonald and she did not recognize what was in her mind. She was clearly thinking 'I'm so bloody useless anyway' and that was why she was for once grateful to the Captain who sat up and protested. But again, and for a moment at least, fortunately, because it gave her confidence, she misinterpreted him. She thought he said, 'No, stay, Mary,' meaning 'I find comfort in your presence.' He did in fact say 'No, stay, Mary,' meaning 'I'd find it more difficult if you left me alone with Flora.' Even at this time, when the Captain was certain he was going to die, even in pain, although it was a little less acute now, he dreaded being left alone with the woman whose affection he could not return. He knew there was no chance of their both leaving him, but he was not sorry about this. At the Private bar at the Moray Arms, his local hotel (not pub), he had actually stated that when the time came he would like to be alone. He used to say, 'Like the animals. They know a thing or two. They crawl away on their own to die.' They crawl away on their own because there is no one to console them. And when the Captain had suggested, so gaily, that he would do the same, he was certain, somehow, that there would be another consolation. But he found none, and he therefore did not want them to go. As sensations slipped away, faster and faster, he wanted to hear voices and see people. As they grew dimmer they must sit closer. As their voices grew fainter they must shout louder.

Macdonald now sat close to him and she began to offer the only comfort she could, which was false comfort. She said the doctor would soon be there; she talked of the doctor, of how good he really was. She said his daughter would be back by breakfast time. The only comfort was in the sound of her voice, not in the things she said. He would rather that she spoke of other people and other things now; it did not matter what. Macdonald, more because the manner of the scene disappointed her, than because her friend was dying, began to get tearful. Her mind could not cope with the tragedy and she fixed on the irritation. She turned again to try to make Mary go back to the farm to make sure that John the police-man had made the phone calls, but Mary obstinately refused to budge. With much effort, the Captain touched the copy of *Treasure Island* by his bedside and Macdonald picked it up. She refused to let Mary read and, in a wan voice, she began at the beginning of the book which the Captain almost knew by heart. It was at the end of the part where the pirates come to the inn that the Captain stirred again. He used to say of his mother 'she was an awfully nice wee body' and he meant to say of *Treasure Island*, 'It's an awfully good book.' But his words were blurred and indistinguishable. They both looked up at him and with one eye, he recognized in their faces his own paralysis which had followed the stroke. It was his left side which was affected, and as he reached across with his right hand to feel his lip and chin he overbalanced slightly and fell against Macdonald, who was leaning forward beside him. They stuck for a moment, in a ludicrous position, their foreheads together like a couple of stags with their antlers caught. Then she pushed him back on the pillows. She looked back at Mary who was staring wide-eyed at the figure in the bed. Macdonald slowly turned back to the book.

At that point, without another word, Mary walked out.

Pink had moved the car along a little from the old bridge in order to try to stop Flossy and the dog in the kennel at the cottage from barking so incessantly, but the sun was rising and Mary soon discovered where he was. She walked across the corner of the field where the stooked corn looked damp and black. The clumps of trees by the river leaning gently with the wind were still without colour. The water itself looked like treacle, but the concrete face of the new bridge was light and bare. A couple of fish lorries rolled along the main road, their sidelights on, their tyres whining against the new surface. The sky was a deep duck-egg blue, with one or two streaks of black.

It was her turn to weep. She did so, hanging on to Pink, who looked very big beside her. He patted her back as she buried her nose in his jacket, and he said:

'The world's your oyster, Lilian. You mustn't forget that.' Then, as she did not recover for a moment, he went on, 'Full marks to old Pinky boy. He funked it altogether.'

At last she paused to take a breath, and tipping back her head she asked, 'Oh God, oh God, why was I no good at all?'

'Purely subjective thing. You seemed to be doing wonders. "Rip his clothes off," I heard you shout. "Don't forget the rings, Nelly——" '

'No, Pink——' she said, meaning 'Don't joke', and Pink said, with a sort of tight jaw, '*De peur d'être obliger d'en pleurer, je me hâ-hâ-hâte de rire de tout*, old mole.' It was something he often quoted.

Mary said, 'Macdonald's not much good either. She would be, mind you, if he wasn't going to die. It's just because he's going to die, I think that's why one's so incredibly bad.'

'Is there something we should do?'

On the main road above they heard a car stop and a door open and close. 'Maybe that's the doctor,' she said after a moment, but when nothing further happened she dropped her head on to his shoulder again.

Pink said, 'Courting couple, you bet. The doc would come right down.'

'Pobbles?' she asked, meaning Peebles.

'Snogging.' He nodded towards the car. 'Really killing them in Covent Garden—"Signori signore", you can't see him for flowers.'

She laughed a little at that. It struck true.

Then she went on, 'I suppose it happens to everybody but I always thought I would cope with death. Should I go back?'

'God, no.'

'He's not dead yet, but he's kind of paralysed.' She gripped him a little harder.

He said, 'Good-oh. No mistake, it's the light fantastic tonight.'

'He was rather brave, I thought. She's reading to him now.'

'What? *Journey's End?*'

'Pink, don't.'

'Well—hell——' he said.

'Actually it's *Treasure Island.*'

Pink's shoulder began to shake. It was difficult at first to know if he was laughing or crying. But in a moment it became quite clear. It was laughter, all right.

'But that's marvellous,' he said. 'What, sitting there?'

'Yes,' she said, 'it's not funny.'

But Pink could not stop laughing.

She started battering at him with her fists.

'Don't, Pink. Don't. We'll both sink into the ground. I'll kill you. Don't.'

But he was out of control now and she too began to laugh, a little hysterically, as her fists began to hurt.

Then, very suddenly, Pink sobered. There was a figure of a man standing on the road above them.

'Oh crikey,' he said. 'Don't look now, old fish, but there's a boy on the Via Flaminia.' He jerked his thumb over his shoulder and she looked up.

'Very strong,' Pink said, as she stared at the figure looking over the low concrete wall of the new bridge. It was David, but for a moment she did not seem to take him in.

'It's nearly light,' she said. 'It must be bloody late.' Then she bit her lip. She looked down at her knuckles and licked a scratch which one of Pink's buttons had made.

'He looks so idiotic there,' she said. 'It makes me rather cross.'

'Are we leaving Macdonald?'

'Yep.' She was still sucking the scratch.

'Shall I go up and tell him the wedding's off?' Pink asked.

She did not reply. He raised his eyebrows.

'It is off?'

She said, 'Why doesn't he come down, or shout, or do something?'

'If you like to bundle into my limousine here,' he said, 'you can bed down with a noted tenor and a hysterical Welsh collie.' For once he tried, quite strongly, to lead her. 'Come on.'

She pulled her hand away from her face, irritably, correcting herself—

'Don't! It's worse than biting your nails.' Then she looked up into Pink's face and said very plainly:

'You take Pobbles home. I'm going to walk.'

He looked more hurt than anxious. Rather mechanically he rattled off another of his imitations—this one of the Sunningdale set.

'You take Jack, Babs can ring Daph, I'll get the Bentley and we'll all go up to town.'

'I mean it.'

'You won't drown yourself, Bubbles?'

'I'm not going to do anything silly,' she said, and took a step away. 'But unless I speak to him he'll stand up there looking idiotic for everybody to see.' At once she turned and rather seriously, putting one foot carefully in front of the other, she walked up the narrow track which led diagonally through the long wet grass to the main road, above. Pink turned away long before she reached David, and with a sniff he climbed into the Humber and prepared to take Peebles home.

*   *   *

Not very far away, nearer the source of the stream, the Humber stopped at a disused slate quarry.

Peebles said, 'I don't smoke because I've got an outstanding tenor voice,' as he bundled out of the car.

Flossy, too, leapt out and waited by the narrow entrance as Peebles, quite soberly, walked farther into the quarry. Pink followed. When the dog saw them relieve themselves, she settled down and put her head on her paws, as if she now understood the reason for the stop. But she sat up again and put her head on one side when Peebles suddenly announced loudly, to Pink and the blue sky:

'Ladies and gentlemen, I should like to give you my rendering of an old Scotch ballad.' He coughed and it echoed round the bowl. He took up his stance like a Victorian tenor, with his hand inside his coat. His moustache looked very small, in the middle of his moon for a face.

The dog settled again, with one ear cocked. She and the sheep had seen some odder things than this, up on the hill, when Peebles had had a drink. Pink, meantime, with his hands clasped behind his back, listened attentively. He seemed to be glad of a pause, at dawn, before getting more deeply entangled in what he called the process of predestinate tragedy. He smiled as Peebles sang, rather well:

> 'Oh my luv's like a red red rose,
>   That's newly sprung in June,
> Oh my luv's like the melody,
>   That's sweetly played in tune.'

PART II

A Breakfast Cabaret

10

THE sun was low across the flood water and it hurt Pink's eyes as he sat, an hour or two later, by the kitchen table. So he turned his seat round and stared blankly at the big white refrigerator. He took a sip of tea from a huge cup and swilled it round his mouth.

'My cake-hole', he said, 'is like a parrot's cage.' But there was nobody else in the kitchen. He moved over to the big cupboard where most of the provisions were kept. On top there was a china jar marked 'Spices'. Inside there were a few of Pink's aids. Amongst other things there were two ball-point pens, an amber cigarette holder, a packet of chlorophyll tablets, a machine for cutting off the ends of cigars, a small hand pump for blowing up a Lilo, a screw-driver with fuse-wire fitted in the handle, two golf balls, a gold watch and a pair of dark glasses. It was these last which he now extracted and put on.

'A little windy,' he said, describing his condition, almost as if he meant it literally, then he put his hand on his stomach and belched. He looked out at the bright sun and knew that it was the beauty of the morning that most unnerved him; that, and the drink, and the Captain, and maybe Mary too. He belched again. 'Just a trifle shaky.'

Mary had not yet returned home, and it was a moment or two before Stephen arrived. Pink had time for two more cups of tea.

When Stephen did come in, Pink pushed the dark glasses further up his nose.

'Hullo, old man, long time no see. What happened to Steve?'

But Stephen did not reply. He took off his green hat (a hat which

Mary hated) and dumped it on a marble shelf in the corner. He looked pale, tidy and depressed. He began to unbutton his coat.

Pink raised his eyebrows and looked at his watch. He was wearing his best one, as he had, in all, half a dozen, but he had forgotten to wind it up. Before he could think of a suitable formula, an 'On the tiles, old man?' or 'Burning that candle pretty low', Stephen said:

'I decided to walk.'

'Really?' Pink sounded enthusiastically interested. He asked, 'Now tell me, did you see our Macdonald as you came down?' and Stephen shook his head.

Pink said, 'I think she's still out at the caravan. Captain's very bad. They were ringing for his daughter earlier.'

Pink said again, 'His dotter,' rather feebly and Stephen, surprisingly, gave a wan smile. He laid his coat on one side and sat down on a clumsy kitchen chair. He stretched his legs out in front of him and, cupping his hands behind his head, tipped back his neck.

He said with a sigh, 'I can't take it in,' and that was the last he said of the Captain.

'There's a kettle on, if you want it, old man.'

Stephen shook his head. He reached in his pocket for his silver cigarette case. It was only silver gilt. He kept his lighter, always serviced, in his sporran.

Pink, meantime, went to his own coat pocket and brought out a half bottle of whisky, which was almost full.

'Something stronger, old boy?' he suggested.

Again Stephen smiled rather faintly. On one note he quoted one of Pink's own phrases, 'Oblivon, old man, or cigar?'

Pink saw that there were no cigarettes in the silver gilt case.

'Of course,' he said, searching his pockets. 'I've got one somewhere.' Out of his pockets he brought three empty packets, one Capstan, one Passing Cloud, and one Player's Weights. He was a splendidly random buyer.

'I don't think I will after all,' Stephen said. 'Have you ever observed the Colonel? Before dinner he drinks and smokes and even talks. After dinner he doesn't do any of these things. He hardly even listens. I've stopped.'

Pink was wielding the half bottle.

'I think you ought to have something, Stiffy, if you've walked all that way. You couldn't come by the river with these floods, could you?' he asked a little obviously. If Stephen had come by the road he could not have missed David's car. 'Did you come over the top?'

'I tramped down the main road.'

Pink nodded, and said, 'Good Lord.'

Then Stephen added, 'As far as the old bridge, from which I looked up and down the river, and saw what there was to be seen.'

That left no margin for error. Pink circled round once or twice then halted with his feet together. He rocked his head from side to side, and suddenly tried another subject. 'Matter of fact I shan't be hanging around too long, old man,' he said. His face looked pale behind the big dark glasses.

'Oh yes?'

'Oh yes, old man. Today or *domani*. Business, you follow. London first stop but I've got Montreal in mind. Oyez, oyez. Big opportunities there.' Then suddenly he leant forward and spoke in an altogether less portentous way.

'Old Stiffy,' he began. 'Look, you don't want to take this thing too hard. Mary's all right. She wouldn't do anything silly. I mean two and two don't make five. She's probably just trying to make you a bit jealous.'

'Then she is succeeding.'

Pink gave an uncertain smile. His language was more important to him than might have been imagined. Pink's way was to humanize things by referring to them as well-known friends: to reduce their proportion. If somebody went raving mad Pink would say, 'Bit of the old basket work,' and faced with a homicidal maniac carrying an axe he might well manage, 'Spot of the old butcher's itch?' To Stephen he said, 'Touch of the green-eyed, what?' His expression was set half-way to a smile. Stephen, at this point, pushing his feet along the hard stone floor, decided to talk. He used a matter-of-fact sort of voice.

'Not much more green-eyed than usual. I suppose if I work it out I'm jealous all the time of all of you—even the Queen's bar lot——'

'Steady on.'

'I'm quite used to the sensation. It comes down to the size of my shoulder and the span of my hand. I'm so used to jealousy and envy that David doesn't seem to make any particular impact. He numbs me, I suppose.'

After a pause he moved a little and said:

'Perhaps I deceive myself.'

Pink sat down by the window, behind Stephen, where he could not see his face.

Stephen said, quietly, 'It's warm in here,' and Pink put the bottle on the floor beside his chair. The kettle on the slow plate hissed as a drop of water ran down to the range.

Stephen's cheeks were now wet with tears. He said, without a break in his voice:

'The ruling emotion is shame.'

Pink tiptoed to the shelf and found a kitchen glass. He poured some whisky into it and pushed it across the table to him. He said:

'Come on. You'd better have a tot. Doctor's orders, old man. You're tired out. Go on.'

Stephen picked up the glass and drank.

'A dram before seven, dry by eleven,' Pink said and Stephen tried to laugh.

'Good man,' Pink said, as the empty glass was placed back on the scrubbed wood table. Stephen turned his chair round, put his elbows on the table and played with the empty glass. He rolled it along the surface.

He said, 'I love her. That's what's so hopeless. That's what it's so difficult to explain. And useless to try, now. But I've looked at it all ways and I love her. I just don't seem able to express it in words, in bed, and now in simple, definite action.'

Pink said, 'Old cock, if you feel it as badly as that why don't you just say so? Just say what you said to me just now. Say it to her.'

Stephen shook his head.

'You could give it a try, damn it,' Pink said.

'It wouldn't work.'

'Can't do any harm, can it?'

'Pointless,' Stephen replied and Pink rocked his head impatiently.

'Damn it,' he said, hopelessly.

Stephen, sitting up again, said, clearly, 'I just don't bother to fight impossible battles.' The tears had all gone.

Pink shrugged. He said, 'I suppose that's sensible enough, in a way. Best generals do that, so they say.'

'Yep,' Stephen replied. 'And I often wonder if they're cowards too. Unsympathetic creatures that they are.'

Pink would have developed that, if only to keep Stephen's mind off himself, but they were interrupted by a noise in the scullery by the back door. They waited quietly as the footsteps came nearer.

'Hello, Mary-bags,' Pink said.

11

Pink said, 'Stephen's just got in.'

Mary stood quite still with her hands behind her on the door.

Pink went on, 'Celebrating with me here: celebrating my proposed departure.' Hearing the lie in his voice, Mary hardly bothered to listen, but his opening remark helped her. She swam in, asking Stephen:

'Where on earth did you get to?'

He said, 'I promised to clear up the classroom.'

'Which classroom?'

'The one we used.'

There was no change in her physical appearance. Her cheeks had been pink before, her eyes had looked as bright. Her hair, when it had been washed, was always the same brilliant colour. In the morning sunlight the down on her cheeks and her forearms always looked golden. Her movements were no more energetic than they had ever been. She did not look happier, or wiser, and her voice was neither higher nor lower.

She said: 'It can't have taken you all night to do that.'

'No,' Stephen looked up at her. His eyes were bloodshot. 'I walked home.'

'What a stupid thing to do.' She did not take her eyes off his face as he looked back at the buckles on his shoes. She said, 'You look quite worn out.'

'I'm quite tired,' he replied.

'We're all a bit whacked,' Pink said, but she paid no attention to

71

him. She was close to Stephen looking down at him, hard, demanding a full answer; almost predatory.

'When did you go back to the classroom?'

'At the end.'

'After I'd gone?'

'Long after; I was the last.'

Stephen was silent.

Pink shuffled forward. 'Look here, old sis, we're all a bit whacked. What say we leave the post-mortems?'

'No,' she said.

Stephen lifted his head and stared at her. Pink shuffled back.

'You saw David go?' she asked.

'Yes,' Stephen said.

'You didn't ask him where he was going?'

'No. I told him where you had gone.'

'God, but I think that's despicable.'

'Steady on,' Pink said. 'You won't do any good this way, old flesh.'

Stephen, forced to it, had found, if not courage, a positive value in his cowardice: a point beyond which he could not retire. Looking at Mary, he said quietly:

'It's all right, Pink. I'll walk away when I want to.'

'But it's horrid,' Mary said.

'I'm not very proud of it,' Stephen answered coldly.

Mary moved and said, 'You knew, didn't you, at that horrid time—when we were all sitting round at the table, before old Fish-face, Captain Fish-face—before all that? And after that when I was going off to Peebles' car, you knew. Yes, you knew.'

'Yes.'

'And you followed David?'

'No.' Stephen frowned. 'I had no desire to do that.'

There was a long pause and Pink said:

'D'you want me to go? Old Pinkie boy to knock along?' But she shook her head. She did not listen to what he said. She put her fingers on the rail by the cooker and talked to Stephen without looking at him.

'If you weren't here I was going to put it in a letter. If you were here I was going to say it all. Lots of things about you, not nasty at all. I don't want to say these things now.'

72

Stephen sat stone still and Pink, his weight awkwardly on one foot, did not dare to move as she sailed in, with the breeze firmly behind her, and destroyed.

'You've done me no harm, Stephen, and I've harmed you. I'm sure you've never said anything wrong about me and at the end I despise you.'

There was a click as Pink put the half bottle down on the table. Then he lifted up his head and listened, looking at nothing, much as if he were attending a funeral service in a private parlour or listening to the Queen at Christmas time. Mary continued:

'I don't feel sorry for you, because I see you, Stephen. Really see you. I feel repelled by you and not just in the way that you've evidently found me repellent. I feel it very suddenly, very strongly, yes I do, I do. And you'll say to yourself, it's because I've slept with David, which I have: yes, as you know perfectly well, although you haven't said so. But it's got nothing to do with that. One day you'll realize that you can't blame everything on that. Bed is only the smallest bit of it and if you go on telling yourself that I left you because of bed, you'll be lying to yourself. I'm leaving you for all the other reasons—the ones that made you stay behind: that made you stroke my hair when you knew: for all the cowardice and self-pity—for the whole "no". For the whole bloody great boulder that I've had to try and shove up the hill. And in ten hours altogether I've been alone with him, never mind the new bridge, in ten hours with him, because I've counted, I've felt—I've felt like a girl and it is a strange and wonderful feeling.'

Her eyes were glistening with tears. Pink held his head low now. Stephen stood up and turned away, at which Mary took a step forward.

For a moment Pink thought she was going to try to undo some of the harm. Her voice had changed. It was pitched a little higher, and the words came even faster. It rose as she spoke, but she was not offering mercy or apology.

She cried, 'I suppose you're going to say nothing? That's it!' as Stephen walked steadily to the door. She shouted after him as he moved away, 'You might say something you'd regret, even something that might hurt me so you won't risk it. You won't. It's just negative.'

Stephen had already disappeared into the house and the door

swung closed behind him. She stood shaking, her head very low.

Very quietly, Pink said, 'It's all right, my love, he's gone——'

'No,' she said, quickly turning away from him, walking back to the rail which she held on to, tightly. 'Don't comfort me. I don't need it. But I feel sick. I don't know which makes me sick, him or me.'

'P-p-punishment,' Pink suggested, in one of his enlightened moments. 'It's got its own stink.'

A few moments later she held out one hand and said:

'Pink, darling, may I have a swig?'

'Of course, old girl.'

'Old girl, old girl. I suppose you hate me now.' She took the bottle from him, and he put the glass which Stephen had used back on the table. 'I know you're fond of Stephen.'

'No, no, no,' Pink protested.

She said, 'Even now I lie. Oh Christ, I lie. Even now. Isn't that awful? I had to do something. I had to charge. I had to look like a woman has to look—am I woman? Aren't I a girl?'

'Steady—steady, love.'

'I had to do all that. I really did.' She suddenly covered her face with her hands and laughed. 'Oh Christ, oh Christ, oh Christ. You hate me, don't you?'

'You're certainly slashing about.'

'Oh darling, Pink. I couldn't bear it if you were nasty. What are you thinking?'

Pink steadied considerably. He poured some whisky into the glass.

'Self observation,' he said. 'The curse of the Fergusons. Thinking, "interesting situation, by God, little woman done by dark stranger, now, what next?" That's the sort of thought. But little woman's certainly rather rough on poor old Stiffy.'

'You don't care about Stiffy,' she said, almost casually, suddenly hitting very true. 'Nor anybody else,' and before he had time to answer she went on:

'Of course it's not true, what I said to him. Of course I don't really feel like that. Not really, really. I just rather wish I did, I suppose. I must have a drink, a cigarette or five packets of chewing gum, I don't know—something to put in the mouth. . . . Pink cares about Pink. A little about me too. Yes, I know that's true. I bet you've been sulking?'

'No.'

'Oh yes, you have. D'you want me to tell about David? I want to tell.'

'Old corruption,' he said kindly. 'Old, old snake.'

'Well of course I was fibbing really, but I wouldn't fib to you.'

Pink tapped the bottle in the palm of his hand and tried to remember; 'You said to me, "Off you go, and take old Pobbles home. I'll walk myself." '

'No.'

'You said, "I'll see him off." '

Again, she shook her head. 'I never did. Pink, don't be cruel. You know exactly what I said.'

'But Stephen's nice.' Pink stretched out his arms.

'Shsh!' she said, and went right to him and sorted out his tie. 'Pink darling, don't huff on me now.'

'I'm falling over myself——'

She interrupted. 'Yes, I know you are. Tell me, though, tell me what I really said.'

' "You hoof it," you said.'

'Yes.'

' "You hoof it and I'll swear I'll be good." '

'No, I didn't say that.'

'You did.' He frowned and spoke again. 'I'm sure you did.'

'No, I can prove it, I didn't. I promise I can. I didn't say that at all.'

'Stephen's nice. He is,' Pink said, almost sang, again.

'I can prove it if you looked. Did you look when you got into the car?'

'No.'

'Then what did you see?'

'I had the hound and old Pobbles——'

'No,' she said, clenching her fists. 'No, no, no, no! What did you see of me—even if you didn't look?'

Pink tried to remember. 'You walked up the bank.'

'Yes.'

'Up the kind of track—footpath, whatever you call it, through the nettles and the grass and that.'

'Yes——'

Pink shrugged.

He said, 'That must have been out of the very corner of the old peepers.'

'What else?' she asked.

'After that, we'd gone.'

'What did I look like?'

'Lady with a mission. Head down. All that.'

'Good,' she said. 'Go on.'

'No,' he said. 'Can't, old thing. Big blind blank. Big blank blind.'

'Quite unnecessary blind, I promise,' she said, then she held on to his coat. 'Darling, I promise I was only like that with Stephen because —because, because, because. Oh, I don't know, that special thing annoyed me, at the table. You didn't see, you were with old Fish-face in the Gents, but it was all rather foul. Everybody kind of knew, at once; David, Steve and me. Everybody obviously knew and it wasn't for me or David to say. I nearly did say. But honestly if you work it out Stevie should have said something. "Veto." "I object." I don't quite know what, but he should have said some-thing. Just as a girl. Just as this shape and no beard and all that; I promise I know. Deep, deep, deep down, I know he should have said something. There was plenty of time.'

'Glands?' Pink asked. 'That's really it.'

She shook her head.

'Not directly—promise,' she replied. 'Maybe connected but not just that. I knew even then, when we all three knew at that miser-able table and when nobody was saying anything. That's the one thing I did know: I was going to lam into poor old Stevie. He asks for it, I promise he does. Be me and you'd know. He really does ask for it.'

Pink pouted.

'All this boulder stuff,' he said, raising his eyebrows.

'Well, I have to push a boulder. I honestly have.' She looked up at him and corrected herself. 'You've been all right but the rest of it—honestly, think of it. Pink, you do look huffy and constipated.'

'Old girl. I'm being most awfully good.'

'Are you?' she asked.

'Yep. Really am.'

'Are you angry?'

'Touchy,' Pink said.

'No need. That's what's so silly. You've absolutely no need to be. I didn't lie to you. I wasn't so wrong with the boulder, I promise——'

Pink could read her like a book.

'You thought it out before,' he said.

She stopped for a moment and he moved to the bottle again.

'A welcome pause,' he said, and nodded. A phrase which he always applied, when she was getting over excited, and speaking so quickly that even he could hardly understand. 'Bang, bang, bang on the lug-hole.'

She said, 'I'll be good. I'll be eminently what'sable. Reasonable and calm.' And she swallowed. 'The boulder. Yes. Complete confession. I did rather think that one up. It sounded awfully good outside. Little me hauling you all up the slope.' She laughed, hopelessly, looked at Pink and then turned away again. She went on:

'It's me that's foul, I know. That only makes me hate him more. And I do hate him. I promise you that.'

'It's not awfully fair,' Pink said.

'Yes,' she said, 'I think it is. And I know what you think. I know, because you said so. You said "glands". And that's such a horrible idea. It's all wrong too, I promise. I'll tell you if you want.'

'If you don't rush——'

'I'll take it terribly calmly, I swear.'

'Tell then. Slowly. In words of one syllable. Not in code.'

'All right,' she said. 'Perhaps we don't love each other after all. You're huffing really.'

'I've been surprised.'

'So have I,' she said. 'Thank God.'

'You don't have to tell, actually,' Pink said.

'Oh yes I do—I have to tell somebody. Now I think of it there's nothing in my life that I haven't had to tell——'

'Absolutely,' Pink said. 'Matter of fact there seems to be quite a few things that never happened in your life that you feel you have to tell, too.'

'Not now,' she said. 'I really mean that. I mean I've always known if I really did live I wouldn't have to think up things. Now life's really going to go, I think I shall find I've absolutely no

imagination. I won't need it, you see, not any more. It's sort of
Lourdes, isn't it? I mean I'm flinging away crutches right and
left?'

'You're sure about David?'

'No, not a bit. I'm sure about Steve. That's what's wrong. One
can't be sure about David.'

'But you love him?' he asked, again extraordinarily responsibly
and seriously.

'I'm not even sure about that.'

'I'd have thought that was rather important.'

'I love Pink as the uncle,' she said. ' "I-should-have-thought"
from Uncle Pink! You must be huffing really, because you wouldn't
be so sane. . . . Mind you, it wasn't awfully true what I said to
Steve, about the boulders and that; about the breath of fresh wind
or whatever I said. Or did I stop myself before I said that? I confess
that's the sort of thing I thought I'd say if ever—well if ever I did
find somebody else and yell and scream and that. But it does give
rather a false picture.'

'You were a bit careless to leave the car there.'

'Oh no, not careless,' she exclaimed. 'I wouldn't have done it
unless I thought I was going to be found out and I'll tell you
something very peculiar. Something rather reassuring, maybe,
except if you think about it too hard, perhaps it's rather ominous.
He didn't mind about that either. He didn't suggest we took the
car up on to the Wade road or in the woods or somewhere like
that. I thought he'd insist. But not at all. He's terribly open about
things in some ways. I mean first ringing me after that party in
London. He knew I was staying with terribly respectable people.
He knew I was married. He didn't even bother to give a false name.
Then following me up here, like that, I mean actually on the same
train. He told the sleeping compartment man, you know, he
wanted the berth next door. And the sleeping-car man knows
perfectly well who I am. It wasn't graft either. Not a very big
tip; I saw. He just persists. Then at the academy. All the others
were there but that didn't put him off a bit. He was going to do
those decorations with me. Then you saw him at the dance.
Extraordinary he is, really. I suppose he's just very bright. But
he's an awful lot of people, isn't he, all at once? Kind of clumsy
turning up like that in a stuffed shirt. But very smooth in not caring

78

a damn. Sometimes he talks in that kind of language these big intellectual wolves do and the next minute I feel after he's paid for a drink I'd better count the change because I'm sure he's incapable really. Anybody who really knew how to cope couldn't be so idiotically scandalous as he really is. But I thought it was rather nice. He didn't even suggest "in the car" which I'd rather dreaded —I don't know if you've tried? He didn't actually suggest anything. We just crossed the road and went down through the long grass the other side.'

'Dialogue?'

She shook her head.

'Not much from him, I mean. Just telling me to shut up. I talked a bit about Captain Gordon and that, you know. I felt it rather a reflection, that; not being able to cope with death. I'm sure that's something to do with not really living. Anyway I was a bit upset and you obviously disapproved so maybe that's what made me go on. We never know quite what does. Anyway I said how foul I'd always been to old Fish-face who was really quite harmless and obviously jolly brave. He just said "Shut up" to all that. Rather rudely, you know, so I followed him down the bank. Then we passed that barking dog and that's when I said everybody would soon be awake and I mentioned about the car being there for everybody to see. He said he didn't care a damn. I thought that was good. But let's not talk about it too hard.' She frowned.

'He's just a bloke who knows his mind,' Pink said.

'Well, yes,' she replied, but she was still quite clearly troubled. 'That's what it would seem.'

'You're doubtful?'

'I suppose there are people who kind of like people to know they're having a great bomb of an affair. Really the affair's not quite all what it should be for them unless they're certain other people know about it. They drop clues all over the place.'

'Who, for instance?'

'Nobody,' she said, thoughtfully, even gravely. 'But there are people, I know, because I absolutely understand. At least I absolutely don't understand, but I can see myself doing it very well. I can see myself making a lover leave a note at my hairdresser and then when she gives it to me I make her swear, get a Bible, or a Koran or whatever it is hairdressers use and say "Swear you won't tell anybody he left this note. Swear!" Lovely,' she said, with a sudden little smile. 'I should almost like to live in London just for that. But I'm sure he's not really like that. It was just a horrible cloud over the moon. I think he's the opposite, after all he's terribly old. He must have done all this a hundred times before. He'll probably sack me, but it'll be living. In a kind of way I think we'll be all right. I can see myself having a row with him in every capital in Europe. Late at the Uffizi, I shall be, and tactless at the Vatican or somewhere like that. I can see his impatience with me. He can lecture, you know.

'But I wasn't lying about the main thing. No. We went down to the river, actually holding hands, but a little kind of cold. I mean 'prose' really. 'Prose' is the word. We weren't at all daisy chain and wild duck, you know. None of your Edinburgh Festival films. I mean, actually, I suppose if you look at it with the grass and the brambles and the two bridges, the flooded river and the dawn, we might be expected to have felt a bit that way. Otherwise I suppose it's a wonderful setting for a jolly old murder. Can you see me floating down the river, nymph in thy orisons, or whatever it is? But we were cold and prose.

'Actually, in the end what was rather odd about it, really, was that it was me that said it. I wasn't very flirtatious or anything like that. I just said, "There's one place, I know", and he nodded. We didn't even hold hands then.'

Pink had sat down at the table again. He was playing with the tea leaves in his cup and now she sat at the table with him. She continued to talk as quickly as ever, regardless of contradictions, constantly almost losing direction yet somehow in the end pulling the story back. After a moment's description of her leading the way along the bank to the cart track and then to the place under the new bridge, she settled for, 'Cattle, really.'

She said, 'That's what we were like. I'm sure it does me good to tell you. It's like an old war song or something. If he was an Aberdeen Angus, then I was a Jersey cow. Oh God, isn't that awful? I only meant that to give you the picture of us walking along, but it really says rather too much.'

She began to giggle. She said, 'Do do that cow look.'

He shook his head firmly.

She ran on, 'You know that awful look, over the shoulder,

rather bored and yet decided. A kind of look of distaste. You'd think it would put the poor bull off for life. But it doesn't actually,' she said. She drew breath and continued more steadily:

'Anyway eventually we got ourselves sorted out towards the top of one of the big concrete support things—the widest beam. But there's not an awful lot of room. We were right up at the top of it, hidden from the track by the uprights, the lorries lumbering along the road above us—cars, for all I know—and the river underneath. All the pigeons flapped away, madly, as we settled down. One couldn't really move to right or left very much, but it was all right, you know. Quite quick. I closed my eyes most of the time and I didn't have to pretend I was somebody else. I was somebody else. God knows who. I felt rather like a pink-cheeked, dark-haired dairy maid, rather soft and fat and seventeenish, I suppose. I don't mean I had to think her up. I enjoyed it rather a lot. Or she did. I'm not explaining myself very well. I shouldn't think boys understand. Do you?'

'I think I can guess,' Pink said.

'Yes, I thought you probably could, but when I tried to tell David this, after, I mean—strictly no dialogue at the time, not a word said until I'd hauled on my pants——'

'Mary!'

'Well, I told you it was prose.'

'Yes, but there's a kind of limit.'

'Oh, don't be so stuffy. I wasn't going to leave them there, after all.'

'I mean there's a limit about how much you tell.'

She looked rather hurt.

'But I wanted to tell.'

'I know,' he said.

She frowned deeply. 'Now you've ruined it. You've made me feel bad.'

'Go on,' Pink suggested.

'No,' she said. 'I'm huffing now. Is there something to eat?' She walked over to the cupboard and found a tin of biscuits.

'For you, slob?'

Pink nodded. 'I wouldn't say no.' She extracted four water biscuits then put back the lid and closed the cupboard door. She gave him his ration and with her mouth full, said:

'After all I'm only telling you. I wouldn't shout it all out in the middle of the main street.'

'I'm not so sure,' he said.

'Come to that,' she said with a sudden laugh, 'I'm not so sure either. D'you think anybody would believe me?'

'No.'

'Why?'

'Charity. They like you round these parts.'

She said, 'D'you believe me?'

'In every detail, old thing. That's what's putting me off.'

'It is true, you know.'

'I know damned well it is.'

'How d'you know?' she asked.

'How do we ever know?' he replied.

'Oh my God,' she said, 'I was rather savage at Stephen . . . Perhaps detail's what makes you so sure.'

'Could be the pants,' he said.

'Oh no,' she replied. 'You're quite wrong there. I could easily have made up the pants. In fact I think I'd be bound to hit on the pants. It only takes a mind with a practical bent. I wonder how?'

'Probably dog's whistle stuff,' he said. 'Unknown accuracy of Pink's ear. I always know when you're lying. And I'm often in the know.'

'Yes,' she said, very vaguely, suddenly. 'Yes, I suppose that's true.'

'Let's take the pants as on,' Pink said.

'Well, then things frankly weren't awfully romantic. Very, very prose indeed. I said about this girl, you know, how I'd felt.'

'He didn't like that?'

'He cut me short.'

'That doesn't surprise me,' Pink said, wisely.

'Well, it did me. I wasn't insulting him. I mean I didn't say I was so bored I had to think her up to give myself a lift. That wasn't true. I just fell into her. It was probably being so flat on my back like that, and concrete's jolly hard. I shouldn't be at all surprised if my shoulders looked like a stucco bungalow; like a bothie wall. Anyway, he wasn't going to talk about that. We walked away, oddly enough, holding hands then, though neither of us felt terribly like it—well, that's not quite true. I did in a sort of a way. I actually asked him to hold my hand. More from kind of wrath of God, I think, than love. I'm sure God's moosh is just like Macdonald's, big, gloomy, hurt, disapproving and so irritatingly patient. But even she's been angry with us once or twice. . . .' She thought for a second, then asked, 'You know that feeling when you keep looking at the sky and feel absolutely certain that your favourite dog's going to die? Like that. So there we were, not going up the bank to his common little car, oddly enough. But along the cart track back towards here, between the red puddles, and the stones those school children fling at each other—he and me, Adam and Eve, picking our solitary way. A likely pair. Only no paradise. Not yet. There will be, though, I think. I'd have the most tremendous row with him, I know, if ever we went to Monte Carlo. Don't scientists have conferences there? I know he'd hate gambling. He's rather puritanical, I'm sure. I'd throw my coins or whatever they're called, all over the board and, goodness I'd boast about Daddy like mad. . . .

'Well, when we came to the garden wall I thought it would be rather romantic to walk along the top of it and he could reach up and hold my hand. "After the ball is over" stuff. I felt like it. I really did want him to pick me a flower. But that suggestion seemed to bring him sharply to his senses. He didn't walk about "mm"-ing and shaking his head like he usually did. He just stood there picking his nose or something. Kind of solidly indecisive. Not crying. But not smoking either.' She broke off for a second. 'Are you still worried about those pants?'

'No, go on——'

'You are rather stuffy sometimes, Pink. And you look awfully silly when you are. You really must fight it. Besides there's nothing wrong at all in girls hauling off and on their pants. It's only our terrible education that makes us so worried about that. Those schools and a touch of poor Macdonald.'

'I'm not worried——'

'Nor am I. I think it's a very good thing, really. I mean that girls should. It's part of what pants are for. So long as they're young—the girls, I mean. Then it's really quite a nice idea.'

'Go *on*,' Pink said impatiently. 'You left him standing at the g-g-garden gate.'

'Yes, well then things did go rather badly.'

'Obviously,' he said, and she knew exactly what he meant. He never missed a trick; recognized at once the meaning of her more hectic diversions. She talked much more slowly as she took the last hurdle.

'I grew rather sulky, mainly, I think, because he looked the way he did. So then I just said, "You'd better not come in now. You'd better go back and then come and collect me. I'll pack a case." '

'Oh yes,' said Pink. 'Nice going. And he said, "I never want to see you in my life again, you forward little puss." '

'No. Not exactly.'

'Spit it out.'

'Important timing,' she said. 'Very.' And she sniffed. 'A split-second first. A kind of light in his eye that might have been shock, but I'm pretty sure it was just the blue sky. I mean, this was only a few minutes ago. It was quite light. I think the look was only in my mind. But it scared me, I confess. Like you, with Daddy, some-times. Kind of absolutely certain that now you're down you're going to get a kick in the teeth. All that rushing through my old nut and I stand there with my toes together, looking a little demure, I believe. That was something to do with the thought about flowers. What's going on in his head I've really no idea. Probably the travelling expenses. He's not very generous, you know. Well, he is, but he grumbles about it, always. In London, he insisted on taking me to lunch at a very swank restaurant then complained about the bill: sort of jokingly. But all this in a split-second and then he's all smiles. Charming and rather formal, and in tails of course, at the garden gate: he even looked rather nice. You know he's got that awful skin that makes him look as if he's spent twenty years down a mine? So useful for a Gaitskellite. . . . Big pores, I suppose. . . . Anyway, even that wasn't so noticeable. Just big black eyes and short dark hair. The answer to my sort of maiden's prayer. He took me in his arms and kissed me and he was really nice: really hopeful. Saying, "You are a good girl" and nice straightforward things like that. I'm afraid I cried like anything. Then I sent him off and came in here, and now you're up to date.'

She said, 'If you have another cup of tea it'll start coming out of your ears. You're getting as bad as Cathie.' Cathie was the maid.

But at the end of all that, she seemed curiously exhausted. Almost panic-stricken. Her face was sad and pale. She looked almost fierce as she took a sip from the flask. She drank another and he made a 'glug-glug' noise. For an instant she did not react.

'Well, don't take it all,' he said. Then he made the 'glug-glug' noise again. He expanded the imitation to a vivid, explosive mock nose trick, and spluttering and coughing she burst out laughing.

'Soaked,' Pink said. 'The fellow's absolutely soaked.'

Mary was holding her sides, coughing and trying to recover herself. The whisky seemed to be coming out of her ears as she cursed him and laughed, at once. She suddenly put her arms round his neck and said very breathlessly:

'Oh, Pink darling, you are the most awful slob, but I do love you and I shall miss you most of all. But you are the most awful slob.'

The last shreds of responsibility were thrown away as Pink now played the slob. A cigarette out of the corner of his mouth, round-shouldered and pot-bellied, he shuffled in a circle, like something out of the sea. 'The smoker' in *Scouting for Boys*.

'Oh, don't, Pink,' she cried. 'It hurts.' Her laughter was very high. 'Don't. It hurts both ways. D'you suppose Stephen's killing himself?'

Pink, very uncertainly, with his hands wide apart, said, 'It's not wrong. It's better this way, isn't it, than being maudlin and that?'

She nodded.

He went on, at first uncertainly, 'It's always the right time for a little celebration. But it won't be a long parting, old trout. I'll see you in the big city.'

'In London?' she asked, frantically encouraging him. 'Will you, Pink?'

'Absolutely. If your old man will let me in.'

'He will. I promise he's nice.'

Pink said, 'We'll have a party, by God. A big get-together in a low-down cellar. We'll trip the light fantastic, Mary and Pink, for auld lang syne and all that cock. Won't we?'

She nodded very hard several times and ran and put her arms round his neck again. She buried her head in his coat and with long pauses in between he slapped her back. It was he who was crying.

A moment later she said rather coolly, as if the thought had just come to her:

'I sometimes think it's rather a pity that Macdonald wasn't our Mum. I mean she'd have had so much more authority, don't you think?'

12

Mary and Stephen slept in the night nursery, a small room that overlooked the haugh, the ha-ha, the river and the floods, but Stephen had drawn the curtains, perhaps much for the same reason that Pink put on dark glasses. ('I somehow feel', Pink once said about dark glasses, 'that Lot's wife could have done with a pair of these jobs.') And Stephen's decision to draw the frilly, gay little curtains was curiously prophetic. The worst scene of his life was later to be played in this sweet room with the big white-washed fireplace and the bright yellow paint.

When Mary had begun to pack she had switched on the light. For a while Stephen had lain, like the effigy of a knight, staring straight at the ceiling, but now he was sitting up in bed reading Cozzens: *By Love Possessed*.

Mary's behaviour in the crisis of departure was marvellously female. Although her husband never took his eyes from his book, she continued to talk to him as she packed, almost as if she were preparing to elope with him, not David. It was as if she felt that pleasant chatter would dissolve an insoluble situation. It was Mary at her most typical, not only refusing to believe in her own actions, but denying reality itself.

'Isn't that the end?' she asked, pressing the clothes down in the suitcase. 'These bloody things just won't get in.'

And then a moment later, she said vaguely, 'I know you don't believe me, but I really don't want to go one bit. I mean, I hate London, and that's just the start-off. I've always come back to this room,' and she put the palm of her hand against the wall. 'It's quite absurd,' she said, 'to talk of leaving it.'

At the cupboard which was really Stephen's but which she used as well, because she had always used it, she said, 'You really have got the dullest lot of ties. I shall make a point of buying you one. That I promise. I'll search and search until I get one just right for you. I'll send it for your birthday. Maybe before. One with nice faded colours, not horrid diagonal regimental stripes like these. I . . .' she paused. Then she said cheerfully, 'You can wear it for lunch when we next meet. We obviously will meet. It would be too childish not to. I mean I'm bound to come north sometimes and we'll have a jolly swank lunch on old Dow's money. That'll be fun. I'd hate it if I thought we were parting as enemies, Stiffy. You see, I do love you, kind of—well, maybe it's not the time to say it. But I really do. We must be friends and I'll write to you and you'll get on much better without me anyway.'

He never took his eyes from the book. She went to the curtains and suddenly swept them back. She said, 'They need some extra runners, we must see to that,' as she looked at the ruffled waters of the flood. There were gulls inland, and a pair of swans. She said, 'It's bright too early, it's going to cloud over and the gulls are inland—that means storm.' And then her eyes clouded with tears.

'Oh my darling silly Juniper Bank,' she said, beginning to cry. 'There's nowhere like this in the world. I know there's nowhere like this.'

Almost as suddenly she recovered herself, bit her lip and grabbed a big handkerchief from one of his drawers. 'Very dramatic,' she said. 'Mop up.' Then she walked straight to the telephone to ring David. She sat on the second bed, a foot away from Stephen, and said, 'I hate the phone.'

David's mother answered first. She was slightly deaf and feared the instrument. She took a moment to understand that the call was for her son. She asked who was speaking and Mary wondered if she should tell the truth. It was not easy lying to anyone as charitable as Edith Dow.

'It's Mary Cameron. Ferguson, you know.'

'Oh yes.' She understood at last. She sounded very worried. 'Is something wrong then, Mary?'

'Well, yes, there is.'

'I'm so sorry. Is somebody unwell?'

'Yes.'

'Not your father, I hope?'

'It's not exactly that. If I could speak to David for a moment.'

She looked up and saw that Stephen's eyes were closed again. She turned away from him.

As soon as David came to the phone she explained as quickly as she could that things were more unbearable then she had thought they were going to be. David did not sound helpful or friendly.

'Really,' he said. 'We arranged——'

'I know we did.'

'It's too bad, ringing this number.'

'David, please, I can't talk here.'

'This is exactly the point; no more can I. It's absurdly early.'

There was silence for a moment then she pleaded.

'I can't wait here as I suggested.'

'Why on earth not?'

'It's impossible.'

'Why?'

'Please, David, please. I can't tell you. You must come at once.'

She could hear him sigh.

He said, 'It sounds to me as if you're acting in a very hysterical way.'

'I'm not.'

There was a long pause. At last he spoke again.

He said, 'Very well. But it seems to me a pity.'

'I wouldn't ask unless—David, d'you mind if I bring quite a big case? David?'

'Let's leave it there.'

He ended the call abruptly. Stephen opened his eyes as the telephone 'clicked' in Mary's ear. Then she slowly replaced it. She looked Stephen in the eye, fiercely, for a second and then walked away from the bed. Although there was still much to be packed, she closed the trunk.

She said, 'You heard all that,' and he turned back to his book.

She stayed in the room, with the trunk and case packed, until David arrived an hour later. She looked exhausted again. She sat still and was quite silent. When she heard footsteps on the steep curved stairs she said very slowly, before she stood up:

'I was thinking of a girl sitting in the gun-field blowing clock dandelions, playing "He loves me" and denying "he loves me not."' She shook her head. 'It's not really like that. I mean love and life and Santa Claus and that. But it should be, I promise you.'

'To prove it,' Pink said, at the door, 'he's arrived.'

'I know,' she lied. Then her energy drained back. Much more quickly again she said, 'I know, I know.'

'Good old Mary-bags.'

She put on a big sheepskin coat that hung behind the door. Rather cheerfully now, jokingly, she said:

'Come on, Pink, you've got to help. Here's my overnight bag.'

Pink was more than astonished by the trunk.

'They'll like that at the Dorchester,' he said.

'Go on, haul! I'll take this end.' She pushed the trunk so that Pink never had to come properly into the room and she herself did not look at Stephen again. Immediately outside the bedroom door she dropped her end of the trunk, and closed the bedroom door sharply behind her, saying, 'Bye!'

'Old Sherpa Pink,' Pink said, lifting up the trunk again. 'What's in it then? The family silver? Warm spooneroonies?'

'Pink, do stop staggering so.'

But at the top of the stairs, he made her drop her end.

'Work study, efficiency, method one,' he said, pointing one finger in the air. 'To hell with the paintwork.'

He slid the trunk on to the top steps and then pushed. With enormous crashes and bangs it somehow slid to the bottom. The banister shuddered. A huge piece of plaster was removed from the wall. Pink was delighted. 'Bloody good,' he said. 'I've always wanted to do that.'

But she did not seem to hear him or notice the trunk crash down the stairs. She walked slowly to her mother's room which was used as the spare room now. She stood just inside it for a moment. There were some sweet peas on the dressing-table but otherwise it looked as blank as any unoccupied bedroom. Pink came up behind her.

'Nothing to do with Mummy,' she said, and as she did so they had the same vision of the mild, stupid little woman who always wore grey to match her eyes.

'Poor pigeon,' she said sadly, and it was as if her mother was dismissed in death as she had been in life, 'nothing to do with her.' She swallowed. 'Just the room . . . It smells of moth balls.'

'Like the Captain's jacket,' Pink said. 'My dotter's doing.'

Flatly Mary said, 'I suppose he's dead.' Then she went on in her lowest tones, 'Horrible. Just now I saw this house quite empty and, Pink, it was all our fault. I don't know why.'

'Old flesh,' he said.

'Old flesh,' she replied, still sadly and seriously. 'I sometimes wonder if we've any bones. Moral bones.'

They wandered out again, and she looked at the ceiling and the curved wall round which the staircase ran.

'We mustn't let it empty itself. I saw myself clattering up the stairs, crying "I'll buy it, I'll buy it", just like in a story.'

'Big stuff,' Pink said.

'Yes,' she admitted with a nod. 'I heard myself say, right on this spot, "I love it, I love it, I love it, because I was unhappy here." I don't know why.'

Then they walked downstairs quietly and once again started to manhandle the trunk. Pink was only serious for one moment.

He said, 'Don't go, love,' and she replied, 'I have already gone.'

* * *

There is a story told in Edinburgh of an old lawyer who never leaves his house and sleeps for only an hour or so at night, sitting in a chair. And he has lived like this for forty years, during which he has devoted his waking time to preparing a brief for an appeal. He is his own client. When he was only thirty action was taken against him for fraud and it was brought by his colleagues. He has, apparently, inexhaustible energy in the preparation of the case which will exonerate him, but although he never takes more or less sleep, in the winter he grows a little tired and it is said that around the end of February or the beginning of March, he will drink a bottle of bad port and confess with a bitter laugh, to his housekeeper, that he was guilty in the first instance. On the following morning, sober by 4 a.m., he starts work again.

Colonel Sir Henry Ferguson appeared to be a great deal more sane, and slept eight hours every night, but behind the blank stare and the occasional charming smile, there lay hidden a not unsimilar obsession, broken only, from time to time, by the appearance of his daughter, whose spectacular beauty appealed so much to his vanity.

His actions could have hardly been less like the unhappy Edinburgh lawyer's, but in principle the obsession was much the same. Born, however, a baronet and not a lawyer, he took a different line, which he followed equally as selfishly. His life was devoted to playing the unaccusing, injured gentleman. He never once mentioned the card game or anything to do with it again, and it is likely that except when he was with Mary, he never thought about anything else.

Apart from his ignoring a wife who slowly poisoned herself to death (for in the end, Lady Ferguson's diet was solely gin and French), there were, every day, many signs of this astonishing self-absorption.

He spoke very little, he avoided company, he was totally irresponsible where his children were concerned, although he often snapped at Pink whom he intensely disliked; he was close with his money but careful to pay all local tradesmen, he was charming to the odd visitors to the farm, and politically he was immovably Right. People meeting him noticed the far-away look in his eyes and instantly felt sympathy for him. They could never have believed, or had they believed could never have blamed him, for devoting his life entirely to Colonel Sir Henry Ferguson.

His routine, incidentally, in this self-imposed exile, was porridge and an egg for breakfast, *The Times* and the *Scotsman* in the morning, a glass of wine with lunch, a little rough shooting in the afternoon, and then tea with the family and the portable television set, which he carried from room to room. After that there was a bath, a pink gin, some light supper, a little more television, check the doors and up to bed.

But in everything he was a gentleman, almost a King in exile, and one of the ways in which this showed itself happened each morning at breakfast, now usually eaten in the kitchen. The Colonel, demonstrating that obsessional eye for detail, supped his porridge standing up. He usually did so by the Aga cooker, but occasionally he wandered about, and this explained his appearance at the bottom of the stairs beside the little pile of plaster which Mary's trunk had broken off the wall.

Seeing Pink, the Colonel turned savagely on him, telling him it was just the sort of bloody stupidly irresponsible thing he would expect of him. Even if he seldom made any moral judgments or suggestions to his children (because gentlemen in exile don't) he never stopped biting at Pink for his bad manners, his scruffy appearance, his slovenly habits and his stupidity. It was a family joke, which Pink did not enjoy, to say that Pink was in the dog-house if the Colonel ever addressed a civil word to him. The dog-house, beside Flush, the Colonel's Labrador, was a step up. Not that the Colonel ever took the risk of getting involved in a serious talk with his son. He avoided him.

So, while Pink was saying 'Sorry, sir' and 'Won't happen again, sir', and Caliban-like, shuffling forward with the trunk, the Colonel turned away, towards the kitchen. As he did so he murmured, 'I don't know what the hell you want a bloody great trunk like that for anyway,' and then with a short 'huh', he added, 'Montreal, I don't doubt.'

Mary had paused on the stairs. She had a kind of clean, morning 'on stage' brilliance, backed by the light from the big staircase window above and behind her.

'It's mine,' she said.

The Colonel stopped and smiled.

'Hello, my mouse,' he said kindly. 'I didn't see you standing there. You're up and about early.'

She took one step down.

'Daddy, I don't want you to bawl me out,' she said, perfectly confident that there was no possibility of this. 'I know it's rather awful of me and I shall miss you, darling, but I'm eloping, or what-ever it's called.'

'Christ almighty,' the Colonel said. 'Well there's a turn-out.' He screwed up his eyes, against the light, as he looked at her. 'You're sure you're right?'

'Not a bit,' she replied, definitely.

'With this Dow fellow?'

'Isn't it awful?'

'It sounds very rash, little one. But I suppose you know what you're doing.'

'I don't really think I do. But actually I've gone. So let's not fuss. It's rather like that awful wedding day. I mean it was too late, wasn't it, by the time we sat in there drinking sherry waiting for the taxi. That was fun.'

'You look even prettier,' the Colonel said.

'You're wonderful how you don't fuss. Daddy, if it all goes wrong I can always come back to you.'

'Always.' He laid down the porridge bowl and she put her arms round his neck. At the end of the hall, by the front door, Pink stood like a frightened butler, moving from foot to foot.

Mary smiled up at her father.

'This time if it's the most frightful muck-up we'll go on that holiday.'

'Fishing?'

She nodded and he squeezed her rather clumsily and tightly. It somehow betrayed his age.

'That is something to look forward to,' she said.

Then she looked over her shoulder and saw Pink and the trunk silhouetted against the bright green lawn beyond.

'Darling, I must go.'

'A little love,' he said and squeezed her again. She batted her eyelids against his cheek. 'A little love' had been a routine for twenty years.

'I'm worried about Stevie,' she said airily. 'You will be kind to him?'

The Colonel nodded as if she had mentioned her budgerigar. 'Tickety-boo' was all he said.

'Daddy, the gulls are inland. D'you think that's a sign of the most awfully bad luck?'

'Oh don't be so silly,' he comforted her. 'You're just a naughty, pretty girl.'

'That's it,' she replied with a delighted smile. 'That's much more in proportion. I knew you'd say the right thing. Come on.' She dragged him to the door by his hand.

He opened the car door for her, but it was Pink who lugged the trunk into the back. David laughed ironically at the size of it, but laughed with Pink, not with Mary, who sat still and upright in the front seat. She said to her father, 'Go away, now please,' and he blew her a kiss and withdrew.

As he walked back to the door, he looked at his watch. He shouted, 'If you get a good run through you should catch the ten o'clock ferry,' and (as Pink later put it) Mary said, quietly, by way of merry reply:

'I feel as if I were going to the gas chamber.'

Cathie, the maid, who had a peculiarly poor grasp of situation, was rather taken by David's looks, and when she gathered what was going on she rushed from the kitchen and threw some rice half-heartedly at the car, wishing them good luck.

'Oh God,' Mary said, dropping her head. 'That is bad luck.' The Colonel sent the girl back to the kitchen saying, 'That's enough of that,' and hearing the command in his voice, Flush, the dog, began to bark.

Mary looked at David as he pressed the self-starter. She said: 'Please don't look angry.'

He took his hand off the steering-wheel and said:

'My sweet, it's your idea.'

She asked very fiercely, 'What's my idea. What is?'

'Steady,' he said, putting both hands back on the wheel, as the car moved off. Pink put his head through the window, held his nose and pulled an imaginary plug.

'Good-bye, old slob,' he said.

*   *   *

Breakfast in the kitchen that morning was a more than usually disturbing meal. Cathie, perhaps because the quiet that had descended rather unnerved her, decided to be cheeky to Pink, who put on his dark glasses again. The Colonel sat staring out at the floods. When Stephen came down he at once began to set the kitchen table, and Cathie, a little heavily but with the best intentions, said:

'I don't know what we'd do without Mr. Stephen, really I don't.'

Shortly after, Macdonald came in, in her cheap fur coat. She and Stephen exchanged glances and seemed tacitly to agree that it was wiser to say nothing. She sat down, away from the table and told Cathie to give her a cup of tea.

Stephen said quietly, 'We'd better hurry, Pink.'

'Oh yes?' Pink asked. 'Why's that? It's the Sabbath, isn't it?'

Stephen pulled in his chair.

'Sabbath or no Sabbath,' he said, 'if you remember, we've got a pack of school children arriving at nine who'll throw spuds at each other and get paid for doing it, unless we're there to shout.'

'By God, yes,' Pink said. 'We'll fix them.'

'You're coming out?'

'Of course I am,' Pink exclaimed.

94

Stephen nodded and said, 'Good.'

There followed a prolonged silence as they sat eating. It became almost unbearable, but just before Pink felt something had to be said, Macdonald began, in her usual gloomy voice:

'Did you see Mr. Thompson at the dance, him with the centre parting?'

Stephen asked, 'The chartered accountant?' But Macdonald did not reply. She looked very tired and dazed.

'There's a story about him,' she went on, as if she were describing a dream. 'When he's on his honeymoon he sends Sheila up to her bed first and after a dram he comes up. He's near fifty when he's married first, and he's got habits. He opens the window just that much—you know, he's fastidious. So he folds his shirt and trousers and all. He puts his shoes, very neat, outside to be cleaned. He lays his dressing-gown, precise, over the chair and he kneels and says his prayers. Then he switches out the light and just before he climbs into bed he says, "And noo Mrs. Tampson," he says, "your thingamy if you please." '

She took up her spoon and continued stirring her tea. There was a terrible, embarrassed silence and Stephen very softly laid down his cup. Extremely seriously and quietly Pink said, 'Very good' just before Macdonald dropped her spoon in the saucer again and burst into tears. Covering her face with her hands she said to the Colonel:

'I'm sorry. I'm sorry. I don't know what came over me. I'm sorry——'

And they all rose and reached towards her. It was the first they knew of the Captain's death.

The Colonel said, 'No matter; one of those things,' and then Cathie, who was by the range, began to giggle.

She said, 'You mean Leslie Thompson? I think that's funny.' She laughed out loud. 'I'm sorry, but I do.'

Pink said, 'Shut up,' then softened the blow. 'Nothing personal, old thing——' He got up and walked out of the kitchen, leaving Stephen to cope with Macdonald who was beginning, in a broken sort of way, to talk about the Captain's last moments.

Pink pocketed his dark glasses and smiled gaily at the walled garden, the big lime trees, the yew hedge, the black shed, the dairy and the castellated steadings behind. He looked even happier when he turned his eyes to the white clouds bowling across the sky. He spoke under his breath.

'You old tragedy, you,' he said. 'You rotten thing.' And then, at once, he underwent one of those extraordinarily swift changes of mood. He froze, with his head cocked slightly to one side and his smile was suddenly false and bitter; even cruel. He was thinking of Captain Gordon. At last he raised his eyebrows, sighed, and by way of epitaph applied Rabelais' last words:

'Tirez le rideau, la farce est jouée.'

13

Cousin, you without morals,

When I dropped the receiver back on its rest, my angelic mother (who had tactfully disappeared into the parlour as I spoke) returned and she looked upset.

'Nothing amiss, I hope? Is it bad news, David?'

I shook my head. I smiled, even, and said 'No.' I never lied to my mother except by silence which is only, sadly to say, that I seldom told her any of the truth. But she understood. She turned away without complaint. I just caught sight of the side of her face and I recognized there exactly the same expression which she had worn ten years before when I told her of my separation. But she never uttered judgment; not after I was grown up. She talked that morning only of tiny creature comforts. Would I like her to prepare a picnic lunch for the road? 'I shouldn't like to worry about you,' she said, and added more quickly, 'Not on that account.'

I think that I must have answered 'no' more abruptly than I realized.

She bowed her head and said again very quietly, 'I would prepare it for two.' Angels are not stupid.

*   *   *

I knew, as I drove to you that morning, along deserted roads through fields of stooked corn, under the huge beeches that reach across the road, I knew I was about to destroy. All that can be said for me is that knowing that, I did not feel excited. I have never felt so depressed. Or is that worse? Here came the bludgeon, shaped by Calvinist hands.

A dear friend of mine's pet otter was once slaughtered by a Scottish workman who saw it on the road. For apparently no good reason he just picked up his long spade and crushed its head. There in Juniper Bank, were you, as illogical, as selfish and as sweet as any otter. It's a nightmare remembered. . . . A big yew hedge, that grows and grows.

You shall not go free. Here comes the spade.

*　　*　　*

There was a murderer's confession that appeared about that time in one of the Sunday papers. The murderer drove the victim to a deserted marsh near Ely, to do away with her, and as she was perfectly able-bodied it was important, for the smooth success of the crime, that he should give no indication of anything except love as he drove through the last village before the fens. In many other ways he proved to be an extremely subtle and well-controlled operator, but he very nearly failed, in this case, because he found it impossible to be pleasant to the girl during the journey. He bickered and quarrelled with her all the way, so that several times she demanded that he should stop the car. In those last hours he could not, in effect, bring himself to deceive the person he knew he was going to destroy.

He might have been telling the story of the Byronic marriage, the one when the groom turns unbearably hostile between the altar and the first hotel.

*　　*　　*

It began almost straight away.

'Be glad,' you said, stretching out a cupped hand in which I placed no kiss.

'Darling, don't be huffy. The ferry doesn't matter anyway. Nothing matters now, does it?'

It was my arm you clasped so tightly now.

'Don't look so black. Look out there, it's terribly pretty, it really is. The smoke's not going straight up to the sky—look,' you said, pointing to a cottage down from the road that led through the first kind, lowland hills. 'It's going downward, the smoke, which isn't a good sign, but that won't matter either. We'll be gone. Will we ever come back here again?'

'You *talk*——'

'You'll have to put up with that,' you said bravely rather than cheerfully, now. 'Everybody does. Darling, I know what you're feeling. I know exactly and I promise I understand. You feel you're trapped. There's a song in Figaro.' You tried a few notes but failed to find a key, then went on, 'You think all the fun's over. That's what it is. I promise I understand.'

'I promise you don't,' I said.

You laughed a little at the trunk in the back seat.

'It is rather excessive,' you said, and then, 'Please, darling, don't frighten me.'

'For heaven's sake——'

'But *tell* me, honestly. Then I'll understand.'

'You sound so bloody cheerful.'

You answered meekly, 'I'm not, if that's a help.'

*　　*　　*

'Please tell me, darling, try and tell me. I'm sure I'd understand.'

Again and again, your voice: 'Darling, I'm sure I'd understand.'

Oh, but I gave myself a score of reasons. I flattered myself at one moment on the theme of the Byronic marriage. Flattered myself that by reasons of birth, of the long line of Protestants and angels, I alone was complicated and made of many men. That now I was forced (I thought of it as 'forced') to live with you I would give away too much of myself and you, dim one, would not understand. I turned it round so that I was the otter and you the spade. That was merely the first vanity.

The other self-flattery, you will remember. I must have shouted it at you a hundred, hundred times. I explained to you, talking almost as fast as yourself, in bed, in cars, in the flat, in night-clubs —God knows where—and grew blind with rage at you, cousin, for your dishonesties, saying, 'You do not know the meaning of love.' You came back like a child asking the same questions again.

Exactly like a child, because, rightly, my reasons for bullying you, as I then explained them, did not satisfy you.

All I did was to shout the same lies again. At the time, I had convinced myself. After all, the explanation absolved me of blame. It explained too, why I spent so much of the time in Classroom IV and in all the other hundred places, getting to the bottom of your sinless lies. I saw you, I said, so amazed, so confused and frightened of life that you would not accept it at all and therefore were incapable of love. There were a hundred examples all like those odd, frightening stories you told about your mother and Arbuthnot—why choose such an extraordinary name? And so I accused. Your hysteria, your skating on the surface, your very imagination was an insult to my love. . . . Do you remember? (And I know the answer to that. You can remember, but you do not.)

I almost beat my chest. My love was something very different. I had lived and come through the turmoils, the girl friends, the harlots, the queers, the wife; my love was real and left unsatisfied. I treated you in bed, when I think of it now, like a clockwork mouse that would not go fast enough.

Oh, cousin, I remember your eyelashes, I don't know why.

And out of bed, I treated you worse. But the explanation, please note, absolved me. I even persuaded some of my more intelligent friends who objected to my treatment of you, that I was the injured party. I did not accuse you precisely of coldness. That would have been too glaringly untrue. Nor precisely of stupidity; for the same reason. I used to say of you, with smiling condescension, 'Poor darling one; she's too frightened to love. It's my mistake. I thought I could help her out of that.'

14

On the Ferry over the Forth, as the sky clouded over, I joined the queue at the ticket office, and picking your way through twenty cars packed closely together, you went aft to the windswept passengers' deck. Half-way across the river, when the ferry passed almost underneath the span of that huge red bridge I rejoined you —remember? You greeted me with such fear in your eyes that it seemed you expected to be murdered, there and then. You held on to the rail and turned to the sea again.

Ignoring the spray that splashed your face, almost enjoying its sting, so it seemed, I remember your nodding towards the Fife coast. Swallowing then speaking even more quickly than you had done in Classroom IV. I can still play it back.

'I never told you, but I went to school down there. I really enjoyed it too. They say those that are happy at school are happy at home, so there you are—that must mean something. Though I don't suppose they approved of me very much. I wasn't actually voted pupil most likely to succeed, I . . .'

I did not help you.

You went on, 'They'd all sorts of silly rules and made an awful fuss when I carved somebody else's name on a desk. Even the other girls thought that was rather off. They all nudged, you know, and looked. I used to lose my temper rather a lot. There wasn't Pink to cool me down. Actually the girl whose name I did carve couldn't have been more pleased. She'd obviously got a crush on me or something. I suppose that's why I carved her name. Lord, there was such a fuss—and about other things. But Daddy was marvellous. He used to come down and look so wonderful that the house-lady or whatever she was called couldn't keep it up at all. Awful, really, I think it was the title as much as the looks. Once he quite turned things round. He came down supposedly to discuss taking me away, which would have been a pity, really, and ended by taking me and two of my chums out for a strawberry tea. A great *coup*. Not this other girl, mind. Two of my healthy hockey-playing friends. I was good at games. You'd never have guessed that, would you? That's one of the reasons they kept me, I suppose. Fanny Blankers Whatsit. I could always run as fast as Pink. I played on the wing at hockey on all sorts of gloomy days like this, then all the same girls that had done the nudging and the looking and the baiting would sidle up after a match and say I was a good sport. Can you imagine? I think they must have got the phrase from their mothers, old frumps that most of them were.'

More slowly you said, 'Oh goodness, I didn't say good-bye to Macdonald.' Frowned, then went on, 'She used to come to chapel sometimes. I once wept when she went away. I was terribly angry about doing that. . . .'

Paused, cousin, then managed to say, 'She used to go and see Pink too, at his ghastly private school. Chuff-chuff, he was then. He went everywhere like a train.'

Paused again, like a diver hanging in mid-air. Then came the fall. Head dropped down to your hands on the rail. Husky and sore-throated:

'Oh God, darling, I hate it, I hate it. Please take me back. I promise it's a mistake. You don't love me and I don't even love you. I don't know why I came. I don't know why I went with you this morning. It's a mistake. We can still go back.'

Other travellers on the ferry, shunning embarrassment of any sort, moved away. Sobbing quite hopelessly now, you leant a little over the rail and let the wind blow your tears into the sea.

'You really do enjoy making an exhibition of yourself.' That is my voice, Oxford cold, that day.

From you, a whispered, 'Go away.'

'Surely,' I replied. 'You'll find me in the car.'

Five minutes later, as the ferry bumped against the quay, I watched you dry your eyes and push your hair off your forehead. You climbed into the car, looked straight ahead, and, bitterly, said something worse than:

'You can bloody well give me a cigarette.'

'Of course. If the cabaret's over.'

We drove on to the border and a T-bone, Scampi-frite type country house hotel. We both got pretty drunk.

*   *   *

Remember the following morning. I always thought of it as one of the happiest times, even if you seemed thoughtful and disturbed. I surprised you when you were still clench-fisted and asleep. I woke without the murderer. For half an hour I forgot the spade.

You woke when I was sitting astride you. You looked so serious. I drew circles round your tummy, playing one of your games, 'Round and round the garden'. You did not trust me, but you were kind.

I remember that as I went and ran the bath I was singing, and I can still see you frown. Disturbed by otter-instinct, you lay with the sheet wound tightly round you, sucking your thumb.

I was pleased with myself. For months, even years, I carried that about as a happy memory. Then one day I saw it in its true light, and it horrified me. The workman was playing at otters. It's, somehow, obscene.

Cousin, forgive.

PART III

The Big City

15

BUT the worst of it came at the end of it, and David, with the expertise of the professional torturer, worked it obliquely. The really nasty stuff was presented to her from the mouth of the one person she certainly loved.

It happened six months later, at about ten o'clock on a summer's night. Pink, Mary and David sat amongst the dirty glasses and ashtrays in the flat in that tatty, curved and concrete block off the Gray's Inn Road. David had shown the last of the guests out not half an hour before and she had spent most of the intervening period abusing his friends rather wildly, calling them hypocrites, parasites, narcissusites, sodomites and Gaitskellites.

It was Pink's first visit. He had come to the party softly, in suède shoes and his best pin-stripe suit, remembering Mary's birthday and bearing a gift of Edinburgh Rock.

David merely prompted. He sat on a cushion by the fireplace and said, all Oxford, 'No, do tell her, Pink. Do. It was really very interesting. I thought you coped admirably.'

It was the third time David had encouraged him and it was obvious that Pink wanted to get it off his chest.

'Actually, they seemed rather interested in the guv'nor.' Pink was considerably fatter.

'How?' Mary asked, and she was correspondingly thinner.

'Well, about the cards and that. This politician chap, David's chum, knew a bit about it. I don't know. Perhaps his old man was involved too.'

'What did he say?'

'Oh, nothing much. Just another card-scandal theory.'

Mary was sharp; a great deal sharper than when she had left home.

'Don't avoid it, Pink. I know they said something foul.'

'Actually, old thing, they seemed very sympathetic towards the guv'nor. Truly. I was impressed.'

'Tell her,' David said. 'If only for a lesson.' Then he turned to her. He always smiled at her now. 'God knows it would help if you had some of Pink's forbearance.'

She said, swiftly, 'I had. And what did you call me then? An unthinking, self-pitying little yes-girl. . . . I believe it was better than that.'

'I hope it was,' David said, again with a false smile, playing the patient, injured party.

She turned back to Pink. David watched.

'What was this theory?'

'Perfectly straightforward, really. I don't suppose there's anything in it, really.' Swiftly again, almost with a swoop, she replied loudly:

'I'm certain there isn't. I'll bet they never even heard about the guv'nor until I came along. Someone'll have made up some nasty story. Probably David planted it.'

'It might be right,' Pink warned.

'Then tell me.'

Suddenly Pink threw the story off as if it were of little importance.

'Suggestion was that there were probably quite a lot of card games in that club, late at night, you know.'

'And Daddy always cheated?'

'No. That's not actually what was suggested. But, you know, those same chaps, more or less the same—one, particularly the same, but I can't remember the fellow's name——'

The more Pink tried to dismiss the story, the more obvious did it become that it had shattered him, only because it had struck him so clearly as true. Mary began to look a little scared. Pink resumed.

'Anyway the same chaps met, most nights. All very influential and rich and so on except for the guv'nor, who they'd kind of taken up, you know—the way these things happen——' he said vaguely and David got up and refilled his glass. 'Well actually, the suggestion is that perhaps they took the guv'nor up for something other than a fourth hand at bridge or whatever it was they played.'

Mary said 'Huh!' almost brassily, a noise she had never made before. Pink looked at her slantwise, wondering if she had already understood the homosexual implication. But she had not quite.

She went on, 'As a kind of innocent. To lend respectability—the fool, I suppose, while the others really gambled illegally?'

'Not actually that,' Pink said, leading her gently, with a kind of low, inadmissible thrill.

'Well, what?'

'Suggestion was that the guv'nor was really rather nice-looking in those days.'

'Go *on*, Pink.' She was refusing to think.

'One of these chaps had taken a bit of a fancy to him. Not exactly for his card-playing, if you see what I mean.'

Mary grew pale as he went on:

'Well, anyway, after a bit of this the guv'nor either fell to it what was happening, maybe even got a little involved, then got pretty worried. Bit of a flutter. Panicky, as one might say. So he turns round and marries the girl from Dundee. She's pretty. Plenty of jute money——. He's a handsome young soldier. Very pleasant. A softness in the voice. That accent, you know. Perfectly right sort of match both sides.'

Mary's voice was much more controlled when she interrupted again. It was as if she spoke along a ruled line.

'That's obviously nonsense. We know perfectly well that they were married when it happened—whatever did happen. You were nearly born. I should think that's the real truth of it even if it would disappoint them. Lots of girls behave in a mad sort of way when they're pregnant. You can imagine Mummy.'

'I should think you're right,' Pink said, unconvinced.

'Of course I am.'

'Mark you, it doesn't mean there weren't those card parties before. Perhaps he got a little involved again. Actually this politician fellow, David's chum, very bright he seemed, discussing this —he had a little theory.'

'I'll bet he did.'

'It could be true,' Pink said. 'Could be. His suggestion was that the guv'nor went back into the lion's den, you see, just to kind of prove something. Either that or to say there were no hard feelings. But if that's true it wasn't the wisest move. I shouldn't think

Mumbo understood—she would never have twigged that sort of thing, poor pigeon. Those Dundee blindnesses, and that. Suggestion was that somebody might have said something in her ear. Probably very vague—"Bad influence" or something like that. But they evidently said something that upset her pretty badly. She was tearful for quite a while. . . . And these other chaps couldn't help smiling, you know. You can see they would. So this night they do play cards and the guv'nor goes a bit far just to win.'

'They wouldn't dare sue him,' Mary said.

'Not quite the point, old love.'

But before he could go on, as if she, too, scented truth, she asked suddenly, coldly, as she got up for a cigarette:

'D'you mean to say you just stood and listened while they said these horrid things?'

'It was a friendly sort of talk. They weren't just being vicious, you know,' Pink said. 'Cocktail party stuff.'

'Of course they were,' she snapped. 'Can't you see that? They can't stand the idea that somebody else might be normal. Didn't you even tell them to shut up?'

Pink looked, for a second, as if he were talking to his father, not Mary. His impediment reappeared. After a little circle of the head he said:

'N-no, old bean. Not much point.'

'Oh God,' she said, dropping her head—a head which she was beginning to learn to use. 'I see. And now David makes you tell me this so's I'll start hating you too. . . . You don't know, Pink darling. You don't begin to understand the way their minds work. . . . Never mind, never mind.'

Pink checked his fly buttons, shifted in his seat, and sighed. 'Frankly,' he said, 'hitting about didn't really occur to me. I was a bit—what shall we say—a bit put out? You see, old cocky, I couldn't help feeling that maybe they'd got a point. I mean the thing's never been quite explained.'

'Oh, don't be silly,' she replied. 'How could they possibly know? They weren't there.'

'One of their uncles evidently——'

'I don't believe that,' she said at once.

'No, no, he wasn't there, but he was in the club. Not in this particular room, you follow. He was sitting upstairs a bit later on.

106

Also a soldier, so I'm told.' Pink suddenly seemed to want to leave the story there. He drained his glass. 'Well, anyway, that was it.'

'What about this man upstairs?' David asked, breaking the silence that fell.

'Well, evidently he was sitting upstairs. Your chumbo told me this, you follow, saying what a terrible thing it was——'

'You bet——' Mary said disbelievingly.

'While he sat there, this old gent,' Pink went on guiltily with pleasure, again, '—he became aware of a rather unnerving noise and at last he traced it to the writing-room. It was late, I gather. He was the last in the club, or thought he was. Well, to cut out the painful details, it was the guv'nor in there, poor old chap. Crying his heart out.'

Mary sat very still, but tears rolled down her cheeks. It was as if the full meaning of the story had only just begun to dawn on her.

'How dare they say that,' she said in a very low whisper.

Pink now seemed strangely disconnected from the story. He did not look at Mary although David watched her tears. He went on, 'There was another odd little point.' David smiled.

Louder, this time, Mary said with pride, 'How dare they say that.'

Pink said, with definition now; with effective, destroying proof positive: 'This chappie in the club. He's the same man who sold us our farm. Oliphant. So there it is.'

And then she broke. She broke in a way that make Pink stand up and then stand back, and very shakily light a cigarette, not looking at what she did, and for a moment afterwards not daring to glance at her face. As a child, both at school and in Pink's presence, she had several times completely lost control of her temper, perhaps as badly as this, but somehow in a child, it is never so frightening. Her voice rose beyond 'How dare!', beyond all words to a single scream as she attacked David, kicking and scratching. When Pink, at last, very gingerly tried to interfere she also kicked at him and called him a coward.

'Darling, darling,' David said softly. He could not have behaved more kindly, trying to soothe her, trying to press her arms to her side but very gently, and also trying to kiss her tears. At last her voice dropped and she began to weep with long low sobs, and then all of a sudden she was quite still as if she were rigid and dead on

107

her feet. Pink was again in the corner, smoking his cigarette furiously when David helped her out of the room to the bathroom where he held her forehead while she was sick. She washed and he came back first.

Pink, with his usual technique of facing a homicidal lunatic with 'a spot of the butcher's itch, old man?' said:

'Everything sorted out all right?'

David replied:

'She'd drunk far too much, anyway.'

But the manner of her return seemed to suggest that she had in the past months quite often been shaken as deeply as this. Her forehead looked higher because her hair was a little wet from the sponge. She still looked pale. But she made it clear at once that she wanted the incident to be forgotten. She did not apologize. She said:

'Where are we going to eat?'

Pink's teeth were chattering.

16

'Come home, Jim Edwards,' Pink said, but she sniffed and shook her head.

'No.' Then she put out a hand to him. 'I'm glad that party was even bloodier. It makes us friends again.'

'Again?' he asked. 'No question of that.'

'No,' she said uncertainly. 'No, of course not.'

'Mark you, you did kick out a bit.'

She brought her fingers together and nodded, firmly. 'That's all it was.' Then she swept back her hair, and asked:

'How's Stephen?'

'Stiffy? Much the same. My jalopy awaits at the door.'

'No.'

'Daddy?' Pink seemed to have to try and remember to whom she referred.

'Jogging along, I think, old thing,' he said, with a frown, at last. 'Square eyeballs. He takes the TV out shooting with him. D'you think that little tale had any truth in it?'

'Don't,' she said sharply.

'Sorry. I thought it might be better to air it. For old Pink, too.'

'It was a stupid story.'

'Lovey, why don't you come home? I'd row you in, I really would.'

'No.'

'Your life, Lilian.'

She nodded. They were sitting on the stairs that led up to the flat door. It was about half past one in the morning. They had left David at the party where they had met all the same guests, one degree drunker. Mary sat a step higher than Pink, who for some potty reason, now lolled back, pretending that he was basking in the sun. He sifted imaginary sand through his fingers as he talked. Light from the hall shone up the lift shaft beside them but otherwise it was dark. A few minutes later, Pink said:

'Give us a statement, guv.'

But she still sat silent. Pink looked up at a small pilot light at the top of the lift shaft.

'That sun', he said, 'is bloody hot. Very dangerous indeed, I'd say. Pass me the Ambre Solaire.'

'God, I love you, Pink. I do. I promise I do.'

'Thank you.' Pink sat up. 'Chumbo, is it always like this?'

'What exactly?'

'I mean all the big guns, you slamming him and that, and then him just ditching you like this.'

She nodded quickly. 'That sort of thing. It may be a bit worse because you're here. That's what he'll tell me, anyway.'

'But why do you stay?'

She shrugged her shoulders.

'Love?' he suggested.

She shook her head. 'I don't think so.'

'Hate?'

'Not always.'

'Sex?'

'Not altogether.'

'Fear?'

'I'm sometimes scared. You're awfully good at asking questions.'

'You're awfully bad at answering them,' Pink said.

She apologized and he suddenly grabbed her hand. He had never had to do so before. They both noticed that.

'No sorries to me,' he said. 'That's not on at all. Why doesn't he sack you?'

'He says,' she said, 'that he loves me.'

'Funny way to show it.'

'No,' she said thoughtfully. 'It's just that he shows it in too many ways. I really ought to be happy. I get everything. He's practically hitting me one minute and the next he's on his knees begging me. He's insulting me or kissing my feet.'

'And bed?'

She frowned.

'It's probably my fault,' she said.

'Oh, Goderooni,' Pink said. 'Not another Stiffy?'

'Oh no,' she shook her head. 'Not that a bit.'

'But you don't like it?'

She, too, had begun to play with Pink's sand. She passed it from hand to hand.

'Very clean sand.'

'Trust St. Andrews,' Pink replied.

'I do at the time,' she said. 'I like it very much indeed at the time.'

'Afterwards, big guilt?'

She nodded. Then, at last, went on:

'What's awful is that I sometimes think I stay just for it.' She stopped and shook her head. 'That really can't be true. It's not guilt because of Stephen, mind. It's something else.'

'A little bit of sin.'

'Well, it can't be, can it, Pink? I mean we've never had anything to do with all that, you and me. If you say "Stuff Moo", Moo really can't worry you, can he? I mean that's not fair at all.'

'Deepers,' Pink announced. 'We've got an awful lot of Moo tucked away. Could be a throw-back to Moo. What's the feeling? Just, shouldn't be doing it at all?'

'No,' she said steadily. 'It's just a bit of a sham. D'you want to know?'

'You want to tell?'

'Yes. Give me some more sand. I'm going to need it.'

'Come home, Jim,' Pink said, but she ignored that. She frowned as if she were collecting herself to take a big hurdle.

'I'm pretty dim, but I think it works like this. We do everything in the book you see and yet in an odd, awful sort of way he's never slept with me, nor me with him. I told you about that country girl of mine on the bridge—well, like that, only different. And I'm sure it's worse for him than me. He's always somebody else in bed. I don't think he sees how different he is. And I either lie there a bit bewildered, you know, because that's really how I feel, or else I kind of whip up an act as well. When we're both bluffing we're capable of big thrills and we can say "nobody's like us" and all the things everybody says, I'm sure. But you see it's a sham, Pink. I know it's a sham. I don't know who he is, and I don't really think he knows who he is. Look at him even tonight, charming at his own party, wily and all kind of cruel when you were talking about Daddy, then arrogant and womanizing at this last do. Yet sometimes, in fact quite often, he's the child. I don't know how he's the energy to keep it up.'

She stopped and looked up.

She said, 'Do you understand any of that lot?'

'You bet,' Pink said. 'Why d'you have to pick the weird ones?'

'There's a question,' she said. 'Why do they hunt me?'

'Because, my love,' Pink said, 'you're the most vulnerable thing on two legs.'

She shook her head, then swept back her hair, again. She wore it longer, now.

'Watch that sand,' Pink said.

'Not now,' she said. 'Not vulnerable now. You should try being a girl.'

'It could be arranged,' he replied. 'This Modern Age.'

'I'll tell you. Now life's getting sorted out. I know now I'm either very soft and breasts and that, or else I'm just a hard little triangle of hair. It's about as simple as that. Only I think I wanted to be soft more than anything. . . .'

'What's to stop you?'

'Me. Once you've started being the other sort of girl, it doesn't seem to be so easy to go back. All girls are rakes, so some Pope said, and that's the truth of it. I used to think I'd get fat. But I'll probably end up like a piece of chewed string.'

111

She paused again, then said:

'Very chewed. Tarts do. . . . There's not much of me left.'

'Oh yes there is,' Pink said very quietly, and she seized and squeezed his hands. 'Chumbo, you'd better come home.'

'No.' She looked disturbed as if she wondered why she was so sure. Then very suddenly she said:

'Lovey, we could talk forever, but I'm tired now. You go home. I'm going to bed.'

She stirred and her clothes rustled. Pink sat upright and when she switched on the light, at the top, by the flat door, he rubbed his eyes.

'Are you going to stick to him?' Pink asked.

Again she frowned, deeply this time, and looked down at her shoes. She had one hand on the flat door.

'I don't know till I find him, really,' she said. Then she told Pink to go away. He went, waving up from each landing, all the way down to the hall.

*   *   *

At the last moment, he decided to leave his jalopy where it was, and take a taxi as far as Piccadilly. Then he decided to walk about a bit. Paddling through Belgrave Square, only a couple of hundred yards away from base, he was accosted by a tart on wheels. He did not know that a modern habit was for prostitutes to ride in well-appointed cars and her arrival at the kerb beside him left him speechless. He looked at her dejectedly, and thought what a plain little woman she was. Any colour she might have had by day was washed away by the street light. She managed a very uncertain smile for a professional as she said:

'Hullo, saucy.'

Pink replied only with a faint aspirant as he climbed into the car. 'Winded,' he said to himself, 'I'm winded, not windy.' For the first mile no words passed between them until at last she asked:

'Where do you come from then?'

Pink replied very loudly, 'France!'

When they arrived at the house, which was large and condemned somewhere in the no-man's-land west of the Edgware Road, Pink looked round the room. He had to go through all the business with the homely maid (two and six will do very nicely) and the welcome-home poodle (he's from France, too), and then the girl closed the door behind her.

'I say,' Pink said, sociably, spotting the electrical stimulator nearby. 'The old Vibro on the couch, what?' and she gave him a look that made him unbutton his trousers, at once.

17

'The last days of Pompey . . .' Your girlish quote. From one of your long letters, which then I dismissed and now wish I'd kept. I can't remember all you said in it, but I remember it was full of apologies, saying you didn't know what came over you to make you bolt at that of all times. You devoted a paragraph to 'good friends' and I was reminded of that tie you were always going to buy for Stephen. You never mentioned my bloodinesses—from the letter one would have guessed that it had been a sunny affair. I can see your upright writing and I remember thinking that it looked as if you had drawn pencil lines across the page, then rubbed them out afterwards. It often struck me as odd that your hands, which usually moved so quickly and competently, produced such child-like writing. But everything was neat and correct. I think you had even checked the spelling, and I'm almost certain you wrote the letter twice. There wasn't a single blot, or scoring out.

I knew much better than you why you left, and at that time I remember telling myself, even if I didn't believe it, that I'd won. Nor was it a surprise when you went. I saw it coming days before. And I knew you wouldn't go home with Pink, cousin. To my eternal shame, I'd fixed that. You frowned whenever I mentioned his name. You may have let him take you back from a party, but you weren't going to go home with him. Not until you'd sorted things out in your mind. I was quite sure of that.

There seem to be only two ways in which the immature—and I am talking of myself, not you—can display a little of their true identity: first in loving someone so much that they forget their own masks and defences, but if they do this successfully they pass out of the category; they are not of the permanently immature. The other way is to fail. And that's really what happened, on a small scale. And apart from that, in the end, after the thrill of the most damnable act of all, namely upsetting you and Pink, the workman was too tired and sad and sorry for himself to lift the spade. The otter approached with safety.

I remember in the kitchen we managed the sort of conversation that only goes with very grown-up people. I didn't quite believe in it, afterwards, but at the time it was genuine enough. I told you all about the experiment that had gone wrong in this lab, on or about the very bench on which I write this now. You never quite understood, but you frowned (which is to say you tried), and I for my part took lots of trouble trying to explain it all to you. One day I'll write it down carefully for you, because I never quite got it across. I gave you a parallel in communication engineering but you didn't understand what communication engineering was so I suppose that only muddled you more. (I can still see the frown as you tried so hard.) In complicated signal and response systems engineers have proved it's more efficient to duplicate some of the signals; to send the telephone message along two lines, because in this way inefficiencies through outside interference are usually eliminated. Still with me? Read it twice. All I was trying to do was show that this happened in animals as well. I got myself a cat most days from the animal house downstairs and carved out bits of its mid-brain through which I knew certain signals were passed. Things called 'righting reflexes', in fact, which means sticking out a leg to stop yourself falling over, or in the case of a cat, if you put it on its back, trying to get on all fours again. If it did get on all fours, or at least tried to do so, after I'd sliced the one telephone line which everybody knows about, then I'd prove that there was duplication in the system.

Isn't it odd, how I go into all that again? I desperately want to get it across to you now because you were right, in a way, about the schoolmaster. In those moments I found patience. I showed, for a few seconds, anything that's nice about me.

You know I always used to tell you that everybody and especially those mixed-up characters, the children of the angelic, are six people at once? Haunted perhaps, by a lot of ghosts of their fathers who have committed no sins except sins of omission, all saying "Go on, take everything, we never did!'? I don't really think the haunted idea bears examination, but I know I feel now, at a moment of peace (although not through the storm like you), most like a rather nice uncle of mine who was once Chief Constable in Forfar. He was patient and steady, he ate too many cookies and buns, and maybe he was on the dull side, but he was a much better teacher than his brother, my father, who was headmaster for twenty years. It's not that I'm cast more in his mould than anybody else in the family. It's just that somehow he arrived, and arriving showed effortlessly, I suppose, all that's best about a Dow, and therefore all that's true about a Dow.

That was what you saw, my darling, in the kitchen. I was weary of bullying you, and I was weary of making simple practical experimental mistakes with those cats. (Isn't it significant that I've never been a good experimentalist in the practical sense? That needs a steady physical touch.) You found Dow. Just for a few moments. And I can see your eyes now, not at all steady and loving but suddenly, very wary indeed, this way and that, as you fidgeted around. Two days later, amazed at yourself, because these were the best two days we had together, even if we never went to bed, you slipped away, not even leaving a note.

Even then, though I see it so clearly now, I deceived myself. It astonishes me that someone (forty was I? Forty-one?) could have been so blind to himself when he was given such clear clues. I saw you funked love, I saw it the minute, the very second you did. (It's the actual bat of an eyelid that I remember, as if it were yesterday) and, at once, I fabricated a whole load of lies. I swore I felt triumphant. When you had gone, and I wandered through the flat alone, from room to room, I whistled. I kept saying, 'You won, David, you won, she loved you in the end. She proved it so. She ran away, otter that she is, but the victory, Davie boy, is yours alone.'

For a day or two I was hopelessly restless, beginning things, as one does, but I made no effort whatever to find you. I was really glad that you had gone—that was the one true thing. And then I rang Phyllis, the wife that was, who I often see, and saw while you were with me, but was damned careful to make sure that she never met you. The ex-wife's life, selling hats in Regent Street, has put pounds of flesh on her. She's Scottish, too, as you know. I'm as cagey as that. Sleeping with her is a little like having a hot bath, and even to me she tends to quote Shelley before she puts on her clothes again.

I remember saying on the phone:

'The most awful thing's happened.'

'Yes?' Very coyly, from her.

'I'm inconsolable,' I said and explained.

She asked, 'Did she say something nasty?'

And I laughed.

'Worse,' I said. 'If she said anything, I'm sure it was nice.'

She promised to try to look in. She always makes it sound difficult. Everything in her life, she's sure, goes wrong and isn't easy.

'At once,' I hear another man's voice that is my own persuade her. 'That's very sweet of you.' She was there within the hour. We even had an expensive meal afterwards with myself at my most gay.

There's the picture, distant cousin, of a man in defeat.

18

Pink was back in Edinburgh by now, at the bar downstairs in the Café Royal doing his best to sum things up. He did so to a young man who had been with him at private school and who was now one of the grey-suited young men in a brewery which was a subsidiary of the Distillers Companies. He was doing very well. Pink confessed to feeling very shaky. Not really expecting to be understood he said, finishing one pink gin and ordering the next:

'*Reductio ad coitum*, chum. The jolly old R.A.C.'

He went to the basement, to the lavatory, on his own. Perhaps initials reminded him of the jolly old F.F.I. His guilt then and always, in spite of any medical reassurances, or advances in chemotherapy, took a physical form. By lunch-time he was perfectly convinced he had a bad go of the pox. He had to stop himself from telling everybody in the restaurant that he had. Weeping tomorrow, he assured himself, with a belch, and frying tonight. When he went up to the bar again he noticed in one of those awful, unmistakable flashes that the young men he had been talking to, no longer thought of him as a funny chap. They exchanged a glance which, in the years to come, he was to know very well. They were not so rude as to go off to their table without returning hospitality, but they seemed to move an extra inch away, and they were now in a hurry. They thought they were avoiding encouraging a friend who was clearly a potential drunk. They were actually avoiding failure, like the plague.

Pink told them, affably, to carry on and eat, and he pretended to be waiting for Mary, whom he knew to be in London. He mentioned her by name. Another gin persuaded him to go along Princes Street and buy a pair of pearl ear-rings. He would present them to Macdonald on his return to the farmhouse. Drink up, Pink old man, he said to himself, looking glassily round the small high room, with the old, marble oyster bar, and the stained-glass windows above. Going through the swing doors, when nobody could hear him he bawled out loud, 'I am afraid. Yippee!'

At home, only a few days later, he got a letter from Mary with her friend Jennifer's address in big capitals written across the top, with a childish joke beside it about next of kin. The letter itself was very short.

Dear Pink,

It was terribly nice seeing you and it did help. Thank you for the Rock which was a comfort when packing and unpacking at Jennifer's. Please note new address.

Am happier: often think of you.

luv from,

Martita Hunt.

Luv to Daddy too. Tell him she's perfectly O.K.

It wasn't her usual style to drop the first person singular and it was Pink's habit, not hers, to sign with a different name.

Very suddenly, Pink tore the letter into small pieces, then he went up to the woods by the gun-field and dropped the pieces in a clearing, where, as children, Mary and he had once buried a dead cock robin.

*   *   *

Mary now trod a well-worn path.

The atmosphere in the new flat was unrestful, even jumpy.

117

Jennifer was one of those girls who do better in war-time. She was thin and quite smart, but with a strong dash of Edinburgh that showed in the shoes and accessories which were bought to last. She had celebrated her twenty-third birthday with an abortion, the father of the child being her husband, and the experience had marked her more obviously than she imagined. She had a rather brittle, gay manner and she walked always as if she were being pulled along by two huge dogs on a leash. She insisted that life was short, and though she always said of her husband, 'Darling he was really very sweet to me', she had also found another phrase to obliterate the memory of a very unhappy two years, unhappy particularly for her, as she had behaved badly, and he had behaved well. She said:

'The milk of human kindness just wasn't strong enough for Scott-Dempster.'

Together, they lived an unreal life made up of realities; of house-keeping, rent, washing things in the basin, of seeing cinemas and offering drinks to young men with cars. Before she brought any-body who did not know Mary to meet her, Jennifer would explain quickly that she had just finished a *grande affaire* with David Dow, and if the guest did not recognize David's name she would follow it with Mary's maiden name, saying, 'You know—the scapegoat man—before the war. The baronet.' Mary, in her way, had name enough. That mattered to Jennifer.

And it was with Jennifer, some months later, that Mary went to a party in St. John's Wood. She only went because Jennifer could not stand the thought of going there, to a nameless party, on her own. It was held in a house that needed repairing and redecorating and a garden that was little more than a weedy rubbish dump. The party was thrown away, rather than given, by an acquaintance of Jennifer's husband, who wrote copy in an advertising agency. He too was something of a name-man, but amongst fifty, hard (gin-cup) drinking guests, there were only three with names. The first was an I.T.V. interviewer, an authority on all subjects, the second a young barrister who had defended a homicidal lunatic and the third a lady from Berlin who made the unlikely claim that she had slept with Brecht. To this group Jennifer was immediately led and Mary landed on the floor next to a man who worked for a serious film magazine, and sang Burl Ives songs like Burl Ives. The party needs no description except to say that it went on and on, until it was enlivened by the arrival of a jazz band who were on their way back from playing in Wisbech. Amidst the noise that followed, the bellow of the songs, the blast of the latest disc and the splash of the unrepeatable anecdotes, Mary watched herself reflected in the huge uncurtained, uncleaned window. Her hair seemed more brown than red. And it was while she was doing this that a very stupid young man said, not with malice, but because it was a smart line, 'Honey, take care. You've got that unlived-in look.' So she drank more seriously.

At half past three in the morning she was standing, for some reason which she could not remember, by a half-opened door to a bedroom, two floors up. She was with an extremely good-looking subaltern who was perhaps less out of water than he liked to suggest. He was considerably the smartest figure there, and there seemed to be no explanation for his attendance. It is doubtful whether he would have found himself with Mary, had he not heard her maiden name. The party was neither elegant enough nor slummy enough for a subaltern of the Brigade. The truth, which in the correct military fashion, he refrained from volunteering, was that he had been to school with the copywriter. They had shared a study together at Haileybury and their rejection of the solid middle-class background, although equally violent in both cases, had taken totally different forms. As he stood in the doorway, staring blandly at Mary who did not meet his eye, the last few people on the landing decided to return downstairs. One of the jazz men wished them luck and with a friend shoved them roughly into the dark bedroom and slammed the door. The subaltern was old enough not to withdraw, but young enough, when he was putting on his felt braces again, to make the mistake of assuming that it all meant as little to Mary as to himself. He suggested within a couple of minutes of completion that they go and find a drink. It was dark in the room but there was light enough for him to see her cover her forehead with her wrist. Like an old and inept husband he said, cheerfully:

'Come on, old ducks.'

She said, 'Please go away,' and that was that.

*　　*　　*

119

The job in publishing was as dull as Mary had been led to suppose it would be, so she could not complain. All the other girls she met outside the office were very envious of her and nothing she could say would persuade them that a large publishing office was duller than a merchant bank. Publishers themselves spend their lives telling girls like Mary this, and she had been further warned that having no shorthand would exclude her from the few more rewarding jobs in the office. So while her friends envied her she hammered away on a typewriter, filed things and kept a little notebook in which all permission payments were entered. Permissions, in and out; that is to say permission granted to other publishers to quote extracts from copyright works and vice versa, took most of her time, but even in this field she was not given full responsibility. By long usage, and with about half a dozen general exceptions, publishers ask the same copyright fee of two guineas a thousand words, but this calculation was not entrusted to a girl. Instead she took all the letters to a conscientious young man who marked each one with the appropriate fee.

What she thought about during all those hours, she could not herself explain. Even her imagination seemed to suffer. For the last hour each day, however, her thoughts were always the same. They were focused on her wristwatch and just as she had done at school, at the end of lessons, she would dash for her coat and escape before the rush. Hating the buses and the tube trains at half past five, she very often walked most of the way home, which was nearly two and a half miles. As she did so, with long steps, her eyes straight in front of her, only very occasionally straying to a shop window which she passed, nobody turned to look at her. Her coat was not very clean, her hair, now certainly more brown than red, was pulled back to a pony tail that was too young for her; her shoes were practical, with low heels. London had swallowed her.

Moreover with the loss of her imagination, facts began to take their toll. Losing part of her own personality she assumed some of the fears and habits of the girls around her, although their lives and natures were quite different from her own. She worried about money. She began to think about age for the first time, and not because her appetite had been whetted by the subaltern at the party, but because the last taboo had been broken, she started going out with other young men. Men know. She met their eye honestly and brightly. She saw several of David's friends. Her name was passed from one to another as worth looking up. She even went out with a married man from her office, in his car.

The extraordinary thing was that the numbness, the feeling of living only in a dream, was not broken when she suspected that she was pregnant. On the contrary, the feeling grew stronger. She was hardly responsible for her own actions.

*　　*　　*

Then, suddenly, life became real again. It took on a direct urgency which within a few hours threw the time she had spent in the copyright department into correct proportion. She knew then that what was little more than a long-drawn-out restless night's sleep must come to a sharp end. She was sitting half-way through one of the letters biting her nails and thinking that the formula was only one away from 'Grant we beseech thee, O Lord, permission to use two thousand five hundred words——' when she was called next door, to a room full of women, to answer a private telephone call on the outside line. As such calls were not encouraged she was already blushing when she lifted the receiver.

Jenny's 'Dah-ling' rang through the room. All the other women in it seemed to have reached a pause in their work. One rubbed out a word she had just typed, another sorted out some papers.

Mary said, 'What is it?'

'Something awful, darling.'

This could have meant that the gas had been switched off, or that Jennifer's current boy friend was quoted by the evening papers as out last night with Penelope Somebody-else. She knew, by Pink's telegraph, that is to say, not by some undiscovered sense, but by some undiscovered accuracy of the ear, that the news was dramatic and affected only her. Just as physical pain can be tolerated by the mind leaping a split-second ahead of the blow, she was balanced ready when it came.

Jennifer went on: 'D'you want this over the thing or shall I meet you for lunch?'

'Tell me.'

'Pink rang. He said I'd better tell you.'

'Daddy.'

'Yes. Look, he said he could cope and you must do what you want. Darling I'm so sorry.'

'I'll ring you back,' Mary said. She replaced the receiver softly and looked up at the four faces round her. All the women had assumed tragic expressions but they could not quite hide their delight that the morning's routine had been exploded.

She went without hesitation to a call-box to ring David, who sounded perfectly delighted to hear her.

'Look,' she said, 'Daddy's dead.'

'Lunch,' he replied.

'Yes, please.'

When she returned, the manager's permission for leave of absence had been granted. The conscientious young man stood by his desk like a very superior travel agent.

'He would like you to ring tomorrow or the next day telling him when you expect to return. I imagine you will be travelling north. I have looked up the trains for you.'

'That's very kind, Eric,' she said. 'But I think I'll go by plane.'

He blushed at the mention of his Christian name and when he shook her very firmly by the hand he could think of nothing better to say than 'Good luck.'

Other secretaries, hanging about the stairs of the ladies' cloak-room, resembled guests at the end of a wedding reception. They wished her good luck with their smiles and a few on more intimate terms said, 'It's more the shock than anything.' She nodded, and she could not say, 'To tell the truth I haven't given him a thought so please don't push me into a false position.' She was horrified by her own tears as she left the place and took a taxi to Bianchi's, where she went upstairs. David, for once, was not late.

'Excellent,' he said. 'We'll eat a great deal of pasta and send you north drunk.'

'I think that's a good idea.'

'Shall we pitch into the wine or have a strong one first?'

'Just wine.'

'You're an excellent girl. I've always said so.' He looked at her carefully and said without smiling:

'It's a shame we can't live together. No, it is.'

Soon after they got the carafe of wine, he said, 'Money,' and she nodded.

'I really don't see why I should underwrite you when you've got a husband and family quite wealthy enough to do so.'

'I do see why,' she replied.

'Air fare?'

'Yes. And three weeks for the flat.'

'You can borrow that from your firm. They'll advance it. Old established firms are famous for it. That's why they can pay their employees less than everybody else does.'

She said, 'I'm not coming back.'

'You're going back to Stephen?'

'I'm going back home, anyway. Whether he has me back or not.'

'Oh dear,' David said. 'I suppose that means twenty-five pounds.'

'You can easily afford it.'

'I know. I'm afraid I can. If you're very nice and cheerful all through lunch we'll go to a bank and get it in new notes.'

'Before three o'clock,' she said.

'You look fiercer,' he replied.

'Do I?'

'It's not unattractive, but I confess it frightens me a little. I believe you've become a tremendous career woman,' he said kindly. 'I'm told this at every corner. You must advise me on my publisher's contract. I must have an account of modern publishing methods.'

She said, 'Are you writing a book?'

'What's called a series of articles. I've done a great deal of work since we've parted.'

He noticed that she smiled a good deal less.

She said, 'Central Nervous System? Communication and Cats?' and he pushed the points of his fork into the table-cloth.

'Not exactly,' he said, and it was a confession. To slip into 'allied fields' is perhaps more suspect than not to work at all. He began to explain himself at length. He was writing the articles for an American journal called *Moral Philosophy*. 'No doubt,' he said, 'they will also be published in the serious German newspapers and the popular Dutch Press.'

'What about?'

'The obligatory scene.'

She ate patiently as he expanded on the subject.

He seemed to be glad to talk about it. Apart from the milkman (with whom he argued on the most intricate subjects) she thought he might have found few people with whom he could discuss the project. His fellow scientists and his intellectual friends would only have given him a wry look if he had admitted to working in a field so far away from neuro-physiology in which he had done all his important work. She seemed to be listening carefully as she smoked and finished her coffee.

He said, 'Can you imagine the playwright's chagrin, if he watched the curtain rise on the first night only to find that one of his principal characters had decided to skip the whole thing? But in real life, nothing could be more natural. That's the difference between life and drama, surely.'

That he might be talking sense was irrelevant. Mary watched him carefully and thought there is a change here, or else, up to now I have been blind. Even if it is correct, this is talk, only talk. It effects nothing.

David continued with enthusiasm. He talked as if he were dictating the paper to her.

'In ninety-nine cases out of a hundred the obligatory scene is never played. The people concerned so dislike the idea of a heavy emotional struggle that they walk off in different directions, one perhaps, rather faster than the other. They leave their problem, whatever it may be, in mid-air. In a year or two, or even a month or two, because it has been succeeded by so many others, equally acute, the situation disintegrates. The traces of it, by a tacit agreement between the parties, both of whom are now convinced that they are older and wiser, are felt, but socially ignored.'

Finishing her wine, she wondered if he were flirting with her: if this were a new beginning. But it was clearly nothing of the sort. He was not tasting the food, or noting the surroundings; not even very interested in her. He seemed to have escaped into words. She suddenly felt anxious for him, wondering what his friends and colleagues would make of him and say of him, if he continued to stick his head so firmly in the sand.

She said, 'If you believe this, what are you going to do about it?'

He looked mystified.

'Write it.'

'But in your own life?'

'Ah.' He smiled. 'I suppose logically, one should stop skipping things. This would be courageous, but I shouldn't think very rewarding. It would be a trial to one's friends and extremely distressing for one's elderly relations. One would be rather like those explosives which do the silly thing: they try and blast the wall where it resists them most. One would spend one's whole time bouncing from one ghastly scene to the next, in search of the obligatory.'

'Yes,' she said. 'David, it's half past two. D'you think we could go and cash that cheque?'

He frowned and wondered why he thought the request was a rebuke. Then he cheered up, pulled himself together and said:

'Excellent. Pay-up. What a nice lunch we've had.'

Standing rather vaguely, moving pound notes in and out of his wallet, he added, casually:

'I suppose we'll probably never see each other again. That's rather how life works.'

PART IV

The Wake

19

WHEN morals are no more, it's time for efficiency at any price, and women, beyond all things, are practical. Mary's own pregnancy, which she divulged to no one, made her more, not less, determined.

They buried the Colonel on a sunny winter's afternoon, in a new grave in a cemetery on a hill. All the men were there except Pink, who felt he could not leave the car, so Stephen took his cord. Pink's collapse, and the wintry sunlight streaming through bare trees, made the burial a more unnerving ceremony than usual. The moment of silence, afterwards, when all the men looked round like actors starved of words, was at last broken by the landlord of the Queen's, an expert at funerals who had slipped in to take Stephen's cord when Stephen had moved to the head. He said simply, 'I'd forgotten there was so much gravel in the sub-soil up this end,' and all the minds were diverted from the unseen figure in the box to the ground itself and to safety again.

After the wake, which in this part of Scotland is no more than tea and a whisky for the road, Mary got straight to work. Cathie, the maid or ex-maid, had been called down from her new house in the estate in the village but she was dressed as if for a queen's funeral, in indirect respect. Her condolences were brushed aside— and 'condolences' was Cathie's word. Mary, who was dressed neatly and smartly in a green suit, sat in the Colonel's place at the end of the long refectory table and Cathie took one of the chairs at the side. The table was still covered with dirty cups and glasses and spread with the sandwiches and cakes that were left over from the funeral tea.

With the hat and the pram and the house, for she had married John, the policeman, the thickening of the neck and the hardening of the hand, Cathie's very language had changed. She spoke now, aggressively, with little nods of the head. Her eyes were much fiercer. She said:

'It's many things that changed me, Mary. It's no joke being married, either way. But a Bobby's the Law and that affects everything. I get the side-long looks. And I'll tell you for why. Just because he's a good Bobby. That's it.'

Mary frowned. She asked, 'Do people object to him being strict?'

'I don't know, I'm sure,' Cathie said truculently. 'I'm not listening to what they're saying. They'll aye gossip about something, some of those. I'm not caring what they're saying.'

'You've got a child?'

Cathie looked at her sulkily.

'A-huh. Alan. Just a year old.'

Mary carefully avoided making the calculation.

'Have you brought him with you today?'

'No, John's looking after him. John's good with him.'

'I'd like to see him.'

Cathie stared at her for a moment, then she seemed to judge that Mary was sincere. She cocked her head to one side and said:

'He's wee, but he's tough. He's going to be a real tough guy, Alan.' Her pride and anger rose together. 'And he'll not be a policeman, I'm telling you that. It's no easy and I know fine. I'm a Bobby's girl and I married one, and you can take it and do what you like with it. They blame John for doing his job and he's no friends that way. They used to blame my father for not doing his job. The watch committee and that was always on to something.'

'Isn't John happy, then?'

'Would you be?' she asked. 'With no friends just to drink with; always that bit out of it, and parked in a wee place like this while there's others better at sucking up and nothing else, climbing up the scale in front of you? Would you? I can't see any man would.'

The difference in Cathie was extraordinary. She talked with one shoulder in front, her eyes filled with resentment.

She said, '*And* there's no money in it.'

'I thought the police were paid well.'

'Tchah!' she said. 'Maybe on paper it's all right and we get a Council house and all the rest of it. But there's boys over there with nothing in their heads at all makes twice and three times the money on the contracts, at the gravel, or up in the hydro-electric. There's others sitting by a petrol pump making more, and that's no' right. I know what they're saying about us, just because we got a television. It's the smallest screen and the longest payment and they all look at us. They watch with big eyes as the man puts the aerial up—Bob Mackintosh it was, and he makes a pile with his van on expenses and that. I came out the back of the house and I said it outright. I says "Why shouldn't we have one like the rest of them?" Why not?'

'Of course you should,' Mary said, like a much older woman, 'if you can afford it.'

'Exactly,' Cathie said, rising to her feet.

'How's John, in himself?'

'Aw,' said Cathie. 'It's ups and downs. I can't blame him. He gets awful moods of it. That's why I was anxious to get the television. He just sits sometimes hours on end, drinking his tea.'

There was the picture of life in the new house, with Cathie, now a bundle of practical energy and the big young man, with his elbows on his knees. Mary asked Cathie to sit down again and, with a glance at the clock, she obeyed. Mary said she would run her back in the car. When she offered her the job back Cathie said:

'It's no good me coming here if the others don't like it.'

'Don't worry about that.' Then, changing her voice with the subject, she asked, 'Are you not going to have another baby?'

Cathie smiled for the first time.

'Heavens alive,' she said. 'Give a lassie time. Alan's no' eighteen months yet.'

'Did you have a bad time with him?'

'No,' Cathie said. Her mind slipped back to the room in the house in Aberdeen which had been used as a still-room, before it was a hospital. 'It was a long time, but not bad.'

'Who was with you?'

'There were two at the end. A nice wee nurse was with me most of the time, but I think she knew less about it than me.' Cathie smiled.

'What did you talk about?'

'You're asking!'

'You can't remember?'

'I can fine,' Cathie said. 'Just as if it were yesterday. We talked about dogs. I said about Miss Ferguson, you know, your auntie that keeps all the poodles. "A hundred and nine?" she says; she was amazed. I remember that fine. In a kind of a way I remember it better than what comes after.'

Cathie had relaxed now, and at last she said:

'If you want to know I'm glad you're back, Mary. Never mind the job like, we've missed you. I have really; I've said often I've wished you were here.'

As Mary nodded and said, 'Thank you,' she realized that her eyes were filled with tears. She said:

'You're the first one to say it,' and the tears fell down her cheeks.

Cathie, putting the tears down to the Colonel's death, said:

'You've had an awful day of it.'

They both got up and after a moment or two Cathie insisted that she could make her own way back. She said again that Mary had had a day of it. Anyway, she went on, she wanted to get some bread on the way, for their tea. When Mary said she should take some from the kitchen Cathie cut her short. She said, with a frown, "No thank you. We're not as poor as that.'

Mary showed her out of the house and coming out of the room they passed Macdonald. It was obvious to Mary that she had been listening at the door. She said rather grandly:

'Macdonald, Cathie will be starting again on Monday. She'll be working in the mornings and those afternoons which she can manage.'

'I'm glad, I'm sure,' said Macdonald flatly, and nodded to Cathie, who returned her look with one that was not far short of impudence.

They passed on, but when Mary returned to the dining-room, she closed the door behind her. Macdonald was putting the plates on a tray.

Mary said, 'I know you were listening.'

'I wasn't eavesdropping. As I passed by the door I couldn't help hearing something you said.'

'What?'

'I don't know what your intentions are, but if you want to keep a secret I should have thought you'd be best not to spill it to a young girl like Cathie.'

130

'I didn't tell her any secrets.'

'No? Well, that's all right then.'

Mary said, sharply, 'Two or three times in the last twenty-four hours you seemed to have been trying to insinuate something, Macdonald.'

'Oh yes? What's that?'

'I wish I knew,' Mary said. 'It's you who's being so mysterious.'

Macdonald said, 'Mary, we used to be very close.'

'I'm not sure what that's got to do with it.'

'I'm not curious. I'm here if you want me.' But she could not help adding, 'I'd have thought looking after you and your mother for near thirty years would make me someone better to turn to than an embittered wee girl like that.'

Mary was rather pink in the cheeks. She gathered up the plates swiftly, as if her hands were saying to Macdonald's, 'You're slow and laborious and boring.'

She used one of Pink's expressions. She said:

'It sounds to me as if you've picked up a fag end. I don't know what you heard.'

'I heard you ask her about Alan being born.'

'Yes, I did. I happen to think Cathie's had rather a rough time.'

'If you don't want to tell me, then I don't want to know——'

Mary said briskly:

'I really can't think what you're talking about, Macdonald. I suppose you're getting all Shetland and mystic. But I do hope you're not going to go ga-ga in your old age. That would be the last straw.'

'A-huh,' Macdonald said, continuing to clear the dishes. 'Lerwick's answer to Cassandra—whatever that may mean.'

The conversation then turned to Pink. Mary gripped the back of the chair at the end of the table as if to anchor herself. She poured herself some tea from the pot which was now cold.

'Did you find out what happened?'

'Yes.'

'Something did go wrong?'

'Yes,' Macdonald nodded. 'I don't know how you knew.'

'I saw him when we left and I saw him afterwards. I saw the boys gather round in here.'

'He didn't have anything to drink.'

'He had a lime juice and soda,' Mary said. 'That's odd enough. But I could have told without that.'

'You can read Pink,' Macdonald said, perhaps with envy. 'You can read him better than I can.' She waited a moment, then she went on, 'Will you not have milk in that tea?'

Mary shook her head.

'You used to have milk in your tea.'

'I don't now.'

'So I see. Mind, I can read you all right. We were always very close.' Macdonald seemed to be taking count of the number of cigarettes Mary smoked.

'Oh, for heaven's sake,' Mary said. 'Is it a crime for me to smoke?'

'No,' Macdonald said. She was standing in her usual place, in front of the fender, at the far side of the table from Mary. She added, 'I don't wonder you smoke.'

'Tell me what happened.'

'It was Wee Alec told me, out there by the cars, when I took him his dram. He told me the episode. Pink didn't manage it.'

Wee Alec was the young man with long hair and suède shoes who ran the Building, Contracting and Undertaker's business.

'Manage what?'

'You know, at the grave. D'you know what happens?'

Almost as if it were a fact of life, not of death, Mary looked down at the ashtray and said, 'I don't suppose I know all the details.'

Macdonald said, 'You've had nothing to eat.'

Quietly Mary replied, 'Go on.'

'They let it down with cords. It's Pink who should hold the main one, but he didn't manage.'

'At the grave-side?'

'Before that, so I gather.'

'Walking through the town?'

'No, he's all right then, walking well, looking straight ahead of him at a point above the flowers on the hearse. I saw him going off. He was fine then. It's when they got to the graveyard, out in the open like. Walking up there on the curve of the hill.'

'What did he do?'

'You know he's got this thing about open spaces now. They've

132

got a name for it. The doctor said——' She could not remember it. She continued, 'When he came away from the cars at the gate Wee Alec said he sort of panicked. Stephen's by him and he turns back to Peebles and Spud Davidson and some of the boys.'

'Then?'

'They come round him and he's dithering, kind of, Wee Alec said. Anyway, they take him back to the cars.' She paused and then added, 'But Stephen coped.'

Mary said, suddenly, 'You're fond of Stephen.'

Macdonald brought her feet together.

She said, 'Yes, Mary, I am. We all admire Stephen, the way he's kept a straight road. The day you went he was out in the fields until the gang knocked off; on the potatoes then. I think your father would be glad it's him, at the end.'

'He always said he was wet.'

'He's not wet. And your father didn't say things like that, at the end.'

Macdonald moved away and Mary began again.

She asked, 'Did Stephen see much of him?'

'To begin with, but not at the end. You wouldn't have recognized him at the end. The last three months he never saw anybody but myself.'

Mary wanted to ask, 'Why didn't somebody send for me?' but was afraid of 'He didn't ask'. She drank some more. Then Macdonald, seeing how weary she looked, said more softly:

'If you'd been here, you couldn't have done anything. There wasn't any hope. He knew that. But he changed, Mary——'

'You must tell me some day,' Mary said, coolly, and Macdonald looked angry.

'I will, some day.'

'I'm sorry. I didn't mean it like that.'

Macdonald did not reply.

'—I promise I didn't. We really all rely on you. I don't know how you managed.'

But Macdonald was not friendly.

'It was useful I'm big, after all. I had to carry him, in the bedroom, like. He never came downstairs again. I lived the two lives, one here and the other up with him. He moved into your mother's room. He was thin, too, when he went.'

'And not quite white,' Mary said. 'And aged about twenty; I saw.'

Then stubbing out her cigarette she went on:

'It's curious, isn't it, how women know nothing about burials. These cords and things.'

'Only hearsay,' Macdonald replied steadily. 'But we know quite a lot about birth.'

Mary felt the colour rising in her cheeks. Her arm was outstretched, reaching to the ashtray, and she let it rest for a moment, deciding whether she should take up the remark. But the decision was postponed because Pink came in.

He looked shiny. His hair was wet and smoothed down. He advanced rather hesitantly, and then as if he were speaking of a dinner party or a wedding reception he said:

'It seemed to go off all right.' He nodded at the table. 'Jolly good tea.' He congratulated Macdonald with a cock of his head.

Mary looked at him curiously and asked:

'Have you had a bath?'

'Sorry?'

He had taken, lately, to prefacing most of his replies like this, as if he had not quite heard what was said. It gave people the impression that his mind was always occupied elsewhere; that he knew no rest.

'Not a bit of it. Just a wash and brush up.'

'I suppose Stephen's down at the farm,' Macdonald said.

'Trust old Stiffy,' Pink winked. 'He never misses a day.'

Pink did not fail to notice the edge in Mary's voice. She spoke as if she disliked him. She did not look him in the eye as she asked:

'Why didn't you go with him?'

'Not really an awful lot of point.'

Macdonald came to his rescue.

She said, 'Stephen's the farmer now. They've got it all organized.'

'Then what on earth does Pink do?' Mary asked across his face.

'Sales, promotion of same; market,' Pink replied.

Mary almost snorted.

'Does Stephen do the dairy too, then?'

Macdonald said nothing and Pink, with an old technique of his, instead of saying, 'Well, yes he does,' said with enthusiasm:

Absolutely, he's a bloody marvel at it.'

'I see.'

'Pink looks after the personnel,' Macdonald said, charitably.

'That's it,' Pink said. 'Sort out their lives for them and that sort of thing.'

Mary said suddenly, 'What have you been doing then?'

'Just now?'

'The others left an hour ago.'

'I say,' Pink said, moving his head sideways and looking at her from another angle, but she did not relax. 'To tell the truth, chaps, I felt a bit lonely, so I wandered in here.'

Quickly sensing that the appeal had failed, he then added, 'But if you want a time and motion study——' He paused, and moved his mouth as he searched for his next phrase. He, too, had begun to talk as if he disliked Mary.

'Then may I inform you that I have just finished rather a tricky interview with one of our ex-employees?'

'Who's that?' Macdonald asked.

Pink nodded mysteriously, and lit a cigarette. She mentioned the name of an Italian, ex-prisoner of war, whom Stephen had felt forced to have sacked. But Pink shook his head.

'Dairy and domestic,' he said at last.

'Cathie?'

'Our Cathie,' Pink agreed.

'Mary's given her the job back.'

Pink nodded but he had not listened. 'Tail very much between the legs,' he said unpleasantly. 'I sent her packing.'

It was as if Chuff-chuff had been made a prefect on the death of the old head-master, and turned out to be rather a bully.

Mary said, 'I absolutely demand that you bring back Cathie here.'

'She's gone now, old girl.'

'Look, old girl,' Pink said. 'Economics. We can't afford to pay chaps to come here for a couple of hours—agricultural rates, mind you, oh yes—and then hoof it back to their husbands with a basket full of ham and eggs.'

Macdonald moved. She said:

'He's right enough, Mary. She wasn't doing much good after she was married.'

135

'If I'm going to stay we'll need somebody else in the house.'
Macdonald contained her surprise.
'Are you thinking of staying?' she asked slowly.
'I may.'
'Sorry,' Pink said. 'The whole thing was thoroughly discussed by the old sub-committee—Macdonald and Stiffy and me.' He smiled. Then said cheerfully, 'Ramsbottom and Enoch and me. Before your time, I suppose.' He put some soda-water in another lime juice and opened his throat. He poured the tumblerful down in one gulp.

Mary said, 'Please go and fetch her back, Macdonald, and tell her my word goes in this.'

'Look, old thing,' Pink said. 'You don't know much about it.'

'I'm not interfering in the farm. Who comes here to help in the house is my business.'

'She's dishonest. She blatantly admitted it.'

'Then she's not dishonest.'

'Oh, come off it, Mary——'

'Please, Macdonald——'

Macdonald hesitated, then moved to the door. Mary's shoulders dropped an inch.

She said, more calmly, 'Do exactly as I say, please.'

'A-huh,' Macdonald said truculently, and when she left the room, Pink said:

'You're playing a bit senior, aren't you?'

'No.'

He said, 'I don't get it at all. Standing there, with all your jacket buttons done up. I don't twig.'

She said quietly, 'Pink, I heard about what happened this afternoon.'

Pink said cheerfully, 'Fair enough. Pink let the party down.'

'I didn't say that.'

'There was a young fellow called Pink,' Pink went on bitterly, with his fattest smile, and she lowered her eyes.

> 'Who did nothing but stutter and blink,
> When they lowered his Dad,
> He made off with the lads
> To the clubs and the pubs, for a drink.'

Possibly he had spent the reception thinking that one out; but not necessarily. He was capable of defending himself with astonishing speed. When she said, 'I noticed you weren't drinking,' he replied, with a big nod:

'All right then. "There was a poor fellow called Pink, Who took buckets of Gordons to drink".'

He thought for a second, but before he continued, Mary said, 'Shut up.'

Pink stretched his neck.

'Pity,' he said, speaking of their whole relationship. 'These things happen.'

'Pink, I promise I'm trying to help.'

'Then give us a limerick,' he said.

She replied, 'Maybe you'd like to go and see how Stephen is. He looks awfully tired. I'm sure he overworks. Maybe you could help him.'

Pink's face swelled up and then seemed to break into a thousand pieces. There was a loud wheezing sound, and for a moment Mary thought he was going to cry. But he changed from the music-hall comedian, laughing at his own last joke, into a prisoner with a phlegmy cough. Then he straightened up.

'Poor old Mary,' he said. 'Quite right!' in a sing-song voice. 'Quite right. Busy hands. Think of the other fellow.'

'Pink——'

He raised his hand. 'All right, Sister. I'll go quietly.'

As he left the room he sang gaily, 'For I'm Popeye the sailor man.' Then suddenly and savagely he slammed the door behind him. The pictures on the wall of shipwrecks and Fergusons shuddered, for a moment, then all was quiet. Ten minutes later, Mary made up her mind.

20

October had been fine, but the first week in November had brought rain, and the steadings were muddy. She therefore wore her gumboots which were lying by the sink in the back scullery, exactly where she had left them, over a year before. It was dark already, and cold enough for her to put on her sheepskin coat.

Four or five minutes later she appeared in the band of bright light outside the dairy. She exchanged a few words with one of the men who were loading the van. He pointed inside, and she nodded her thanks. With her fingers but not her hands in her pockets, she disappeared into the dairy.

Changes had come fast. There were many signs of heavy new capital investment. There was a new bottling machine. Before there had been a circular affair holding about eight bottles which had to be put in place by hand. They were shifted automatically now, in a continuous process, and the cows, too, poor things, had been 'time and motion' studied. They were not milked in their own stalls any more. They came in at one end of a special milking byre, which held three or four at a time, and went out the other. They had been milked by machine before, but now the milk was weighed and tested straight away. It ran directly to a larger tank which fed the bottling machine. Stephen had not wasted his year.

But the noise in the dairy, and then the smell in the byres, never changed. The clatter of bottles and the throb of the machines made talk impossible but Mary waved back to one of the girls who recognized her and shouted a greeting. The other girls looked at her oddly, as if she were some sort of actress dressed for a Technicolor serial, that had strayed on to the wrong set.

Stephen, at work, looked much more the factory manager than the farmer. He was still in his grey suit and black tie, but in gumboots too, and he was showing some visiting farmers round the byre. They turned out to be New Zealanders, staying for a week or two in Scotland. They were narrow men, one with thick smooth grey hair. But for their accents and odd manners, as if they had pins and needles in their feet and backs, they looked like a couple of Cavalry officers. Stephen, very calmly, broke off his lecture to introduce them to his wife. As soon as they had said 'How-do-you-do' (although they both avoided the actual expression of 'How-do-you-do' as if it stank of 'actually' and all the other gong words) Stephen continued his talk on the process. Even the feeding was rationalized, if not mechanized, now. In the byre, a little further away from the din of the dairy machines, Stephen still had to raise his voice. The visitors stood nodding and pouting, demonstrating that they were impressed. One of them often looked at Mary who was watching a hose, held by a dark young boy, as it played between the stalls at the other end of the byre that held a hundred cows. A couple of bulls were in their places in the last row, safely chained, separate from the cows who were ambling, in threes and fours, to their stalls. Above each place, marked in white chalk on a little blackboard, was the name of the cow. They had the same fascination as racehorses' names, historical, topical and private. 'Soraya, Mary IV, Greta, Hilary, Margaret Rose, Lolita, Kirsty . . .' Most of the cows were in their places at this time; they had been washed and milked and now they found some turnips in their troughs. The shed looked busy and colourful. But in the early hours of the morning when they were turned out to the fields the byre looked like an illogical penitentiary, all concrete and metal, bathed in thirty arcs of direct white light.

At last Stephen parted from his visitors and he came back to find Mary in the corner where he had left her. She watched him as he came. He passed some cows as if they were people in whom he had no interest, dawdling about in an Underground. He shoo'ed out a dog that had strayed into the byre. But then Stephen, who was shaping up to be one of the best dairy farmers in the country, disliked all animals and was not particularly fond of the outside life.

He approached her with the same smile and in the same bright, slightly official manner that he would have, had she dropped into the byre a year before. He approached her as he had the New Zealand farmers. It was a sort of works manner, developed by a manager who was not absolutely confident of himself, but was certain that he knew more of what was going on around here than anybody else. His manner somehow betrayed that he had no capital interest in the place and his first words to Mary were, 'Have you come to take a look how I'm mis-spending the family's money?' said, may it be added, with the confidence of a man who knew he had spent every penny of it well. As he explained to her, without her asking, some of the improvements he still wanted to make, asking, in an oblique sort of way, for her support where he needed no support, because Pink could sign the cheques, she said, suddenly:

'I don't suppose I ever would have married you, had I never seen you at work, and had I only seen you at work, I don't suppose I ever would have left.'

He quite ignored the remark. But she was right. It was not only a question of his decision and authority here. There was a social factor too. Such things as the fastidiousness of his dress, the over-perfection of his Highland dancing, even the care with which he mixed a cocktail for Pink and her, had an uneasiness. Only here, of all places, in the cowshed, and perhaps in the office too, did he have any social confidence because it was here, alone, that he lost his self-consciousness. It was impossible for her to talk to him here, but by a dart of the eyes it was obvious that she knew she would get more out of him on his own ground. She therefore guided him carefully and as they strolled through the comparative quiet and complete privacy of the calf house, a wooden building just a few yards outside one of the side doors of the byre, she led the conversation away from those words which only farmers recognize as agricultural: cost, margin, return on your money, subsidy, loan, rate of interest, plough back, overhead, turnover and acres enough.

There were eight calves, in open boxes, the youngest ones trembling where they stood, and Mary leant over the first gate and let the calf suck her four fingers. The shed was lit by two unshaded bulbs which threw double shadows on the walls, on the straw and the roof. Although Stephen had plans for a new shed, Mary, who was usually quite unsentimental about the farm and the animals in it, was glad that it had not changed. It smelt the same; more powerfully and much more sharply than the main byre.

She said, when at last he paused, 'You're going to be furious with me.'

'Oh yes?' He was a little nervous.

She smiled and said, 'It's nothing too awful.'

'You'd better own up.'

She did not see how much pain she had already inflicted. By her friendliness, more than by her breathtaking beauty, for in her own country, it was nothing short of that; by her smile alone, she had brought back the months when Stephen had the promise of her love, and the hope, not the task of its satisfaction. Not by a flicker of an eyelid did he give this away.

She said, 'I've re-employed one of your ex-employees without reference to the sub-committee.'

'Oh God,' he said. 'I know. Cathie?'

'I couldn't help it, Stephen.'

'You know she got into the habit of lifting half the housekeeping home?'

'Yes. But I think she feels she deserved it. Anyway it wasn't for herself. It was for her John and her Alan.'

'He's a dreadful little child.' Stephen had grown to the habit of thinking of the employees' children much as he thought of the animals: necessary evils.

'Why?'

'He slobbers,' Stephen said. The curious thing was that when Stephen was truly negative, in the sense of being totally cynical rather than simply without hope, he had a certain rather humorous charm.

She said meekly, 'Anyway I've done it. I think Pink was rather cruel to her.'

He too leant over the stall but only to give the calf a long, uncompromising stare.

Then he said, 'I'm not in the least surprised to hear that. Why anybody ever calls Pink unreliable I cannot fathom. He's the most predictable man that I know.'

He moved to look at the next calf, and went on:

'Pink's got too much conscience to look someone in the face after he's done them a bad turn——'

'Don't say that,' she replied.

Stephen misunderstood. He raised his eyebrows, he said:

'True enough. He refused her. So she went away and married the Bobby.'

'I mean about looking people in the face.'

Stephen had obviously feared the moment when they would leave other people's problems to talk about themselves. It was not a step he would willingly ever have taken. Eight months of work from dawn to dusk had almost seen him sane again. In the last five months he had been, he believed, as happy as he would ever be again. She was now looking him full in the face.

'You seem to manage,' he said.

She replied, 'It doesn't mean I haven't got a conscience.'

He said, in a sensible sort of tone:

'I told you at the time, or tried to, not to blame yourself. It was less your fault than you imagine.'

141

'In which case you can't have much of a conscience. You manage to look me in the face.'

He smiled slowly and said:

'That's my Boy Scout's training. Patrol Leader of the Bull's Patrol; hardly appropriate,' he added. 'I've got the firmest handshake north of the border. It's a question of interview technique. Those New Zealand gentlemen are still sorting out their knuckles.'

She laughed and he went on, excited by her laughter. 'I could stare out John Knox, and wouldn't mind having a try.' Then suddenly, he did not say, so much as hear himself say, 'It is also because it's a long time since I've seen your face.'

If it had not been plotted before, it was now that the intention formed hard in Mary's mind. It was so clear to her and seemed to be so necessary to her that she feared her anxiety might show in her face. She turned away and moved down to the smallest calf at the end of the row, perhaps with what she hoped would look like modesty. Then she turned her face back towards him and asked, quite loudly, 'Has my face changed?'

When he said, 'Yes, I think it has,' and followed it quickly, in a low, dry voice with, 'It's more beautiful, not less,' she frowned and turned back to the calf. She shook her head.

He said, 'I don't imagine you want or need compliments from me.'

'Stephen, I'm rather frightened. Would you mind if I stayed on for a little? At home.'

'Of course not,' he said. 'Anyway, it's your home, not mine.'

'Why am I frightened?'

Stephen replied sensibly, in a low matter-of-fact sort of voice.

'I don't think you are frightened. You're nervous. Death's unnerving, anyway.' He did not look at her.

Calmly, not really thinking what he was saying, he went on:

'You just don't know whether to take the plunge or stay at home.' Then he said quietly, 'I know you've left David,' and it startled her, because somehow she was certain that he knew nothing of her year away. One of the calves began to moan and she went across to it, as she asked:

'How did you know?'

Stephen said, 'I told you. Pink's a completely reliable character. I think I know everything you've done, while you've been away.'

She paused and calculated, then her shoulders dropped. Calmly she said:

'I left of my own accord. It didn't last very long, you know.'

'I thought you said he'd seen you to the air terminal.'

'Yes, he did. We're quite friendly. But I've been on my own for a while.'

He stood up straight and banged the little gate on the stall.

'I know this job now. It wouldn't be very difficult for me to get a place elsewhere: maybe a better job. I've been asked more than once. If you want to come home for ever, say the word and I'll make the arrangements.'

'No, don't be so silly, I wouldn't think of it. I didn't mean that, I promise. I meant something else, Stephen. I meant would it matter if I stayed here with you?'

'Darling,' Stephen rested his head on his hand. 'You're not using your brain, or your eyes.' He looked straight at the calf's back as he went on. 'I love you. Even if I've never been able to show it very much, that happens to be true. It wouldn't be possible for you to live your own life with my sheep's eyes following——'

Then she said it in one breath. 'I didn't mean to live my own life. I meant to come back to you.'

'No. After David,' Stephen said, 'after all that you couldn't be happy for long——'

'Yes, I could. I would be, I swear. I know it. If you didn't want me in bed, it wouldn't matter.'

Stephen wagged his head from side to side.

'It wouldn't, darling,' she insisted. 'I haven't come back for that. I don't expect a miracle. I've no right to come back, but I want to very much.'

He would not turn to her.

She said, 'Believe me, I'm tired of all the whipped-up passion. I promise I am. Please, Steve. It wouldn't be like last time. Really it wouldn't. Don't worry about that. I expect nothing.'

He kept his hands covering his face.

She said, 'Everybody's told me how wonderful you've been. You say you're not particularly clever and look what you've done here. You said you were a coward and that's not true either. I did my best to ruin your life and you didn't let it be ruined.'

Stephen was pressing his eyes very hard, as if they were painful.

He was like a school hero, appearing from the headmaster's study, determined not to cry.

He said, 'Let's get out of here,' and moved out of the shed into the dark. Just outside, there was a pile of coke for the boiler that heated the shed, and it crunched under their feet. The noise of the dairy machines sounded far away.

Outside, Mary stopped and leant back on the door. She suddenly said, guided by infallible instinct:

'I'm here, in the dark, by the door. My eyes are closed.'

He was trembling very badly when his hands first touched her face. His fingers passed all over it, for he too had closed his eyes. Soon he brought his hands down to her arms and, leaning forward, he lowered his head until it rested on the wool in the lapel of his coat. She brought one hand up and held the nape of his neck, and as he wept she said: 'Don't, whatever you do, be ashamed.'

She stroked his hair softly and as she said again, 'Don't be ashamed. Don't be sad, I'm back,' she opened her eyes. To one side was the dark shoulder of the byre, to the other the huge skeleton of the open hay loft. Behind, the cars' lights followed each other up the main road, past the bothie. Above that, the woods, and higher still the Pole star. It was Stephen who at last broke the silence. He squeezed her arms and looked at her. He kissed her firmly and quickly on the lips, saying:

'It will be all right?'

Mary nodded.

'Of course it will,' he said.

'Yes,' she replied, almost absently, and she let him slip back a little. She looked at him curiously as if she had never seen his face before. He was smiling and he took out a huge clean handkerchief to dry his cheeks. She looked very perfect, pale and cold.

He said, 'I've done some batty things.'

'Such as?'

He whispered, 'I got them to chop down our damned silly monkey puzzle tree.' He had carved their initials on it, before he had even proposed to her.

'You didn't,' she exclaimed, in a sudden lively voice, and she began to move away. Their feet crunched over the dross and coke until they came back to the muddy track: a track which Stephen was going to improve.

144

Still talking of the monkey puzzle, he said:

'I didn't know you'd come back.'

She gave him her hand and rather cheerfully, she said:

'Poor Steve, what else, batty?'

'I read Gibbon's *Decline and Fall* from cover to cover.'

The thought of it made him say 'God help me!' and laugh at himself, and an instant later she laughed too.

She said quickly, 'Oh dear, you must have been upset.'

'And you?'

'Batty things.'

'Weren't you happy?'

'No. Then I didn't really expect to be. I wasn't in love for very long.'

White lying has a curious, curving effect on how things are said. The words run smoothly together and the voice rises or falls at a different place.

'. . . I think for a little longer than he was. That's never very nice.'

It occurred to her that even if she were making up this story, there was no language to explain what happened with David.

'After David?'

'After David? Well, I shared a girlish flat. I got a job too.'

'Publishing.'

'That's what I liked to tell people. It was filing and copy-typing. Not much else.'

'And men?'

'After David?' Coolly, 'None, darling.' She paused, then excitedly she said, 'Oh yes, one. My boss in the office. My very own big white chief,' and she gave a description of Eric, her boss. Stephen said:

'He sounds very nice.'

Stephen did not know much about lying. He did not know that when a Customs man hears a girl say with a laugh, 'Well, I've got a horrible jar for me Mum,' in just the same sort of facetious voice, he knows there is also something else.

'No one really,' she said. 'Except the odd friend of David's being kind and standing me lunch.'

He clasped her hand very tightly and said:

'Darling, it will be all right, it will be all right.'

Again with a coldness, almost a brittleness, she laughed and said, 'Scout's grip.'

But he was talking very seriously. He said:

'It'll probably be as miserable as before, but you won't have to copy-type.'

She stopped and shook her head. They were at the edge of the pool of light that came from the dairy. She said:

'I don't expect miracles. You mustn't either.'

'I never have done,' he replied honestly.

'Dig my down-beat man,' she said, and was surprised this time by her own voice. Trying to find herself again, she said more steadily:

'There's a sort of hopeful pessimism, isn't there, that's you? It's better, I think, than poor Pink's hopeless optimism.'

'Saner,' he said, and she nodded as though she were learning things.

Then, suddenly, she reached for his hand again and she was glad to hold it. It was cold. In this fashion they picked their way back through the puddles which reflected the dairy lights, until they came to the house.

*　　*　　*

Stephen was quite childishly excited about the reunion and he went through the sitting-room to tell Macdonald and Pink the news. Mary, who was altogether more apprehensive, remained in the kitchen where she was joined, a few moments later, by Pink, who was struggling into his duffle coat. He wore a pork-pie hat, poised on the top of his small head.

Mary was by the Aga. She was preparing, or at least pretending to prepare, some supper. She said, 'You've heard?'

'Sorry, old girl?'

'Stephen's told you.'

'Not my business, old girl.' He shook his head and said with an infuriating smile and little bow:

'Some of us mind our own business, Miss Popham.'

'Aren't you glad?'

Pink said, 'I wish you every happiness in your life together. But as a matter of fact, old thing, it won't have much to do with Pink.

146

Oh no. I'm expecting a most important letter. Canada, as a matter of fact. Oyez, oyez. You can ring those bells.'

He checked his fly buttons then pushed his feet into an enormous pair of flying boots. 'There's a nip in the air,' he said happily. And then he laughed a noiseless laugh which shook him, and pointed one finger in the air. He raised his eyebrows and cocked his head to one side as he said, 'And high above, a long piercing note . . .'

'Pink, darling,' she said, much more softly. 'You're not going out, tonight?'

Pink pushed back his head and again raised an eyebrow. He spoke with undisguised hostility.

'Does a chap have to sign out, now, eh?'

She shook her head. She said, 'I mean, I want you to stay.'

'Sorry, old thing. Just a bit late.'

'You're huffing.' It was the first thing she said which penetrated, because it was about the only thing she had said since she had returned which was couched in their own language.

'Me, old girl? Not a bit.'

'You were, earlier. Sitting staring into nothing. All that.'

'No.' He shook his head. He would not acknowledge the corners of her mouth which were ready, whenever he was, to break into a smile. 'Not a bit,' he said again.

He nodded and leaned towards her, using his most confidential tone.

'I don't know if I should say it, but I'll tell you the truth, old love. I don't feel bad at all. Pink feels a lot better.'

She looked at him oddly and he nodded again.

He said, 'I don't want to be hard. Of course he was a tragic character and that, our mutual friend, but I'd be fibbing if I didn't say it was a load off my mind.'

'Of course it's a relief,' Mary replied warily. 'If it had to happen——' and Pink waved that aside with his hand.

'It's a relief,' he said. 'Better this way: all that stuff. Baa!' He bleated like a lamb. 'It's the truth. You can like it or lump it. Now he's gone I feel a sight better. Better already. Stevie and I've got the old place ticking over—mainly Stevie, I grant you, oh yes— Well——' He splayed out his hands. 'Things aren't at all bad, you know. Matter of fact we never had it so good, like the gentleman said. Things are looking up.'

147

'Go out tomorrow,' she said. 'Stay at home and cheer us up tonight.'

'Not actually poss.'

'You're not going down to the steadings, are you?'

'No. Not actually the plan.'

'Well then, where?'

'Questions! Power!' Pink suddenly exclaimed, violently. 'Macdonald's asked me all this. Women! Power!' he said again. ' "Num" questions. You're not going out, *are* you? When will you be back? Who with?' Pink smiled. 'Dear little things,' he said, very quietly. 'Gorgeous sweet charms.'

When Mary began, 'Are you going into . . . ?' he interrupted at once.

'As a matter of fact I am. Anything I can do for you there?'

'No.' She shook her head. She said, 'Peter Forbes, and Peebles and Blue Boy and that crowd?'

'It's Saturday night,' Pink replied.

'The Queen's? Pink, you can't. No, honestly you can't. Not the very same night.'

'Why not? Eh? Private party. Private room.'

'Even then——'

'Now,' Pink warned, 'don't play the heavy with old Pink. What's the alternative, Pink asks? Sitting through there watching TV, or sloping off to my own fart-sack half an hour after the scoff?'

'Just tonight,' she said. 'We could talk.'

'Windy?' he said, looking at her.

'It would be nice.'

'Maudlin,' he replied with a shake of his head. 'Well rowed, maudlin. It would be maudlin talk. But don't get me wrong, old duck, there's no question of a fellow getting high. Peter said it. Wee Forbes. He said, "Now, Pinkie, we've been there every Saturday night for years, now, and Sir Henry'd be the last to stop us, I'm sure. He'd want us to carry on, and that's just what I votes we do." No drunkenness, no singing. No sobbing.'

'It sounds a bit boring,' Mary said.

'Just chums getting together in the quietest possible way.'

Mary knew nothing would shift him. She nodded and said, 'Don't be too late,' and he turned by the scullery door.

'Don't you worry your pretty little head. Not about anything.

We've got it all tee'd up, Stiffy and I. I tell you, this is something really different. Sad and that, but I feel a new man. It's going to be a great ranch, little girl, a great ranch. You ask Steve.'

She nodded.

'Oh, yes it is,' he cried, slapping the pork-pie further on to his head. Just before he left he said, as much to himself as to her:

'And great ranches need great men, eh? Chin up. See you, angel-bum.'

Mary was still standing watching the spot from where he had vanished when the kitchen door opened again.

Macdonald came in. Seeing Mary, she stopped for a second, then walked across the room, keeping to the far side of the big kitchen table. She said:

'I think it's wicked. I'm not saying more or less than that.'

21

The same false quality which had been in Mary's voice when she had said to Stephen outside the dairy, 'Dig my down-beat man', and 'My very own big white chief', often came into play in the days that followed. Pink must have noticed it, because it was the sort of thing he recognized before anybody else, but if he did hear it, he made no comment because he, on the other hand, was far too involved with the Pink problems. He seemed to want to make it quite clear that he was suffering great mental anguish and presented them each meal and each evening with all the physical clues. He assumed an air of ferret-like rather than poetic distraction, rushing at his food then staring blankly out of the window for ten minutes at a time. He counted the cigarettes in his packet most times when he took one and when he was not drinking lime juice and soda he often rushed to the kitchen and grabbed a lemon. This he would eat like a monkey, biting at it savagely and sucking out the juice. Whenever he went to the village or as far as Forfar or Perth, Coupar or Aberdeen, he brought back another couple of bottles of lime juice, a dozen lemons, fifty or sixty cigarettes, the odd cigarette holder, and on one occasion, a clay pipe. He was both secretive and careless. He never mentioned these buying sprees but never failed to leave the objects where they might be found by one of the others. He seemed to enjoy his food very much, but after the heartiest meal he always stuffed in a few vitamins in pill form. He was growing rather paler in the face as he now never ventured out of the house, except in the car. He was also growing fatter. Most of the time he wore too many clothes, and his brow was usually covered with a gleaming surface of sweat, which he mopped from time to time with one of several handkerchiefs he carried, 'just in case, old chum'. Because he was also consuming a large number of Amplex pills and making profligate use of every deodorant on the market, Mary said that she was sure he was drinking. But this was not true, at the time. He was just wildly worried that he stank like a polecat. Once or twice a week a huge parcel would arrive from Trumper's packed with lotions, spirits and eau-de-Cologne. Where all the bottles went was a mystery which none could solve. But the annoying thing for them all was that when they tried to help him he denied stoutly that anything was the matter.

'Old bird, I don't know what you're talking about. Never felt better. Don't I look too good, then?'

He said this to Mary one afternoon when she returned from a walk round the farm with Stephen. She had found Pink at four o'clock in the afternoon, fast asleep in the nursing chair.

She replied, 'Pink, I can't be expected to help you unless you tell me.'

Just then the telephone rang and Pink rolled across the room to it. He landed with a thump in the desk chair and, picking up the receiver, said in the quiet, slightly sapsy voice of a gentleman publican:

'Farm house here, Sir Charles speaking.'

As usual, it was somebody complaining about an error in the local milk delivery. Pink called her Madam, and patiently noted down her requirements.

Still prissily he said:

'In point of fact, delivery isn't my particular pigeon but I quite understand your distress. It shall be seen to immediately. Your cream, Madam, will be at your door by 17.50 hours this evening. There's a van goes to the station at that time. Thank-you!'

He replaced the receiver and made a note. His handwriting was wilder than usual.

Mary said, 'I never knew a van went to the station at six.'

Pink said, 'You don't know everything, chumbo, oh no!'

She asked who was driving it. The usual milk van would be at the dairy at that time.

'Service,' said Pink. 'I shall drive it myself.'

'But, Pink, that's terribly inefficient. You can't drive ten miles just to deliver a quarter of a pint of cream.'

'Service,' said Pink again. 'It counts.'

He rang the dairy and, mock military now, instructed one of the girls, at that time due for one of the few breaks she had during the long day, to deliver to the house, without a moment's delay, one quarter-pint carton of single cream. When he put down the receiver he sighed, took up the pencil and ticked the note he had made.

Then suddenly, in his sulkiest tones, he said:

'You two are all right, so it would seem. I'm surprised you even notice me about the place.'

But Mary had lived too long with him to accept jealousy as the cause of his uneasiness. That he was pretending to himself, just as his mother might have done, long before, that people did not show him the love due to him, was perfectly likely, but Mary was not deceived. The change had come over him not when she made it up with Stephen, but when the Colonel died. His father's death had had the opposite effect of what he himself had anticipated. He thought his disappearance would leave him free to live and he had found, in a curious way, that it had left him free to stop trying altogether. But he did not confess this to Mary.

She said, 'If you're not going to help yourself, there's not much I can do. If I were you I'd ring up and say that cream won't go until tomorrow.'

When the door closed behind her Pink sat for a while, doodling on the note-pad. In truth he did not know what he wanted, and in this he was much like that poor pigeon, his mother. He just expected more of life; that one day, something would happen that would make it all better. He was reduced, he knew, to believing in a miracle, and vitamin pills, foreign travel, deep sleep, even shock therapy, about which he knew an unhealthy amount, occurred to him as the possible forms which that miracle might take. He some-

times put his hand to his ear, and as it was now his habit to avoid
the word God, he would say, with a horrible laugh:

'Moo, I hear thee not!'

*   *   *

And when, at last, it happened, Macdonald was there, on the
landing, in the middle of the night. Instinct had kept her awake,
and the sound of voices, rising, brought her from her bed.

She stood, breathing very quietly, just outside Stephen and
Mary's bedroom door. The lights were on within and a shadow
flitted across the bar of light at the bottom of their door. A moment
later there was the noise of somebody crying, and expecting it to
be Stephen, Macdonald was at first unnerved by the noise, which
was pitched high. Only as it continued, and as it was broken now
and then by the repetition of a single phrase, did she realize that
it was Mary's voice. The noise of the anguish of frustration, as
any gaoler, as any nurse or nannie knows, when it reaches the
extreme, loses identity. It becomes a note on its own, disembodied,
and profoundly alarming. It is a note that passion never reaches,
even if, for obvious reasons, it is close to the note of that dream of
passion that sometimes rings in the ears. Hearing its wail, Macdonald stood very still, listening for the sound of movement or of
another voice, below it. The final exchange between Mary and
Stephen, as Macdonald might have guessed, was merely childish
reiteration. At first with frenzy and then hollowly Stephen said
many times, 'I can't.' The words that Mary was still repeating
from time to time, as Macdonald heard only indistinctly, were
simply, 'You must.'

Macdonald stood back as Stephen came out: things were quieter
by then. She did not try to hide and Stephen said nothing to her, in
explanation. He neither ignored her presence nor acknowledged it.
It was as if he had passed her in the landing, at any time, as she
walked from the bathroom back to her room. For some reason,
rather absent-mindedly, he unhooked and closed the nursery gate
at the top of the stairs, as if to complete his dissociation from an
unbearable, carnal mess. Then he disappeared into the darkness of
the hall and corridor below.

Macdonald, without hesitation, as soon as he had gone, pushed open the bedroom door and went in. The picture that was presented to her more than confirmed the situation. It showed, in agonizing detail, the story of the preceding hour.

Mary had stopped crying. She was on the single bed farthest from the door and the near bed had not been disturbed. She lay on the flat of her back watching the shadows on the ceiling which were cast by her elbows, arms and interlocked fingers, held above her head. The sheet was lemon, not white, and it matched the paint-work in the room. This, and the darker tone of the wallpaper affected the quality of the light. It was both yellow and bright although it came from only a single bedside lamp, which had been placed on the floor between the beds and partly covered by Stephen's woollen shirt. The bed clothes of the bed on which she lay had been stripped off and hung over the bottom of it. There were usually two pillows. One lay on the counterpane on the other bed. The other did not rest under Mary's head, but under her hips. Her red hair looked extremely untidy and long and her body looked thin and white. She was not quite naked, as she had chosen to wear a pair of very dark stockings which Macdonald had not seen before. She did not seem to object very strongly to Macdonald's entrance, which showed that, in her mind at least, Macdonald was still con-siderably more the servant than the mother; but as Macdonald approached she lowered her arms slowly and covered her eyes with the backs of her hands, her fingers still interlocked. It was all there, but for the Vibro.

From the look of distaste on Macdonald's face Mary might have thought that she was going to forget her usual infuriatingly steady manner, but this did not happen. After one short glance at the slight, anonymous body, Macdonald moved to the cupboard in the corner and unhooked Mary's winter dressing-gown. She picked up her bedroom slippers and moved across the room. By then, Mary had slipped her legs round, and was sitting at the edge of the bed pushing her hair from her face. Macdonald bent down and put the slippers on her feet, then helped her into her dressing-gown.

As Macdonald tied the cord tightly round her waist Mary expected her to say, at the very best:

'Either you're going down these stairs, or I am.'

She turned round and looked up at the huge white face. The

cheekbones looked as big as ribs. She felt a little afraid, and it showed in her eyes.

'Away you go, now,' Macdonald said very softly. 'Away downstairs, and tell him the truth. It's a game of consequences, so it is.'

Mary nodded gratefully. Before she had even left the room Macdonald had put the lamp back in its place and started to make the bed.

*   *   *

Mary and Stephen did not talk about what was going to happen and when they parted things seemed to be left more in the air, not less.

With the unswerving instinct of a Colonel's daughter, she made for the dining-room, expecting to find him sitting there, consoling himself with a man-sized whisky and soda. But Stephen was too modest and too honest to settle for this pose. She found him at last in the kitchen where he had poured himself some coffee from the pot which always sat in one of the ovens of the Aga. He was adding milk from a bottle when Mary came in. He was cold, and as he sat down at the little kitchen table by the window, in his trousers and pyjama top, with no dressing-gown, he began to shiver. She sat down at the other end of the same table and said nothing for a while. Meantime he drank his coffee.

At last, in quite a steady low voice, which she addressed to the toes of her bedroom slippers, Mary said:

'If you haven't guessed already, I'm pregnant. I know I should have told you before, but I just couldn't.'

She glanced across to him, boldly, but he did not attempt to say anything or even to turn his head. He continued drinking coffee from the huge, deep cup.

She said, 'If it had worked I don't suppose I'd ever have told you, so I can't really make any excuses. Only you haven't been a girl. It seemed the only thing to do. The only practical thing. If it had worked you'd never have been the wiser and it would probably be a happy family. That's what I'd hoped. But it didn't work, so that's that.'

He said, 'That's why you came to the dairy that night?'

They were both glad that she managed the truth.

'Yes, Stephen, it is.'

154

'I must say, it makes sense of quite a lot of things I didn't understand.'

'It doesn't mean that I'm not very fond of you——'

She stopped there.

He said, very coldly:

'I don't think that's a line we should follow now.'

For a moment they were silent again, then Mary said:

'I think it is. I can't persuade you it's true. I can only tell you. I'm sorry it's all such a muck-up. Most of the things I've said to you since I've been back have been perfectly true.'

He started stirring the last of his coffee and he sipped the sugar at the bottom with the spoon. He turned suddenly and looked her straight in the eye.

He said, 'Are you hoping that I'll strike you?'

'No.'

'Or at least shout and slap your face?'

'No.'

He said, 'If it's a comfort to you, the performance was spectacular.'

She put her fingers over her eyes and shook her head, saying another sort of 'no' this time.

He went on, clearly:

'It never occurred to me for a moment that you weren't telling me the truth. Then, as you know, conception, gestation and birth only crop up in my brain if they're connected with the farm. Even if you had made a mistake or two, I probably wouldn't have noticed.'

She sat quietly.

He said, 'I suppose the real reason why I am so calm is that I just can't believe it now. I know it's true, but I can't swallow it.'

He got to his feet, and went on:

'If you like to stay down here for a few moments I'll get my clothes out of the room.'

'No, I'll go.'

'I'd rather lie down on the sofa. I'll be going out early, anyway.'

She nodded and said meekly:

'All right, Stephen,' and that finished the conversation.

For want of something better to do, Mary, too, drank a cup of coffee.

155

When Stephen went upstairs there was no sign of Macdonald but both beds were made with the corner of the bedclothes turned back. The chairs had been tidied and Stephen found his clothes neatly folded. He took them down to the nursery, where he would be less comfortable than in the sitting-room. He did not even notice himself take this monk's choice. He pulled a footstool up to the nursing chair and switched out the light on the desk. He lay there, wide awake, until at last he heard the steps on the stairs as Mary went back to bed. That the strain had been passed from one to the other was now clearly shown. Mary fell asleep within a few minutes, and Stephen sat tensely, alarmed by every board that creaked and startled by the hoots of owls.

*　　*　　*

Wherever Mary found her story of Uncle Arbuthnot's death, it certainly was unlikely to have been complete invention. It held the essential truth about suicide, as opposed to attempted suicide. The method a person chooses for killing himself is strictly in character, if he truly means to go through with it. And Arbuthnot, the tidy boy, equipped himself with a bucket as well as a knife. There is a reason why a student chooses to hang himself in a college lavatory, why a girl drowns herself in a pretty stream, why a distracted housewife picks the gas oven and the retired Colonel shoots himself in his den. Stephen must have known that he was bluffing.

His approach to suicide demonstrated the astonishing difference between David and himself. They had not after all come from very different homes and they had both taken scholarships to small public schools. Thereafter Stephen had accepted the environment of the idea: patriotism, enterprise, integrity, leadership and all the rest, although he was very conscious of falling short of the ideal. David, on the other hand, perhaps because he came from a home which was very, very slightly lower in the social scale, or perhaps because he was more mature at that age, refused the new environment. His school days were a running intellectual battle against a system which he refused to accept as desirable. Duly extended, it can be seen very easily that even if David ever reached the point of contemplating suicide the possibility of his doing so in Stephen's gentleman's way did not exist.

As soon as Stephen took the Colonel's shot-gun from the cloak-room which, in itself, was a tricky operation, as he was certain that Macdonald was awake, he found himself in difficulties. The Colonel had locked up his cartridges but, after searching his pockets, Stephen found one, in an old hacking jacket, behind the door. It was dawn when he arrived outside the house and he was at once embarrassed by the enthusiasm of the Colonel's Labrador, who appeared from nowhere, barking madly, certain, on seeing Stephen with a gun, that it must be the morning of the Christmas shoot. As quickly as he could, and savagely, Stephen shoved him into the first place he could think of, which was the black shed where all the apples were kept. He then proceeded on his way, more than ever determined to do the right thing, quickly, before he had time to think.

He went up to the woods above the bothie, but in the end, for reasons which were later very obvious to him, he walked right through the wood, where the trees creaked a little in the wind, to a rough patch of moorland at the edge, which long before this incident and for some forgotten historical reason, had been called the Hospital. Perhaps some keeper, years ago, protected wounded birds there. When the moment came, and the woods were behind him, Stephen behaved less like a gentleman and more like a school-boy. His movements had the formality of a Fascist officer who had come to pay himself a debt of honour, by the grey light of dawn, under the cloud-swept sky. One detail in the following swift physical action which closely resembled the first movement of 'shoulder arms' was highly important. When the gun was cradled in his arm, and his head tilted slightly to one side, he was careful at the last instant to save his eye. This pushing forward of the head would probably in itself have saved his life, but the important fact was that the cartridge was in the first barrel, and it was the choke barrel that dug into his skin. The result was more or less serious than the spirit of farce invited. The best thing that could have happened would surely have been that he missed altogether, or alternatively blew off his head. What did happen was that he shot a considerable hole in his head and collapsed unconscious, with the softness of failure, on a large clump of sphagnum moss. The keeper who found him, not very long afterwards, used this as a first emergency dressing. By mid-day he was conscious, comfortable and silent, in the room in the cottage hospital which Captain Gordon had been so determined to avoid.

The news was brought to Mary by someone who was almost a stranger, and fortunately she heard it when she was alone. How that happened was fairly simple. The gamekeeper, who was employed in the neighbouring estate, came down to the bothie to ring for the ambulance and, before returning to Stephen, told the woman who ran the bothie to go across to the house and tell them what had happened. This woman, however, was of an extremely nervous temperament. She found herself catering for only half a dozen girls, in the heart of the country, because the task of running a small boarding-house at an east coast seaside resort had reduced her to a winter of poverty and tears. She could not possibly have faced the prospect of telling a young wife that her husband had shot himself, and she used as a double excuse, the imminent arrival of the baker's vans and a nose-bleed which she had been trying to control since breakfast-time. One of the girls, therefore, who cannot have been more than sixteen, volunteered to run across to the farm. Like anybody of that age, she enormously enjoyed bearing illtidings, even if she denied this to herself.

All this was relatively natural and honest. It was the interview between Mary and this long-faced, bright-eyed girl, that had its bad moment.

Mary was over by the garage, outside the back of the house, when the girl arrived and called breathlessly:

'Mrs. Cameron, oh, Mrs. Cameron. I've terrible news for you.'

At that, before her mind had time to calculate what the news might be, Mary looked duly alarmed. She looked at the girl severely.

'It's Mr. Stephen—Mr. Stephen's shot himself.'

Again, nothing went wrong. Mary grew paler and placed on the ground the bucket which she had been taking to the hens.

The girl went on to say:

'They're taking him in the ambulance, Fyvie the keeper's there. They're taking him to the cottage hospital. You're not to worry, Fyvie says. He's going to be all right.'

The girl smiled, but even she was a little mystified by the expression which in that instant passed across Mary's face. Had Pink been there he would have defined it. In a second it was gone, never to be seen again, but Pink would not have missed it. It was an expression of bitter disappointment and it was a moment or two before Mary could find words. The girl thought her confusion was understandable, but she would have backed away had she understood it.

In the next few moments, Mary extracted all the details and immediately afterwards made the necessary telephone calls, but it was that moment of self-revelation, not Stephen's condition, nor, as Macdonald thought, the events of the previous days, that winded her so badly. She never came near to weeping, but for an hour or two after the first frenzy of activity she seemed to be literally struck dumb. Even Macdonald was alarmed by her condition and went into the dining-room where she sat and coaxed her to take some coffee. Macdonald's expression as she did this was cagey. She seemed to be saying, 'Even if I do give you a warm drink, do not imagine that I have changed my opinion of you. It is only by the grace of God that you are not a murderess.' With that last sentiment Mary, for quite different reasons, would have had to agree.

Pink also tried to cover up his first reaction when Macdonald went into the nursery to tell him what had happened. She was by this time generally impatient of his behaviour so she did not stay to examine his reaction. She simply put her head round the door, announced the news, then went back to the kitchen where Cathie stood, petrified with excitement. In fact, Pink, at first, looked deeply offended, rather as if his understudy had been given all the notices. Then after a moment or two he shouted angrily to the closed door:

'Well, there's damn all I can do about it, is there?'

*   *   *

Stephen was kept in hospital for several weeks, and Mary visited him practically every day. Their meetings each afternoon at half past three would have been of interest to David, in his preparation of 'The Obligatory Scene' for *Moral Philosophy* and the Dutch popular Press. They never approached the obligatory in all the weeks Stephen was there and yet, on his return to the house the change had been made, the decision had been taken, the future was as settled as ever it can be. Mary's attitude towards him during these weeks might also have reminded David of his own angelic mother. She never referred to the attempted suicide, or to the days that preceded it, nor did she ever substitute for them some convenient euphemism. It was Macdonald, when she visited, in hat and fur cape, cluttered up with parcels of sweets, shortbread and grapes, who referred to the 'accident'. Mary did not mention it. It was as if she disapproved entirely of his action, never forgot it, but quite forgave it, and was determined to show, as his closest relation, that it did not in any way affect her liking for him. The visits were never cheerful and the two of them often sat in silence, but over the weeks they found the bond between them. Stephen saw very clearly that Mary's attitude to him was identical with her attitude to herself. It was as if she were saying to him, as a request so urgent that it was nearly a command, 'Make no mention of what has gone before and it is possible we will find a way. Mention it once and we are done for.' There was a severe see-no-evil conservatism in her attitude more common in older people, that is often mistaken as mental laziness. It is in essence, a refuge, a tight-rope of compromise, a narrow plank on which it is necessary to walk without saying a single word about the gulf that lies below.

The most cheerful visit, curiously enough, was Pink's. He only came once, at the wrong time, without being announced, but during one of his enlightened days. These grew fewer and fewer now, but when they came they had an extra warm quality. Coming in, as he did, in dark glasses, a week after the New Year, he looked to Stephen as if he were at the bottom of the trough. He brought as a present a 'make it yourself' transistor radio.

'By God,' he said. 'This'll make you wild. Guaranteed to whizz you round the bend.'

And seeing Stephen's dismay, he burst into a long wheeze of a laugh and tucked his dark glasses into his breast pocket, in which, that day, he was sporting five propelling pencils and pens, and a tyre pressure gauge. He looked round the room, which was like any small private room in a hospital, except that it boasted new, plastic, Venetian blinds, and he said:

'Everything, old man. I could take everything except the bed pans.' It was as if he were talking of wild animals. 'They'd get me in the end.' Pink dared subjects which everybody avoided. He approached them with a directness that would have horrified the nurses. He started to laugh again, leaning back, and holding one knee between his hands.

At last he managed to say:

'Old Flush,' which was the name of the Colonel's Labrador, 'Old Flush in the apple shed, eh? That's what got me.'

For a moment he could not manage to say anything more, because he was laughing so much. He pushed his nose to one side, then the other, like a performing seal. He said:

'He was in there seven hours before we found him, tossing Cox's high and low.'

Stephen too began to laugh. He said:

'Don't. I'm not meant to shake about.'

'That's excellent,' Pink exclaimed, and Stephen recognized that he was referring to one of his favourite subjects, laughter in church, when he said:

'Old Stiffy in the front row of the choir, eh?'

Stephen, in his most miserable tones, which delighted Pink, said, 'Well, I couldn't help it. The bloody dog must have thought it was Boxing Day. Started howling around.'

'You should have taken a bang at him.'

'Too British,' Stephen replied, and Pink said:

'Mind, you'd have probably missed him, or taken a lug off. That wouldn't have been at all nice. You'd never have got back in the house that way.'

Then Pink's mood changed. He grew intensely serious and pulled his chair along the polished red linoleum, closer to the bed.

'Mind,' he said again, 'I don't see how that happened. Didn't it put you off, I mean, bloody dog bounding round and licking you? Enough to ruin murder, far less suicide, isn't it?'

Stephen shook his head, very gently.

'Well, come on,' Pink said. 'This is Your Life.'

Stephen said, 'Once you've made up your mind that sort of thing doesn't matter. Lots of tactical difficulties you have to overcome, but you've made up your mind, you've told yourself you're going through with it, INTENTION to annihilate private enemy number one. Things get in the way but they don't stop you. If Flush had wandered into the nursery a couple of hours before things might have been different.'

161

'Now isn't that fascinating?' Pink said. He shook his head, grasped his knee again, and went on:

'By God, that's good. I get it, though, I get it. D'you suppose murder's that way?'

'Premeditated. More or less.'

'Good old Steve. Ever thought of doing somebody in?'

'Yes, often.'

'Really? I find that most interesting. Thought of murdering me?'

'No.'

'Oh,' Pink said, disappointedly. 'Steady on. There's no need to be rude.'

'How's Flush, by the way?' Stephen asked.

'Joggin' along,' Pink replied. Then he assumed that curious, secretive smile which usually heralded some devastatingly intimate confession. In this context it alarmed Stephen, and he was greatly relieved when Pink merely said, 'Apples', and put one finger in the air. He opened his mouth several times as Stephen, guessing what was coming next, began to smile.

'No, no,' Pink said. 'Serious animal study. Real Pavlov stuff. Interest to Mary's boy friend: old smelly Dow. I've been trying Old Flush. Oyez. The other day he chewed up one of Cathie's ghastly hats, and I went right up to him.' He demonstrated excitedly, 'Like this, hands behind my back. Then I faced him with it. The biggest Cox's I could find. I held it right there in front of his nose. I did.'

He nodded, triumphantly, and leant back again. He seemed inclined to leave the story there.

'What happened? Was he frightened? Tail between his legs?' Stephen asked.

'Well, as a matter of fact, old man,' Pink replied, rather stuffily, 'he ate the thing.'

Soon after, a nurse came in and it was the end of the visit. Stephen never saw him again until he was let out of hospital, though he got a Valentine card from him with a shot-gun through a bed pan, as device.

*   *   *

But if there was a moment during Stephen's long convalescence which could be counted as a turning-point it must have occurred one afternoon in February when Macdonald came, instead of Mary. It was thawing. Through the window, as gloomy afternoon turned swiftly to night, the patches of snow on the banks of the lawn outside still showed long after the features of the miserable little garden had faded away. The light was already switched on, in the room, when Macdonald arrived, and by this time Stephen was tired of lying still. At her first glance Macdonald could see he had arrived at a state of what she called 'natural depression' which, in its way, was a subtle definition. She meant by it the sort of straightforward schoolboy depression which comes to everybody who is bored and lonely, as opposed to the type which Pink favoured. Stephen's barometer was at low, but with ordinary cheer and new subjects of interest the needle would gradually creep round again. No outside influence on the other hand, had any effect whatsoever on Pink's storms. It was only possible to wait until the needle hit the buffer at 'low' and bounced back to 'Oyez, oyez, ring those bloody bells'.

Within the first five minutes of her visit Macdonald was afraid she had put her foot in it. As he was lying so quietly she searched for subjects and picked on the roads being better, as they had been icy for nearly three weeks. She mentioned that Mary would find it easier driving back from the specialist in Dundee, assuming that Stephen knew where she was that day. Neither she nor anyone else quite realized the narrowness of the plank which the two of them walked together. The attempted suicide was never mentioned, nor the return from London, nor the bedroom, nor the bed, and although Mary was now obviously pregnant they never mentioned that. Macdonald now realized this, too late, when Stephen asked her questions. Macdonald said:

'I shouldn't have mentioned it, maybe.' Neatly she found a reason. 'She wouldn't want to worry you with it, Stephen, you know what men are when they hear about specialists. But there's nothing wrong at all. He's the best gynaecologist round about, that's all there is to it. If she goes to him he can get her one of the private rooms at the hospital and that's not nearly such big money as the nursing homes. Most of it's on the National Health.'

'When's it due?' Stephen was lying back on the pillows. He was playing with his watch, which rested on the sheets over his tummy. He buckled and unbuckled the strap.

'Not till May. There's time yet.'

'Does David know about it?'

'I don't think so,' she replied, and she watched him carefully. Macdonald took some big risks sometimes, which she never felt to be risks, herself, because her instinct was so strong. She used to say, 'I just tell the truth, that's all it is,' but this in itself could not have been less true. She often told lies. But she had an unerring sense of timing. She knew when the truth would be most effective. She tried it now.

'I don't see why he should, either. It's got nothing to do with him.'

Stephen thought she was being kind, not truthful. He shook his head and said:

'Nothing to do with me.'

Macdonald, unwrapping a box of Meltis fruits said, almost casually:

'That doesn't mean to say it's got anything to do with David, either. Mary wasn't too happy in London, you know.'

Out of the corner of her eye she saw she had said the right thing. Jealousy does not work like fear. One cannot measure oneself against the unknown. The sharpest pain comes when one sees the person who has been preferred. Stephen pushed himself up with his elbows.

'Do you know that for a fact?'

'I know nothing as a fact, Steve. But you've only got to look at David Dow, and where he came from. Even when they're tear-aways like that, there's some things is always saved. She'd have gone to him if it was his—I'm certain of that.'

Then she put a parcel on one side and said more cheerfully:

'Come on now, Steve, I've no right to be talking to you like this. The walls have ears. D'you want more books yet? The man at the library here says you've read all he's got. We'll have to send up to Foulis Lending, to keep you in stocks.'

That was all there was to it, but when she left him he looked much happier.

Macdonald did not confess to Mary that she had had this conversation, but then Mary no longer confessed things to Macdonald. Yet the hostility that had existed between them when Mary first returned, gradually disappeared. Macdonald, herself, seemed to grow much older that winter, as if only now, after the Colonel's death, could she relax and admit to herself that she was nearly sixty. She would occasionally sit and talk to Mary, and they even began to laugh together, about old times. Mary learnt of her father's last months, indirectly, in this way. Macdonald joked about the terrible things Pink had said to the local minister who had come very often to visit him, because the Colonel turned to God at the end.

'What is it he calls God?' Macdonald asked one evening as they sat on the leather fender, drinking sherry. 'Is it "Moose"?'

'Moo,' Mary said. She always wore a fur hat that winter and she played with it as they talked. Then she stopped herself fidgeting, with a conscious effort and put the hat over with the parcels she had brought back from the shops in Dundee. She bought all the things for the baby, by herself. She knitted none. She brought things back each Tuesday and Thursday when she went to the clinic in Dundee. She never showed them to Macdonald, but put them straight into the new white chest of drawers in her bedroom. That Macdonald and Cathie looked in the drawers when she was not there did not upset her. Indeed, she might have been disappointed if they had not done so. But Mary said very little, these days, that was not absolutely necessary.

'Moo,' Macdonald repeated. 'Pink was terrible with the poor man, waving him good-bye, shouting "love to Moo!" or something like this; you know what he is. He got really aggressive once or twice, mind; I was worried he'd attack him at the bottom of the stairs, shouting at him, "If a man does not love his brother whom he has seen how can he love Moo whom he hath not seen? Eh? Answer me that!" Pink looked really angry, you know. The minister's very patient, mark you. He never complains about this Moo thing, and he just says where the verse comes from, one of the Epistles, I think, and says he agrees with the apostle who wrote it.'

Mary nodded. 'What did Pink say to that?'

Macdonald raised her eyebrows.

'That infuriating laugh of his. You know, the one he always gives when he claims he's won an argument. It used to drive you crazy as a kid.'

Mary filled Macdonald's glass again.

'You said you'd tell me some day,' Mary said, and Macdonald nodded. She knew what Mary meant. At last she replied:

'You'll have guessed the most . . . with the preacher calling and that. He wasn't the same man, your father, at the end. He was brought down with grief and no' just fear either. Mind there was no jokes with him. I think that's why Stevie and I had to have a laugh at Pink. Your father didn't know it but he had a kind of dignity at the end. He didn't come downstairs much and he'd just stare at the television but he saw nothing and heard nothing. You could turn the sound down and he'd never notice. The preacher'll tell you, Mary, he went very bravely, and very humbly too. He was kinder to me in the last weeks than he'd ever been in the years before.' She said, 'It was kind of worth it for that.

'We didn't know when he was going. It was sudden at the end. Your mother, you know, she drove herself to it: she made herself go. Your father just let himself go. Very suddenly. I think cancer's like that. It can linger or not. There's no telling.'

She seemed to leave a gap. She looked at Mary, then away again, and at last she continued:

'As soon as he moved into your mother's room, and he was insistent on doing that, mind, he didn't think of anyone in this world any more. He was on his way, then. But he went over two incidents in his life. Over and over them, to the minister and me. Over and over again, his hand pumping up and down on the arm of his chair and his eyes quite watery. He'd say, "God forgive my soul." '

Macdonald took a sip of her sherry. Mary looked at her own toes. She sat alongside, on the leather fender. When she leant forward she could clasp the back of one of the oak chairs at the side of the refectory table. The lights were low. Two brackets on the wall were lit and the faces of the Fergusons in the portraits were lost against the sheen of the heavy Victorian gold-painted frames. The silver on the sideboard caught the light.

Mary said, 'When I was in London I heard a horrible story about the card cheating. I mean what led up to Daddy doing it. I should think it was rot.' She swept back her hair and looked at Macdonald who was staring at the wine-glass that looked very small in her huge, bony hand.

Quietly, Macdonald said, 'I shouldn't think it was. But it wasn't that that worried the Colonel. Not in the end. He was like all the best men, so the minister said. He was worried only about the negative sins, that's what you call them, the things you leave undone.

'Evidently when he came back from that club and it was old General Oliphant brought him back, kind old soul he was, your father had a talk with his wife. I know he did, as a matter of fact. I heard their voices and wondered what was going on. It was only an hour past dawn. As you know, your mother was a wild kind of frightened wee thing, and she'd never have gone to that club unless she'd got herself into a terrible state. I'm only sorry I didn't know her better then. I'd have stopped her. I wasn't long enough with the family. . . . But, let's not deny it, she could be real infuriating, your mother. She couldn't lift a finger to help herself. That was the drawing-room training—Dundee style. She couldn't boil an egg and I don't really think she'd grasped the difference between a cock and a hen. She certainly can't have understood what was going on, but someone must have put the wind up her good and proper. She got the feeling that it was something really sinful and she wasn't far wrong. I fancy, too, her own life wasn't going so well. It was a mystery to me how either of you two came about. A gesture to convention, I'm sure it wasn't much more than that.

'I shouldn't speak ill of the dead, and mind, I don't really. She was a harmless enough body, your mother, but let's just say she wasn't top of the class. Not the brainiest. Your father therefore thought it best not to tell her anything, even in the state he was. So she kept asking him questions mainly whether he'd cheated at the cards, because she wouldn't have known how to frame the real questions, at all. I sometimes think she thought the gambling was the sin and it ended there. Anyway, she went on and on at your father, who as you can imagine was feeling pretty dithery and she kept saying, "All I want to know, is did you cheat?" And evidently, so he said to the minister and me, he said "No." Isn't it odd? You've got all these awful things happening and when it comes to him dying he's worried about that lie more than any. He says that's what cut her out. If he'd admitted that, he might have got round to admitting everything, getting her to understand and making a marriage out of it. But he failed to tell her—he went on a lot about this, Mary. He failed to tell her and that was maybe the beginning

167

of what happened to her. She needed a hand in life and he just didn't give her it. Even before she started on the booze he'd never say a word to her, you know, except "Good morning" and "Good night." You wouldn't remember that.'

Mary said, 'I understand, I think.'

'It was his own arrogance,' Macdonald said, 'that he was so worried about.'

'What was the other thing?'

'Och, it was the same thing. Just another scene. Evidently one night when I was out, I'd a night a month off in those days, she went as far as his dressing-room. She asked to be forgiven. She said a funny sort of thing. She said, "Let's just pretend we love each other." I can see fine what happened. He just called her a stupid woman and shoved her out the door. She went along to you two that night and woke you up, and later on I found her on the rug in the bedroom, fallen asleep beside the dog.'

Macdonald put her glass down on the table in front of her, then sat back on the fender.

'That was the first Flush of them all,' she said. 'He was a nice enough dog.'

'Oh God,' Mary said, suddenly, and then she put the question she had held back for three months. 'But didn't he ask for me?'

'Of course he did.'

'Kindly?'

'Of course. He was kind about everyone at the end. But before he went into your mother's room he asked for you every day. I was mad, trying to trace you, Mary.'

Mary frowned.

'What d'you mean, "trace me"?'

'Well, I knew you'd left David but none of us——'

She interrupted.

'Pink——' she said. 'He had my address. He . . .'

And then she stopped herself and in a curiously awkward way she put the heel of her hand over her mouth and pressed it very hard. Slowly, Macdonald began to understand. And she knew, too, at that moment that Mary was going to cry.

'It'll not matter, Mary, it'll not matter. . . . But he was funny about it, your father, I mean. He wouldn't take any steps to find you, the police or that. He wouldn't let me do that. He said it was a kind of judgment on him——'

'No.' Mary spoke almost under her breath.

Macdonald said, 'He talked a lot about you. And then he made his mind up and moved into your mother's room.'

'Was he there long?'

'Just a week.'

There was a short pause and Mary clenched her fists very tightly. At last, Macdonald said, 'Did Pink not even tell you he was sick?'

Mary looked very frightened and pale.

'I didn't see him.'

'Of course you did. In London, with David at your birthday time. That's why Pink went down.'

At first it was a moan, a dry sort of moan, and then at last she began to weep. When Macdonald held out her huge arms she fell against her and pressed.

'Old Rock,' she kept saying. 'Bloody Cassandra. Oh, darling Macdonald. Old Moo-Morality!'

22

She came down later that night and found him sitting in the nursery, staring straight in front of him, playing the *Marche Funèbre* on the radiogram, behind which he at once hid his glass.

She approached him and knelt in front of him but he did not turn down the sound. She put her hands on his knees and said:

'Pink, love, if it's about not giving Daddy my address; if that's what's really eating you, it doesn't matter, I promise.'

He stared at her stupidly.

'I beg your pardon, old flesh?'

'I wouldn't harbour it. I love you. I do.'

His expression never changed. He reached out, but not to turn down the volume. Instead he retrieved his glass.

'In point of fact, old thing,' he said, 'I'm a trifle predestinately pissed.'

A moment later she turned round and left.

'California,' Pink said, as the door closed, 'here I come.'

PART V

From the Lab

23

ALMOST the last picture is of her standing in front of a swagger golfing hotel looking quite exhausted, her eyes washed out with tears. She is oblivious both of the porters by the swing-doors who stare at her and of the broad-beamed business men who look over their shoulders at her as they pass by, pushing trolleys of expensive matching sets of golf clubs in enormous bags. There has already been a shower of rain, and the porters' two big striped umbrellas lie open, on their sides, by the front step. Mary herself looks a little heavier. She is in a cotton frock and a suède coat with a dark green silk square tied loosely round her neck. She is not looking at me, but staring blankly at the mauve clouds, at the formal borders of flowers by the perfect lawns, at the fountains, and beyond, at the first green Lowland hills, and she is saying flatly:

'I've sinned. This time, I've torn it. This time I've sinned, I know.'

And I reach out and seize both her hands and shake them but I have no argument. I close my eyes and say again and again:

'No, no, no! We have. Not you.' And I think I meant both Stephen and Pink in that 'we'.

*　　*　　*

Let me take it from the telephone call. I suppose it was about eighteen months after the Colonel died: a little more, because they were hay-making at the edges of the fairways on the course, that morning, before it rained. It must have been June. I rang from a box in the internal Post Office. It was that sort of hotel.

Her voice, then, was flat enough.

'Who is it?'

'David.'

She sounded weary and asked only for facts. I told her where I was and why. I was staying at the hotel by invitation, with all expenses paid, to read a paper at a Conference on Management in Industry. I talked brightly and made it sound as if I were enjoying myself. The title of my paper, believe it or not, was 'Work and Play', and the invitation to prepare it had followed the successful publication of *Obligatory Scenes*. In the allied fields, in and around social science, I promise you, one can get away with murder.

'Oh, yes,' she said to all that.

'Hundreds of brisk business men,' I said cheerfully. 'Pretty Wildian pages and happy Dickensian boot-boys constantly at one's service. All with Glasgow accents. The Secretary of the Conference calls me D.D. You must come at once and rescue me from unqualified success.'

'It's not very easy,' she said at last. 'Stevie's got the Jaguar.' I remember particularly that she did not just say 'car'.

'Oh come.' My accent, I suppose, as usual, grew more affected and 'Oxford', as I sensed the possibility of failure. 'Let's be pals. You can't leave me to the sharks. I'll give you the hell of a lot to drink.'

She replied, after a pause, 'Macdonald's out in the fields just now. They're hay-making.'

'I'll come and fetch you, I've got a car.'

'No.' She was very definite about that. 'I might catch a bus about twelve.'

'Excellent. It only takes an hour.'

'Why are you inviting me to lunch, David?'

'That's not allowed. No. That's a wrong question. Because I want to ask you to lunch. You must come.'

'All right. Things need organizing, that's all. There's Pink trouble. I won't be able to stay very long. And there's a baby-feed at two, but Cathie might manage that. All right. I'll come. How are you?'

'Bloody,' said with a loud laugh.

'I thought you must be.'

'One o'clock then.'

'About then.'

It is easy, and oddly enough, comforting, after the disaster, to write it all down in the dark hours and passionately blame and abuse oneself. It gives one the same kick that drives young people at those horrifying Retreat week-ends to confess publicly to sins which they never committed. This I have already done in a pile of unposted letters to her, now burnt along with the dead cats. But this I am determined not to do, for a simple reason. I blame my breed almost as much as myself. Some of the responsibility, after two years of exhausting self-examination, I place bitterly and sadly on the angels.

Before I rang her from the hotel, I was very certain of my position. I rang her because I wanted to put things right. I wanted to see her so that I could explain; which is to say, apologize; which is to say take the blame; which would have meant abusing myself. I had had nearly two years in which to try to find out why I had been so unbearably cruel to her, because when I was with her, I had better make it quite plain, not a day passed without its cruelty. I never lost an opportunity to damage her self-confidence. I actually struck her on several occasions and in the end, of course, I went to great lengths to break her faith in the two people who loved her. But last of all (a point which I failed to notice on my first examination), I somehow got it across to her, at the same time, that I was myself shocked by my treatment of her. By a look a day or a word a week I managed to tug at her sympathy, and this, because it made her stay on, was perhaps the most cruel of all.

I now wanted to tell her the curious conclusion I had come to. On all previous occasions, when she had asked me, like a child (she would simply ask 'why' again) what made me treat her so, I had talked a little mysteriously of *odi et amo*, and all that. I accused her, quoting all her fabulous fibs in evidence, of skating on life's surface, or refusing to be real, and therefore of being unable to love. As my love, I explained and flattered myself, was real and fundamental, I reacted violently against all her falseness. I honestly think I convinced myself. And of course love is complicated for the complicated just as it is simple for Romeo or Juliet. But so conditioned was I by the arguments and discussions of my mind-bending friends that the utter absurdity of the suggestion that we hate those we love, as it were, by definition (and if you don't hate her, then, my

173

goodness, you had better whip up your passion) did not occur to me. That we are capable of this hatred is undeniable: but that is to say something quite different.

Gradually I came round to the workman, the spade and the otter and very gingerly, because it was far from comforting, I began to face the fact that the most passionate affair of my life, with Mary, had very little to do with love and much to do with envy. Mine was the bite of the dog in the manger. 'You shall not be free.' With a nasty cold feeling in the very middle of me, I began to see that I was acting out a very old play.

For many years, usually when drunkish, I have bored my friends with the suggestion that the Scots, of all people, are misunderstood. A glance at their history or literature (and especially if you count Byron as a Scot, which after dinner, at least, is permissible) reveals what lies underneath the slow accent, the respectability and the solid flesh. Under the cake lies Bonny Dundee. But even as I put forward these theories with enthusiasm I was doing everything in my power to suppress the one contemporary sign of that splendid vitality which I had ever come across. They christened her Mary. I cast myself, perversely, as Knox.

This much I realized when I went north to read 'Work and Play' for big business in the swell hotel, and the reasons for my envy seemed clear enough. Anybody who has shared the heavily moral, non-conformist upbringing knows how the hoodoos stick even into middle life. Mary, although she was due for just such an education, had, primarily by the accident of her father's indiscretion and her mother's subsequent death, avoided these troubles, even if she and poor Pink had run into a load of others. Nor do I withdraw any of these conclusions, now. But they were not enough, because knowing this much, and already loving Mary in the way which is truly best described by her own 'cousin-style' I then waded in again and probably, in that one afternoon, did more damage than in the six months that had gone before.

What is perfectly horrifying is that I now believe I knew I was going to do this as I waited for her in that plush cocktail bar which looks like the waiting-room in a Warsaw brothel. There is always a clue. When I had said, on the phone, 'I've got a car. Shall I come and collect you?' she had said, at once, quite definitely 'No,' meaning 'Don't show yourself here, at the farm.' I can at this moment, still feel my heart leap.

That we are the perverts and the peeping-toms, the sex maniacs and even the murderers, we, the sons of the righteous, everybody knows. But we are something else, whose childhood was stolen from us, who never, without correction (not necessarily punishment) told Mary's splendid stories; who never went with Alice through the looking-glass. It is the curbing of our imaginations, the firm guidance back to the grammar and the prose, that make us so hungry now for experience. But for a special sort of experience; a kind of imagination of the flesh. We are the tinkers, who move on; who invite experience but flee from consequence. At the last moment our eyes turn furtively away. This is to say that we are the most dangerous of all: the permanently immature. And for that I blame the angels.

*   *   *   *   *

Physically there was quite an alarming difference. She was already sunburnt and her hair was at its lightest red. Her eyes, therefore, looked their most brilliant green, and none of the other men in the American bar failed to take a second look at her. Rather blandly, she stared them out. Her movements seemed to be slower. Her shoulders, barely covered by the loose cotton frock, looked heavier, and she was wearing a pair of brown sandals with no heels. There was something more than careless in her dress. It was a slovenly quality, which in the ordinary way I might have associated with a Lesbian. She had developed the same off-hand manner as if she felt it no longer necessary to please. And yet, by the looks on the faces of both the men and women round about, it was clear that she now caused considerably more stir, wherever she went. We played the name-game.

'Not Mary,' I said, after a long pause.

'Brenda,' she replied. It was not the only time that she seemed to take pleasure in disparaging herself, but I shook my head.

'No,' I said. 'What about Georgina or Margaret?'

'You tell me.' She ate another olive.

'I think it's Georgina.'

'Heather,' she suggested.

175

'You really mustn't be so rude to yourself,' I pleaded, 'it's embarrassing. Tell me, in one word, if we can't get it in a name.'

She looked at me for a moment, then said, 'David, if I'm to get back before tea-time we had better go in to lunch.'

From a huge menu, she chose a straightforward meal, without delay or hesitation. The last time I'd lunched her, even on that day at Bianchi's, she had been unable to decide on a meal. It used to infuriate me when she made me decide first, then chose exactly the same menu. There was none of that, and I thought I had found the clue.

'Ah,' I said, 'you lunch here often?'

'No.'

'This sort of place?'

'We often go out on a Saturday,' she said.

'To a country club?'

'That sort of thing,' she replied. 'Or one of the hotels.'

'Fair enough,' I nodded. 'For a dinner dance?'

'That sort of thing,' again, she replied.

'Money,' I said. 'You've come into money.'

'I hate to think what I look like,' she said slowly. 'You're staring at me as if I'm something out of a museum.'

'You look very beautiful.'

'But not so vulnerable,' she said.

'Not so obviously,' I remember replying (and how wrongly), adding the academic 'I confess.'

24

Vulnerable one, cousin. If all these things were revealed to me, if I wasn't in love with you and knew it, if I could not give before I ever came upstairs that afternoon, how, you ask, did I continue to make physical love? But there is no problem here. Those of us who have failed to break the bonds that tie our hearts, still manage, by a trip to the big city, by a journey back to *boue* to cure the rest. We may have no passion, but we are wanton enough. Give us a girl, a boy, a prostitute, give us even a scone for a wife, we can perform and do. Stephen is no Scotsman there. His fastidiousness is foreign to the line that leads back to the wynds of old Edinburgh and to your friends Ina and Elspeth and all the others in that inaccurate, timeless, fanciful but true tenement in the back streets by the Tay. His troubles are surely the responsibility of the more civilized successors of Dr. Arnold; the makers of agnostic monasteries.

I go through the scenes in the swell hotel, often, often, usually late at night in the lab when I wait for the cigarette to burn down, the Pentothal to wear off, or the cat to right itself. My lab's on the top floor now. I look down on Mill Hill and Hendon and the lights of London beyond and am transported back, wondering what trick it is that brings all the ghosts of passion that make a soul so fluently to the surfaces of the skin and into those special tears that are never shed. For a moment, or an hour, they brought a sweet and unfathomable depth into your eyes. There was an ocean sounded by a deep bell. I heard it from the shore.

I sat for a quarter of an hour as you surfaced. The white sheet tucked round your waist made your skin browner than I had seen it before and I remember that my thoughts for moments on end could not leap beyond the sensation of colour. Your hair looked darker red against the big pink coral shells on your breast. You slipped noiselessly into shore.

Cousin, to watch you and look after you was almost enough. Then, at least, I felt a strength, a protection, which I had never known was there. If not a lover, I was a man, and am thankful.

But to be loved like that, deep bell, is frightening. And as soon as you awoke, I was afraid. The ponk-ponk of the tennis balls came back, the jazz pattern on the curtains, the horrid wardrobe, the glass that still said L.M.S. I remember the little white chair which I'd taken from the bathroom squeaked as I moved back, ashamed that my eyes had woken you. Oh, this time it was David who spoke.

I can't go through all that again. The meaningless piles of words, none as imaginative as yours used to be, but even greater fibs. I used every Dundee cake of an argument. Even facts. Money, my own divorce, the child, Stephen, even the differences in our age. Forget me walking up and down; forget me standing, drymouthed, by the window, quickly trying to think of a new argument, a new card to lay on top of the house that I had built. I was shaking, not in the hand but right in the middle of me.

177   HG—M

At the end of it, when somehow I had returned to your side, you drew an arm out of the crushed summer sheet and touched my cheeks with your finger-tips.

Do you remember saying, 'Your guttersnipe face'?

Once in Classroom IV, I spoke for you when you asked me to. . . . But in the swell hotel you had the courage and the faith to give me my lines.

'I'll tell you what to say, Davie. Say "I want you to marry me. I don't think I ever want to let you out of my sight again. I want to look after you always. I don't want anything or anybody else. Say that." '

I think you already knew. You said it with the same conviction with which you used to speak of your father and mother in those splendid fibs. You were saying it against yourself and I knew, I knew that we were sailing headlong for the rocks. I could hear the noises of the wreck. So could you.

There was no possibility of a reply. There was no hope of explanation. I stuck. Just stuck. How long after? You'd begun playing with your fingers, stretching a long red hair, scowling up at it, with your head still on the pillows.

Very calmly, you said, 'We condemn ourselves out of our own mouths, David.' It was not Davie, then. You were quite matter of fact. You looked at me, and you went on, 'It was I who was the teaser, that's what you said. It was I who was the tamperer with life. So you said.'

I remember biting my finger: sticking again. For ten minutes, was it? It might even have been more. I jumped up cheerfully in the end.

'Let's go down and get some tea.'

A pause. 'Fine.'

25

It only remains for me to write down what I said and did for the rest of the day. I do so with a coolness, an attempt at objectivity which is false. The worst was to come.

When she was dressed, we wandered downstairs to the huge lounge where the palm court orchestra was reducing itself to tears.

178

I sat, sweating slightly, ordering tea, and she went and telephoned home. She used no guile with Stephen.

She said, 'I was having lunch with David Dow, darling, and it's gone on. We'll be coming back soon. How's things?'

Stephen trusted her implicitly. He was very cheerful, he had had a good day in Perth. At home, so she said, the combine had not broken down once. The gun-field was finished.

Back in the lounge, the orchestra and the central heating had reduced the guests to such depths of apathy and depression, with a kind of nostalgia for nothing, that they took no interest in us. I drank several cups of tea but I gave my cake ration to her and she ate, in all, five chocolate éclairs.

I said, 'I must have lost my balance altogether; I want to give you five more.'

About five minutes after, she swore it was only the music and the cakes, and apologized for becoming a schoolgirl again. But she began to cry so badly that I had to take her out. Everything in the hotel was miserably depressing as we moved down long corridors, trying to find something to cheer her up. She would not let me buy anything for her in the little shops by the main entrance. We went and looked at the empty ballroom and the billiards room filled with industrialists who had done their eighteen holes that morning. Both were equally depressing. We watched two boys who could not really play, banging about in a squash court, and somewhere else we heard the hydropathic click of ping-pong balls. In the swimming-pool, four children were yelling their heads off and the attendant was nowhere to be seen. Mary was still crying hopelessly so I ushered her into the spray room where we stood on the wet cork matting, along from the marble stalls. Steam swirled about the ceiling and I held her firmly by the arms. She looked younger then than I had ever seen her.

I tried to comfort her.

'You've done more good for me in one afternoon than the twenty-five years that went before. That's not bullying to say that.'

'No, darling.'

'Come on then,' gently.

'I promise it's only that awful music. I know it was only that . . .' Then she broke down again. She put it back to front in mirror

179

writing. She spoke as if she had refused. 'Oh, Davie darling, I can't, I can't. There's Stephen, and—I promised. I swore. I can't.' She sobbed very loudly as I held her. She tried to stop crying until she said it made her throat sore, and then she cried again. 'I'd give anything to be able to, don't you see, but I promise I can't.'

For a second poor Lucy Ashton came to mind. I wondered if it were possible, after all, to drive somebody mad. She had no idea what was going on round about her. She asked me what the spray was for.

I sat her down on an old, gilt cane chair that had found its way from the ballroom to the sprays, and I unfolded a huge white handkerchief and said, 'Blow it to bits.'

Then I said, 'I refuse to do more damage, darling.' This time it was not mirror writing. With a great wail she replied, 'God damn you, Davie, or damn whoever made you, or spoiled you, so you can say a bloody silly thing like that. Don't you understand what you're doing?'

'Darling, calm.'

'No,' she cried, 'I shan't be. I shan't be calm. It's a horrible dream, one of the ones when your feet stick to the ground. What else do I have to do for you? Don't you see I've really found you? I've reached through all your faces and edges. We're there!' And then with a laugh, 'No, we're not!'

Then, for a moment, she tried to control herself again. She pressed her head down and wiped her eyes and forehead with the back of her hand. But she was losing grip again.

'It'll break—Davie, I promise it'll break. My heart will break.'

She flung back her head suddenly and her whole face was wet. Her eyes looked curiously light. She said, 'I shall have to go to Moo.'

I replied, hopelessly, 'It's just—you must have been working up to this.'

'Oh Christ,' she said, rolling her head again in a curious, almost bear-like motion. 'Oh Christ, I shall have to go back to Moo. Don't let me go there—we could live, darling. I don't care where. I'd have your babies, with keely faces too. . . . It's hopeless!' She said quietly, like an older woman now, 'I wouldn't lie any more. I wouldn't have to. I'd keep you sane. You'd keep me sane. Just that?'

And as I still could find no reply, she said, looking hard at the floor, 'I'm not sorry I spoke—I shan't be ashamed.'

'Of course you mustn't be,' I insisted, very quietly, but there I stuck again. I held her shoulders. I believe I was afraid lest she might literally break into pieces.

Then all the children came running, from the baths, to the sprays.

But by the time we got back to the main entrance, where I had left my car, she was much recovered. She still was frowning. We stopped for a moment to look at the conference's Notice of Events and she asked me, then, if I had anything to do that night. 'Work and Play' had completed my obligations that morning, and I said if I did not simply eat and sleep I would probably drive south. But I added:

'Don't ask me to supper.'

She said, 'No. I was going to ask you a favour.'

'On you go.' The Oxford accent had vanished.

'I'm meant to be doing something terribly depressing tonight, and I really feel too weak.'

She was red about the eyes. The porters watched us with undisguised curiosity.

'What?'

'I said I'd run Pink over to Arbroath. He's to go into a place there.'

'A place?'

'It's not as bad as all that. Looking round,' she said, 'I should think it's much like this. Anyway it's about the same price. It's voluntary and so forth. He's all right about it. But they might be able to do something for him. Make baskets, I suppose. Would you do that?'

She was quite calm. A hostess asking a favour.

'Go with you, you mean?'

Firmly she replied, 'No. Alone, please.'

'What about Stephen?'

She brought her finger down her face, pressing the bone of her nose. 'He's working so hard. I don't really want him to drive late at night.' Then she added, 'Anyway, I want to be with Stephen tonight. Would you?'

'For you.'

181

'And for old Pink,' she said carelessly. 'I think he'll be pleased it's not me. Together we might get terribly gloomy . . . A little dodgy, I think.'

*   *   *

It was soon after that, just outside, that she stopped and spoke of sin while I cried, 'No.' I could not find the words to say 'Now that you are there, that you feel love, that you have given, don't already start making rules and feeling sin; just be glad.' And not finding the right words I made a pompous sort of statement.

I think I said, 'It's better to start just with life and find out about right and wrong than to be burdened with so many hoodoos that you spend all your time in revolt, and miss out on love and life altogether.'

She cut straight through that.

'Do you love me?' Then, under her breath, 'Can you love me?'

Why couldn't I have lied? I do, in a way. Cousin, I do. But then came the furtive look. I moved a step forward. Something was sticking in my throat.

In a horrible stony silence, we climbed into the car.

*   *   *

A big mauve thunder cloud came up from the west as I drove her home, still in silence, and when we arrived the house had a bright, clear, well-washed look. From the gravel, it was like a child's painting. Directly in front, one could not see how far back it stretched, and in the odd bright light, it looked oddly two-dimensional, with the door in the middle, a square window either side, and three windows above. The roof did not look quite straight. To the right were the chestnut trees and the yew hedge, to the left the small lawn and the walled garden. Flush came up to be patted on the head. The windows, too, were full of faces, just like a child's drawing. They were all waiting for Mary. Pink waved supremely gaily from an upstairs window. Cathie came to another with the baby in her arms, and tried to make it wave to its mother.

'My goodness.' The tinker was beginning to regret the visit. 'I'd nearly forgotten about that one. He or she?'

'It's a "he". A boy called Harry,' she said. 'Don't worry, you won't have to meet him. If he's up there, he's been fed.'

Just before she reached the door she said, 'Do I look a wreck?'

'You could have been crying.'

'It doesn't matter.'

The last private thing that she said to me was, 'Do I look a bit more Mary?' but I was still too cold and stuck to do more than nod. She was much more relaxed than me: curiously, calmly resigned.

She said, 'I'm glad about that. The only girl I knew called Georgina was a kleptomaniac.'

*   *   *

In the sitting-room Cathie recognized me, but it took me a moment to remember her. She had developed a more aggressive, impudent manner which barely covered a sense of happiness. Cathie was gradually replacing Macdonald, and although she was meant to leave at four she evidently always stayed until six or seven at night. Macdonald herself seemed to have slipped gradually but certainly into the background. Telling all seemed to have left her without wind in her sails, as if those evenings with Mary had completed a life which, more obviously, might have been expected to finish with the Colonel's burial. Age seemed to be catching up with her, all of a sudden. She had even lost confidence with the baby and Cathie, unthinkingly, had stepped in.

Cathie asked me fiercely, 'Have you not been offered a drink?'

Before I had time to reply she said, 'A fine house you'll be thinking this is, and you're given no hospitality.' She looked up at me and went on, aggressively but not unpleasantly, unsmilingly but not without humour, 'And a fine sort of guest it is, too, who doesn't even go up and see the son and heir. Mary says you've to go in the dining-room and pour yourself a whisky.'

'Thank you. I'll manage that.' But I could not then remember her name. At the door, she said:

'Pink'll be down in a moment. We're trying to persuade him to take a reasonable amount of stuff. You know what he is with all his things. He's everything there but the kitchen stove. You'd never get your car up the hill.'

Soon after, both Mary and Stephen arrived and we all had a drink together. She had made up her face again. She looked me perfectly warmly and friendlily in the eye, as if I'd become, in an hour, an old family friend. Stephen looked brown and well. He greeted me with great enthusiasm and even asked me to stay the night. The cut on his forehead rather improved his looks, I thought. What might be called informally formal, he was correct, but did not stand on ceremony. His manner was energetic and verging on the hearty. He was in shirt sleeves, and he was meaning to go out again after supper, because the hay harvest had prevented him doing a thousand and one things round the garden. But he still had the old habit of throwing all his worst cards on the table. I can't remember how he came to it but one self-disparaging phrase sticks in my mind. 'Well, well,' he said. 'I've got a 3.4 Jaguar and oil heating throughout. I can always tell St. Peter that.'

Pink, when he appeared, was dressed for the city. He was in his best suit and Old School tie. He had a case in each hand and an umbrella under his arm.

'V-very good of you, old man,' he said to me, making the best of his stutter. Then he stood looking into thin air. He would not even accept a lime juice and soda and silence fell, as we stood round the door of the dining-room. As Stephen began to ask me about the conference, Mary hurried us along.

She said, 'David doesn't want to be late. Let's put these cases in the car.' We took them outside and it was then that Macdonald appeared for a few seconds. She stood at the back of the hall, and stared. We bundled Pink into the car and Mary nodded quickly to me so that I should not wait any longer. Pink was looking white and strained. The gay wave from the upper window was already forgotten.

Then, at the last moment, as if Pink were going off to school, Mary suddenly dashed into the house, and when she returned she slipped him a five-pound note. His last remark to her before we left had a curious, triumphant lift to it, but I did not see how she reacted. I could no longer look her in the face. As the wheels turned on the gravel he smiled and wound down the car window.

'*T-tirez la* whatsit, Belle,' he said. '*La farce est jouée.*'

* * *

'It's most awfully good of you,' Pink said to me as we approached the huge baronial mansion, on the outskirts of Arbroath. 'In point of fact it's nothing much more than a five-thousand-mile check-up. Thirty-fifth year, I am. Oyez.'

*　　*　　*

The Superintendent of the baronial nut-house (as Pink would have it) was uncertain of himself, it seemed to me, only in the sense that he could not quite make up his mind which part to play. There were several alternatives that went with an actor's hoody face and a thick shock of white hair. To the patients, I fancy, he liked to present himself as, frankly, an angel. He had a way with him, everybody agreed, and if one of the male nurses was having difficulty with a patient he would not fail to go and help, and usually he did good. Sometimes he used a slug of Pentothal or Soneryl, or one of those with more or less Biblical names, but occasionally he just talked. That was what he called, 'a little touch of Hector in the night'. To the patients' relations he was the brilliant scientist—'We're mapping out the mind, Mrs. Robertson, we're charting it.' He talked of deep sleep and physical methods, of analysis and occupational therapy. To the visiting scientists, officials, students or professors he was the prophet and the poet. He played all these parts with great energy, and his real genius lay in the fact that he persuaded himself he was being entirely honest in each.

The interview with Pink and me gave him full scope for his powers, and it was not until the end that he discovered that I was a scientist. Even then, he bluffed it out. Most of the conversation was directed to Pink who was more than prepared to discuss, in painful detail, the methods that they used. Hector then insisted on showing us round the place although I was anxious to go as quickly as possible.

'I say,' Pink asked him. 'Have you tried any surgery?'

'Oh, no, no, lad. We don't have the bad boys here. No bad boys.'

The Superintendent cleaned his glasses. He did not appear to enjoy the suggestion.

Pink said he was glad about that and then, alarmingly suddenly, both he and Hector started roaring with laughter.

Hector said, 'Were you thinking we might be chopping out hunks of your grey matter?'

Pink giggled and Hector slapped him on the back.

'I'm glad you've come, lad,' he said. 'I can see you'll be an asset to the place. You've got to have a sense of humour, you know. It's exactly like on board ship.'

But it was a curious, unnerving, sort of ship. Mary had been nearer right in the hall, that afternoon, when she had suggested it would be like the alco-pathic golfing hotel. I trailed from room to room, and did not smile. It was agonizingly depressing. Some of the rooms were bright and filled with people, playing bridge, listening to records, making rugs or dancing the cha-cha. There were several Buns and Belles playing clock golf and they looked at us as if we were men from Mars. In no case could the Superintendent define the nature of the patient's complaint.

'Nervous,' he said, certainly. He made a very dramatic speech, in one corridor. The rhetorical questions bowled along the vaulted roof like buckled wheels.

'What is a drunk? Or a dipso? Or an alcoholic? Or an unhappy fellow, eh? I defy you to define it, eh? Doctor, I defy you.'

One or two men and women, in spite of being jollied along by Hector as he passed, still sat alone, firmly determined to remain within themselves. But whether the faces, as they passed, were miserable or ludicrously happy, they filled me with the same terror. I saw one red-headed woman there, and wondered whose cousin she was.

Pink behaved as if he were being delivered to his private school. He seemed to find the whole idea of the place so awful that he made himself live entirely in the present. When I left him, with a sudden, strange, personal sadness, he was happily accepting a cup of cocoa from a trolley wheeled by a man with a handlebar moustache.

*　　*　　*

'Smoking,' Hector said to me, as we passed back to the main entrance of the huge converted Victorian house, 'is allowed everywhere. Send him cigarettes, eh?' Hector put an arm round my shoulder. 'Of course you're depressed,' he said. 'But your brother'll do well here. I'm sure he will. We don't guarantee things. You know that, as a scientist.' I fear I only wanted to get away. Hector had a curiously cynical phrase for it all.

'God, bottle and bed,' he said. 'That's what brings them here——But Bedlam? No. Not if I can help it. It's a question of organizing them. Just giving them things to do.' He went on about Pink, at last. 'But we'll do no harm. And I bet we do good with your brother. I bet we do. You never can tell, but I bet we do good. It's not all science, you know. There's a bit of water-divining too. A lot of it's instinctive. We look into the dark, we do that. "We look into the dark and there's always someone there." That's Yeats, you know,' he said.

I felt very tired. I shook hands rather hurriedly and walked back to my car. I did not stay at the hotel that night. I picked up my things there and drove through the night, south to London again. The road passed Juniper Bank, and as if to mock me, the clouds drifted away from the moon as I came down past the bothie. The farm lay below, neat, toy-like, by the old hooped bridge and the bend of the river. As I swung round the corner and crossed over the new bridge I saw the house at its own level, and it looked solid, safe, permanent and un-neurotic. For a moment, it seemed to me unbearably beautiful.

*　　*　　*

We look into the dark and there's always someone there. We look into the dark and see the faces of those we have already destroyed, by our own ignorance of ourselves; our immaturity.

We look into the dark, sweet cousin, and no wonder we are afraid.